Lost

Rose

By Elinor Battersby

Chapter 1

"What about Kerberus?" Charlie suggests, staring adoringly at the drooling face in her lap.

"Kerberus? Is that a name?" Luke asks from his position slumped on the bed, scrolling through '100 unusual dog names'.

"You know, the big dog that guards the gates of hell?" Charlie explains.

"That's Cerberus. It's an S sound at the beginning," I chime in.

"Are you sure?"

"Definitely."

"Maybe you can say it both ways," she suggests.

"You can... but one of them is wrong," I tell her firmly.

Luke laughs and Charlie sticks her tongue out at both of us in a distinctly disgruntled manner.

"You could call him Cerberus," Luke points out.

"I wanted to call him Kirby for short," she explains in a huff.

"Yeah, that wouldn't really work so well. Nice idea though," I say with a grin, turning my focus back towards my laptop screen.

"How about Fluffy?" Luke suggests.

"Harry Potter reference? Definitely on brand for us being massive nerds."

"I thought that was the *plan*? Massive nerds doing amazing at A-Levels and getting the hell out of here?" he reminds her.

"Yes yes, I do recall, it is *my* plan after all," she replies in exulted tones.

"I'm pretty sure it's the school's plan actually, but

OK. Are you saying you don't want a nerdy name?"

"I don't know! It shouldn't be this hard to name a dog!" Charlie cries in frustration, causing said dog to raise his head and whine gently in response.

"Any good options over there Penny?" Luke asks me.

I sigh and try to find the correct tab on my browser.

"She's not looking at Dog names Luke, she's back on the message boards," Charlie tells him flatly.

"Nooo! Why?! They just make you mad!" he exclaims, getting to his feet and stretching.

"I just want to see what they're saying now," I mutter defensively.

"And? What's the verdict?" Charlie asks with only the slightest edge to her voice.

"One thousand three hundred and twenty six people have liked this post saying that *I'm* the one who kidnapped you and dad was just covering up for me. Apparently I'm a crazed killer."

"Well it's good to know that you're not allowing strangers on the internet to dictate who you are. It would be rubbish if you let them get to you," Luke points out with a smile.

"Well I'm not going to suddenly start *offing* people!" I snap.

"Well that's a relief! Since I'm so desperate to 'play the victim' I would *definitely* get killed if you went on a rampage!" Charlie shrieks happily.

"Can you both please stop looking yourselves up online?!" Luke demands.

"Sorry Lukey boy, but that analysis of me was in the newspaper! A wonderful critique of myself to read over my morning coffee and eggs!"

"Since when do you start the day with a newspaper and eggs?!" I demand.

"I told you! Massive nerds! We have to be the best versions of ourselves this year guys! Penny, if you're going to be a psychotic killer, you have to be the *best* psychotic killer that you can!"

"Ok, we've officially deviated from the school's plan for us," Luke comments, burying his face in his hands in despair.

I can't help it, even with the words of a thousand plus internet strangers running through my veins, I laugh. Charlie and Luke seem to act like a magic spell, pulling me from my melancholy when nothing else can.

"If this goes to trial it's going to be a nightmare," I sigh, a small smile still on my face.

"I don't know, people would at least know it wasn't you," Luke points out.

"Yeah, but they'll absolutely *crucify me!*" Charlie exclaims, burying her face in the side of her still unnamed dog.

"And I'll be a psycho-kidnapper's daughter," I add.

"But they'll know he didn't kill Rose."

Charlie says the words softly and they settle on my skin like summer rain, but I don't know that I believe them. Luke doesn't either, I can see it in his eyes. Until we know what actually happened to my sister all those years ago, my dad is going to be a suspect. It feels like its own tragedy, that he went so far outside the lines to try to get her case reopened, and in doing so made himself look guilty of the crime.

"I vote that we don't look at anything to do with the whole 'kidnapping thing' for the rest of the day!" Luke declares, folding his arms across his chest as though the matter is settled.

"Seconded!" Charlie agrees.

I sigh dramatically as I shut down the web-page and turn to face them.

"What are we going to do instead then?"

"Instead of unhealthily obsess? Literally anything," Luke replies.

"Oh. Um. I have a suggestion. How about we take this beautiful creature for a walk? He's got that expression again," Charlie pipes up, looking at her dog in some concern.

We run through the house but he still manages to leave a small puddle in the hallway before we can get to the front door. I shout a quick apology to mum as she appears armed with paper towels and disinfectant spray, but then we make our escape. Since Charlie picked him up two weeks previously, an inordinate amount of our time has been spent cleaning up her dog's pee. It got old very quickly.

"How long does it take to house-train a dog?" Luke queries, not for the first time.

"Depends on the dog. Some dogs are really intelligent," Charlie tells him happily.

"And, *this* dog?" he presses, watching as our four legged companion bumps into a wall it was endeavouring to sniff.

Charlie doesn't answer, she's watching her pet with a besotted expression, her attention utterly absorbed.

We move up the road at a snail's pace thanks to the plethora of smells that need to be investigated. It's only once we reach the woods that we pick up the pace, the dog gambolling ahead of us in sheer delight. That's probably the biggest change effected by the inclusion of a canine into our lives- the woods have completed their metamorphosis from a nightmare into something bright and green and beautiful. They feel more like the woods from my childhood summers than they have in a decade. I breathe in the scent, letting in seep out, sinking into every inch of me. I'm not afraid any more. How's that for personal growth? My therapist is very proud.

We chatter happily about Charlie's plans for our year as perfect students, acing our exams and stunning everyone with our brilliance. The only thing that interrupts the calm good-humour of the outing is the occasional dog walker. Their eyes find us quickly, their own conversations dry up or fade and stutter to a close as they watch us warily as we pass by. My instinct is the same as it's always been, to shift my gaze to the floor and appear as small as possible, but Charlie is still Charlie. Thank God. She gives them broad smiles and stubbornly friendly waves but I can see it grating, their expressions grazing her closer to the bone every time.

"I know what it is!" she declares suddenly after our fifth such encounter.

"I look at her enquiringly, waiting for whatever

revelation she's about to impart.

"We need ugly fleeces!"

I'm not following.

"Ugly fleeces?" Luke queries, also confused.

"Yes! We don't look like normal dog walkers! We stick out! We need the official 'I'm walking my dog in the woods' uniform!"

"I have an ugly fleece already," I remind her.

Said fleece has been a source of some contention for years now. It's oversized, slightly tattered and made of fleece- Three things Charlie has previously been vehemently opposed to.

"Luke?" she asks eagerly.

"My parents have a farm, of course I have a fleece," he tells her a little defensively.

"We only need one for me then!" she concludes cheerfully.

"Isn't it a bit too hot? Not really fleece weather," I point out.

"It will be soon! We only have a few days of summer

left! I'll ask my genetic donor to buy one."

Charlie's dad. A figure of myth and mystery throughout our childhoods- a figure that she reached out to for a relationship only to be ruthlessly shut down. It was this rejection that set Charlie spinning and sent her to my own dad looking for a relationship of some kind. If it wouldn't be totally hypocritical given my own parentage, I would blame Charlie's dad for a lot of what happened. If I'm honest, hypocrisy or not, I do blame him. He wanted nothing to do with his own daughter, until suddenly she was in every newspaper and on every news station, at which point 'estranged daughter' was better for his image than 'rejected estranged daughter'. They still don't have a relationship, but he has given them the money for the dog, is providing a small allowance and there has been talk of him buying Charlie a car if he can find something that he feels to be appropriate. I'm honestly not sure how Charlie feels about the whole thing. She certainly isn't talking about the man in warm and fuzzy terms but based on what she's said so far, I'm not even sure they've actually spoken directly. I'm desperate to know of course, but through a monolithic effort, I'm not asking. Charlie knows I'm here if and when she's ready. Again- admirable personal growth!

I'm counting down the days until school starts again. It's a deadline that fills me with dread and I've been attempting to keep it at bay through sheer willpower. I did try to convince mum that home-schooling might be the best option for me but she wasn't even willing to consider it. Apparently she doesn't feel equal to the task of educating me though my A-Levels. Although she works at my school, she has zero teaching experience. She was given the position out of pity by the headmaster, Mr Danes, when she quit her job in marketing after Rose went missing. She works admin four days a week, unless she's going through one of the 'phases' that don't allow her to leave the house, or even get out of bed. Then she doesn't work at all and I suppose the admin just waits for her to feel better, the same as the rest of us.

The last few weeks, since I found Charlie, and dad was exposed as her abductor, mum hasn't left the house at all. At first my step-dad Coop and I had to split the duties of looking after my little brother Oliver and mum just cowered in the house avoiding the news and staring vacantly into space. Slowly she's been coming back to herself but she seems fragile and her moods are erratic. I understand, I really do, the things that people are saying about our family are unthinkable, but I do wish it hadn't hit her so hard. I would have liked a bit of time to fall apart myself.

"So, ugly fleeces, fancy morning routines, excessive studying, what else is on the agenda for this year?" I ask.

"Your mum has a Nutribullet, right? We could have green smoothies!" Charlie suggests brightly.

"I vote against green smoothies," Luke counters quickly.

"You're out-voted. I have additional votes because I was a kidnap victim."

"Penny was a kidnap victim too!"

"Yes, but Penny hates being a tiebreaker. Besides, she knows that I can wear her down if she disagrees with me," Charlie tells him.

"So basically I'll never win?!" he exclaims in horror.

"Nope, sorry!"

I slip my hand into his and give it a squeeze.

"Sad but probably true. Sorry," I admit.

"You're lucky you're worth it," he mutters to me under his breath, sending a pleasant shiver down my back.

"So, green smoothies. Does that mean there's going to be other health related aspects? Exercise?" I query.

"Is this about netball again?" she asks with a small gusty sigh.

"Yes it's about netball again. I don't think you should go."

"You've been clear about that, and I hear your

concerns. It's just- I like netball. I like being on the team! Some of my friends play! And if I can just remind you, Coach Dan had nothing to do with my abduction."

I take a moment, trudging along the path behind her, trying to pick out the perfect words. The right selection in the right order to make her understand. I've tried before of course, I told both Charlie and Luke what happened when I broke into Dan Cosford's home, but they still couldn't fully comprehend it. There's no way to make someone grasp the look of terror on Tina Cosford's face or the sense of disquiet that permeated the whole house. The way Dan kept the back door key in his own dresser draw. The fact that her clothes and personal knick-knacks had been relegated to the wardrobe of the guest bedroom. The box of women's underwear in Dan's own wardrobe. None of it was overtly threatening or dangerous, it was just... wrong.

"I know he wasn't involved, but that doesn't make him innocent. I'm sure he isn't a good person."

I want desperately to tell her that I think Dan

Cosford is dangerous. I think he's more than capable of hurting someone and I wouldn't be at all surprised if he already had. I want to say that Dan Cosford is evil, but I know that the melodrama would only make Charlie scoff.

"My dad had him on his suspect list for a reason. And he lied to me about being part of the search party when Rose went missing."

I stop there, carefully toeing the line. This reminder is already a risk- Charlie is understandably reluctant to admit that my dad has a single leg of reason or sense to stand on. To her he is a monster and nothing more. Pointing out that my father didn't trust him is as likely to turn her in Dan's favour as turn her against him. The fact that he lied to me however, that's a difficult one for her to reconcile. In the first weeks following my daring rescue we talked it through on a loop- everything that we'd learned, everything we knew, the mystery car. Charlie had tired of the topic before I'd even begun to sate the itch and Luke just seemed anxious, wary of saying anything at all. Dan Cosford's proven lie is the only thing that they both agree absolutely is suspicious. It's the only thing that they don't try to explain away.

"I'm still thinking it over Penny. But I promise, if I stay on the team I'll be extra careful and I won't ever be alone with him," she tells me consolingly.

It's not enough.

"When are we going to have to drink these green smoothies?" Luke cuts in, always keen to diffuse the tension.

"Hmmm, good question. We should create a schedule. We need to make sure we allocate time for everything. We should block out time for studying, time for sports, time for healthy green smoothies, and of course time for vocations."

"Vocations?"

"Yeah, vocations. Like Luke's boy-nerd stuff. And my history pursuits. And your investigating."

"What?" I ask quickly, stopping in my tracks.

"My history plans. I definitely want to study it at uni

and I want to get into a really good programme, so I'm hoping to find some sort of extracurricular that I can do to bolster my resume."

"No, not the history-"

"Ah you mean Luke's boy-nerd stuff? I'll admit, I'm not exactly clear on what that consists of. I imagine there are conventions to attend, costumes to make and online fan-forums to add to."

"I don't go to conventions! And I don't dress up!" Luke snaps defensively.

"You are on the forums though aren't you," she counters with a wicked smile.

"I talk to people who like the same shows as me..." he reluctantly admits.

"Online. You go online and post about Star-Trek." she ruthlessly elaborates.

"Yes. Alright, I do. But I don't write any of the weird fan-fiction!"

"You do read it though, don't yo-"

"Not that either Charlie! What did you mean about

my investigating?!" I demand.

"Just that."

"Investigating what?!"

She stops walking, her dog straining at his leash, and turns to face me.

"Penny. This is our last year here, and then we will be leaving town. You have all your dad's notes and pictures. You have your own theories. You know there was someone else around that day, you know about the car on your driveway. You're closer than you've ever been. Closer than anyone else has ever been. Are you really telling me that you're not trying to figure out what happened that day?"

I stare at her, searching her face before turning to Luke and then back again.

I have been trying to figure it out. Of course I have. On the night I found Charlie drugged and locked up, I took all my dad's papers with me when I carried her out of there. I wedged them under a fallen tree in the woods and first chance I got after I was released from the hospital, I went back for them. I've been sifting through them every night since, trying to mentally sort them into some sort of order. I've been scouring them for clues, waiting for a pattern to emerge but nothing has.

"It doesn't just apply to murdering people Penny. If you're going to be a detective, be *the best* detective you can be."

They're both watching me intently, their expressions calm and focused. I realise that they've talked about this between themselves and I stifle a small pang of hurt. They both knew I was still looking into things- a fact that I had been carefully concealing.

"You know? You know I want to-"

I falter, still not feeling that I can say the words aloud. I'm afraid to give the thought such definite form and weight in case it drags me down.

"If you don't try, do you think you'll regret it?" Luke asks evenly, not wanting to push me one way or the other.

I think about that for a moment. I've been mulling

over ideas and sorting through papers, but I've been doing it almost on auto-pilot, without any real thought or consideration. But if I stopped? If I just walked away and let the whole thing go?

"I couldn't not *try*!" The words bust from me almost in a panic.

"Alright then," Charlie tells me with a small but firm nod.

"Alright?"

"Alright. We're here for you. We'll help however we can. You don't do anything alone," she explains.

"And no more breaking and entering," Luke adds.

That sounds fair.

"But- it's crazy, I can't just... figure out what happened to Rose after all these years!" I tell them.

"Penny, you got into my secret email account!" Charlie reminds me.

"You figured out something weird is going on with Dan Cosford," Luke offers.

"You *saved* me," Charlie whispers, reaching for my

hand and giving it a squeeze.

It's true. In a very literal, not even being dramatic way, I saved her life. When I got to Charlie she was barely breathing. Days of being drugged, no food and hardly any water had left her on the brink. The doctors were very clear that if she hadn't been brought in when she was, she likely wouldn't have made it. This fact catches in my chest every time I think about it, bringing stinging tears to my eyes and a wave of revulsion for the man who did that to my best friend. My dad.

"But it's been ten years," I point out.

"You mean he might not still be here? In town?" Luke queries.

That isn't what I mean. Something, some sense buried deep within me, tells me that the person responsible for Rose's disappearance *is* here.

"No, but... what clues can I hope to find after all this time? My dad gave his entire life to this case. He obsessed over it. He never thought about anything else, but he still didn't solve it."

"No offence Penny, but that's because he went nuts. We won't let that happen to you. You can investigate and we'll keep you sane."

This is better than anything I could have hoped for. Permission to go deep into the madness of my dad's research and follow up every lead I can find, complete with a tether to keep me safe and sound of mind? That's too good of an offer to refuse!

"OK!" I tell them, hoping that my eyes tell them everything I wish I could explain about how grateful and loved I feel right now.

They both smile at my reaction though I still think that Luke looks wary. I promise myself that I won't do anything to cause him any undue alarm. I can investigate what happened to my sister and still be safe. I'm sure I can.

Chapter 2

Sleep is a funny thing. It's been elusive and vague ever since Charlie went missing and didn't return once she was back. I've spent nights trying to piece together my father's thought processes, reading though his messy scrawl and scanning the pictures he'd taken. As soon as I lay down in bed, my mind would start to race, wondering what he might have seen, what he may have found out. Before long I would find myself back at my desk, his papers in front of me.

With permission secured to investigate fully, you'd have supposed I would redouble my efforts, stay up all night and pour over every scrap of information, but as soon as my head hits the pillow that night, I'm asleep. It's my first full night of rest in weeks and it feels like coming up for air. I wake refreshed, hearing the sounds of normal life clattering along downstairs.

I can do this.

First things first, I need sustenance. I head downstairs, the unmistakable audio of the CBBC channel leading me to the lounge.

"Olly Wally!" I sing song, reaching over the back of the sofa and hoisting him into my arms with an effort. He's not as small as he was but I can still throw him back onto the cushions making him squeal with delight.

"Penny! Do it again!" he demands, his arms reaching up to me.

I oblige a couple more times before distracting him with the offer of pop tarts.

"Strawberry pleeeease!" he calls to me as I make my way to the kitchen.

Coop is perched on a stool at the counter, slowly

consuming some buttered toast while he reads through the morning paper. Charlie would be very impressed.

"Any new articles about us?" I query, keeping my tone light.

"Nope, nothing."

I'm not surprised, the initial feverish interest has died down. No doubt there'll be a resurgence if there's a trial, but I'm still hoping that it won't come to that. Dad's lawyers are 'in negotiations' but if he pleads guilty to abducting Charlie then life would be easier for everyone. My biggest concern is that the police may think like the rest of the general public seems to. There's a lazy assumption that if my dad abducted Charlie, he must have killed Rose too. I don't believe this for one second, but if the police do, then they might file charges against him for murder and there's no way he would plead guilty to that. A trial might turn up new leads in Rose's case, but I'm not sure whether mum would survive it.

"Good, good..." I mutter to Coop.

I try to keep my voice sounding normal, but the very effort to do so sends it cascading up and down octaves with abandon.

"You alright Penny?" he asks gently.

"Yeah, yeah I'm fine. Last week before school!" I say with a shrug and a half smile.

He replies with a half smile of his own and shifts his attention back to the newspaper. I make tea and pop-tarts while silence seeps from our skin, coming off us in ripples and waves, leaving the air thick.

"How's mum today?" I ask when I think I might choke on it.

He gives a small, sad sigh.

"Not a good day today, but I'm working from home so you don't have to worry."

I give a nod of thanks and then depart with a mug in one hand and two plates balanced in the other. I deliver Olly his breakfast and then retreat back to my room.

Coop and I used to be close. Long before my dad

turned out to be a deranged psycho, Coop had taken over in the father role and I had been more than OK with it. Coop was kind, calm and dependable. We had a great relationship! But that was just one more casualty in my dad's fight to find my sister. The issue arises from the fact that Coop is on my dad's suspect list. Admittedly, it's a fairly comprehensive list, including pretty much anyone who lived in town or knew Rose and didn't have an alibi. Dad spent years figuring out where everyone was the day Rose disappeared, while delving deeper and deeper into the dark and sinister world of child abduction and human trafficking. There are lots of people still on his list- lots of people whose movements that day couldn't be tracked or couldn't be verified, but most of them don't live in my house.

I carefully set down my tea and pastries, then throw myself down into my chair, setting it spinning. I want to just push the thought away, but it's always there, humming beneath the surface of my conscious thoughts.

Everyone has something to hide. Everyone has

something to hide. Everyone has something to hide.

I massage my head with the heels of my palms and take a deep breath. I need to focus.

The huge stack of papers is locked in my bottom desk draw. It was the only one big enough to fit them all in. I dig them out and set them on the desk in front of me. Hundreds of pages of disconnected reports and ideas. So let's see if I can connect any of them.

I'd been keeping the papers in the same order, as close to the order dad had them in as possible. When I'd grabbed them from the house, I'd swept them into a bag, but the bottom papers had stayed at the bottom of the pile, and the top papers at the top. I'd kept the same arrangement, looking for some significance, trying to follow whatever distorted path my father had been on, but it's time to stop. I need a new approach. My dad didn't find Rose. He didn't figure out who was responsible. *I will.* I'm done following his lead- this is my investigation now.

I scan through the first sheet and set it aside. Then

the next, and the next. I slowly sort the pages into piles, making order from the chaos. First, I group the photos together, sorting them into a neat stack of illicitly snatched images. Maps get their own pile. There are maps of Upper Chalfont and the surrounding area, with specific buildings and other locations marked. I've already checked a few of them out. They're mostly abandoned houses, like the one my dad used to keep Charlie in. Some aren't even there any more, consumed by the beast that is new development in the years since my sister vanished. There are also maps of London, Birmingham, other cities and even other countries. My dad tried to track down anywhere that stolen children get taken, but that turned out to be a monolithic task and it took him further and further away. I plan to focus closer to home. I just hope not *too* close.

There are lots of pages of rambling notes and half formed ideas. I put these in a pile too, but I silently promise myself that I won't give them much time. I don't need my dad to do this.

Then there are the pages on different people. A list that he printed again and again, whittling it down from hundreds and hundreds to, well, hundreds. It's still a big list. Every generation of the list is here, from the original with its numerous annotations, to the most recent version - just the people still unaccounted for on that day, with my little stars drawn beside familiar names.

Dan Cosford's name is on that list.

I keep coming back to him. He told me that he was out of town when Rose went missing and the official searches were taking place, but he wasn't, he lied to me. His name is on the list of the searchers - he signed in. Why would he lie? Why is his wife terrified of him? Why does he have a box in the back of his wardrobe full of women's underwear in various styles and sizes, like they all came from different people?

I searched that box myself and I couldn't find anything in a child's size- nothing that pointed to Rose, but I didn't have time to look properly, I can't be sure there wasn't something there.

I can feel it in my bones that Dan Cosford is dangerous.

I collect together any of the papers that relate to him and any of the pictures of him too. There are candid shots from years ago, pictures of Dan leaving his house, pictures of him getting home. He used to live right on the edge of the woods, his house as close to the trees as ours is. My dad obviously followed him on occasion, hoping to witness something suspicious or something that would clear this man and allow him to move on. It's been ten years and he never managed to clear him. Once I've gathered all the details related to Dan I add my own notes to the mix. I add print-outs of his social media, the notes on my conversation with his neighbour and my interaction with his wife. Lastly I print out a single page with the words 'He lied. He was at the search.' and set it on top. It's a hefty pile and I feel quite pleased with my efforts though I'm aware that none of it would stand up in a court of law.

There are lots of reasons to suspect Dan Cosford.

Coop has been my father for ten years now, he's been living in the same house as me! If he was involved I would have known! I would have felt it!

No, Dan Cosford is a much better suspect.

I'm not really sure what to do next. I need to figure out a plan of action but I have no idea where to start. I need to find out more about Dan Cosford. Ideally, I need to talk to his wife, Tina. I also need to figure out a way to identify the car in my driveway the day Rose disappeared. My mum has always maintained that she was home alone that day. My dad was away at a conference - she called him to come back but he missed it and didn't arrive until that evening. Until then, it was just mum at home while Rose and I played in the woods like normal.

So who was the owner of that car?

Charlie saw a silver car outside my house. It might be nothing, but...

I need a plan of action.

I start a list of steps I need to take and the first one is to pin down as much of a description as Charlie can give me on the car- That way I can start to narrow it down. I wonder briefly if I should ask mum about it, but her fragile state relegates that option to last resort.

So I have- get description of the car, talk to Tina Cosford, find out what Dan was doing when Rose was taken.

I'm aware the list escalates quickly from a manageable task to a potentially insurmountable challenge, but that can't be helped. I fire off a quick message to Charlie asking if she'll be around at some point today and then I make myself close my laptop and move away from the desk. I've spent enough time with the notes this morning, it's time to do something practical. I shower and dress, pleased that shorts weather has already passed and I can pull on some full length jeans and a t-shirt once more. Piecing together the essentials, phone, money and keys, I leave my room. I stop on the landing for a moment, listening out, but there's not a single sound from my mother, still safely ensconced in her room. I take the stairs slowly, breathing deeply in preparation for meeting Coop. He's in the lounge with Olly, working together on a sprawling Lego creation. I affix a bright smile to my face and raise a hand in greeting.

"I'm heading out to meet Luke," I tell them.

"Any plans?"

"Nothing in particular, we'll just stay around town. We might meet up with Charlie later too," I tell him vaguely.

"Alright, well keep me posted and let me know if you'll be home for dinner or not, ok?"

I agree, my smile straining my cheeks.

"Have fun Penny," he tells me, his expression inscrutable.

I hold my breath until I'm out of the house but he doesn't say anything else. I keep waiting for him to ask me what's wrong, what's changed, but he never does.

I message Luke as I walk, letting him know where

I'm headed, but then I silence my phone and stow it in my pocket. The sun is still warm and the day is bright, but every step into shadow is a brisk chill. The weather is cooling quickly and by school on Monday I suspect it to be practically autumnal. Charlie's right, ugly fleece time is imminent.

My first destination is only a few streets away. Careful studying of my dad's photos and some time on Googlemaps street view has helped me to identify the precise house that I want to see. Number three Chestnut Drive. The house that Dan Cosford lived in when Rose went missing.

It's a simple, red brick affair, on the end of a terrace. It's small and boxy. Smaller than the house he lives in now. It's not far from mine, but the street looks totally different, except for the dark cluster of trees visible between the end houses.

He was right next to the woods.

I don't know what I was hoping to find, I think I just wanted to see it. I wanted a visual on where he was then and what his life looked like. Ten years is a long time, what was Dan Cosford like back then?

I allow myself a minute, to just stand and look up at the house. I wait for it to speak to me but clearly it has nothing to say. It stares resolutely back at me. I'll need to find my own answers.

I stuff my hands into my pockets and continue on, walking further into town. I know the rough direction and I let my feet carry me; I want to look as calm and as natural as possible. I'm just a normal girl doing entirely normal things.

I repeat this phrase to myself as I near Dan's new house.

Normal girl. Normal things.

I try to walk with a normal gait, paying particular attention to the casual swing of my arms. I'm just a normal girl, walking down a random street with no particular significance. I slow a little as I draw opposite the house, risking a quick glance up at it. I find the same stretch of wall that I perched on a few weeks ago and I settle down, pulling out my phone with every appearance of nonchalance. I intended to sit here, waiting for something to happen and pretending to scroll aimlessly the way people do, but when I enter my unlock code I see a message from Luke. From the tone, I don't think he's particularly happy. I stifle a sigh as I begin my scrolling, sneaking furtive glances at the house across the street every minute or so. Day one and I'm already causing Luke concern. So much for my excellent intentions.

Before long I make out the sound of footsteps and Luke comes into view. He's fantastic at walking normally, I note. I bet he isn't even *thinking* about his arms! He does need to work on his expression though—he definitely looks annoyed.

Before he can reach me and say something indiscreet at an audible volume, I raise a hand in silent greeting and try to broadcast my sneaky intentions to him with my mind. He clearly picks up on my signals as he gives a slight, disgruntled shrug, but doesn't say a word until he's reached me and slumped onto the low wall beside me.

"Spying?" he asks in a low voice.

"Just keeping an eye on him!" I counter.

"Is he even in there?" he asks.

It's a good point. For all I know I'm keeping an eye on an empty house.

"He might be. Or Tina might be," I tell him.

"Which is why you should have asked me to come with you!"

"To sit outside in broad daylight in a public place?"

"Penny! I'm serious! You think he might be the one who took your sister, right?" he presses.

I almost shrug but turn it into a lurching nod at the last minute.

"You think he's dangerous. You shouldn't be here on your own."

His tone is flat but his expression is so serious that I can't help but lean over and kiss him. I don't mean to dismiss his concerns, on the contrary, it feels really nice to see him concerned about me. My life has suddenly shifted, from a state of close confinement and endless oversight by my mother, to abrupt and unsettling freedom. She doesn't ask where I'm going when I leave the house. She doesn't message to ask when I'll be home. She's so like a ghost of her former self, that I'm afraid to reach out in case my hand passes right through.

"What's the plan then?"

"Plan?" I ask.

"Yes Penny, the plan," he repeats.

"Well, just this really," I admit uncertainly.

"Just creepy lurking?"

"Keeping an eye on things!"

"Well keeping an eye on things looks a lot like creepy lurking."

We both scroll mindlessly on our phones for a bit but Luke is clearly restless.

"How long are we going to stand guard here over a potentially empty house?" he asks after another twenty minutes.

"Just until I hear back from Charlie," I tell him soothingly.

He raises an eyebrow in enquiry.

"I want a better description of the car. I need more details so that I can begin to track it down," I tell him.

"You think it was Dan's car?"

It's a fair question but it isn't one I have an answer to. Honestly, I don't know what to think. Why would Dan's car be in my driveway that day? Why would anyone's? But Dan lived just minutes away on foot, so why would he of all people have been driving? And why to my house? Looking for Rose?

In lieu of a mad, rambling monologue of incoherent thought, I just shrug and lean against Luke's shoulder. He feels reassuringly solid.

"So we're just waiting to hear from Charlie," he repeats, resting his own head gently against mine.

"Yep, just waiting for Charlie."

Waiting for Charlie turns out to be a more lengthy process then I'd anticipated. Eventually, we're forced to give up and move on, walking into town together to get some lunch.

"Next surveillance trip, I'll bring snacks," I tell Luke apologetically as we walk.

"Next creepy lurking trip?! *Next*?!"

I ignore his words and carry on. I know that he doesn't understand my urge to sit outside the Cosford house. It's not something that he could comprehend- possibly because it is a bit insane. I just feel anxious, knowing that he could be doing anything at all if I'm not there, and I wouldn't even know about it.

"Maybe I should take up netball," I suggest.

Luke snorts and I give him a shove.

"Sorry Penny, but... a group sport?"

"I could be good at it! You don't know!"

"Yeah, but I'm guessing you don't know either."

He has a point there. I've actually exerted quite a lot of energy to avoid any kind of group sport; at least as much energy as the people taking part, I'd say!

"Alright, you may be correct, but that doesn't mean

the idea has no merit whatsoever," I grumble.

"Because it would give you a chance to be around him? Other than lurking outside his house?"

"Exactly."

"Do you think that's a good idea? Particularly after the less than friendly conversation we had with him a few weeks ago? You did sort of accuse him of sleeping with Charlie," he reminds me.

I chew my lip uncomfortably at the memory.

"True, but it's not like he could say 'I don't want her on the team, she thinks I sleep with students,' is it?"

"I suppose not... but he still wouldn't be thrilled to see you, and he could probably keep you off the team for another reason. Like- you don't play netball."

It's a valid argument but it's still not the sort of response I need. There's no room for negativity here, my chances of success are too low to survive it.

"Fine, what about cross country? He coaches that too, right?"

Luke doesn't have a response for that one beyond a

deep sigh.

"I run! I could totally do cross country! And it isn't a 'group sport' as you phrased it."

"Do you have to get that close to him?" Luke asks in a small voice.

I feel a pang. He's worried. He's had to be worried about me for weeks now, in fact pretty much since he's known me, and here I am looking for ways to get closer to danger.

"I'll keep my phone on me all the time, with Find My Friends on. I'll text you at the end of every practice and again when I get home so you know I made it."

He thinks this through, turning the suggested precautions over in his mind, testing them for weaknesses.

"Alright, so long as you keep to those strictures," he agrees, taking my hand in his, his grip tight.

We choose a table at the cafe and I take a seat while Luke goes up to order. The gentle hum of conversation around changes cadence, grows barbs, but no one approaches so I just keep my head down and send another message to Charlie letting her know where we are. She sends a thumbs up but nothing more expansive and I feel the familiar tug of concern through my navel. That nauseating uncertainty. Is everything alright? Is everyone safe?

I push the thought aside as Luke returns with a decadent hot chocolate for me, topped with whipped cream and marshmallows in a fluffy pink and white cloud of pure sugary joy.

"Oooooh!" I croon as he sets it before me on the table.

"Toasties are on the way too," he informs me, settling into his seat.

"What did you get?" I ask, peering over at his cup.

"Latte."

I recoil slightly, expecting a familiar smell to set my heart racing, but it doesn't.

"It's alright?" he asks me with a smile.

"What did you do?"

"I had them add caramel syrup," he explains.

I give another tentative sniff. Caramel. Overall, the drink smells more like the candle isle of TK Maxx than the Americano dosed with rohypnol that my dad treated me to. I grin and pull Luke in for a quick kiss, appreciating the sweet caramel taste clinging to his lips.

"Thank you," I mutter, millimetres from his face.

"Ahem!"

We break apart and spin round quickly.

Trish is waiting ready with our toasties and is looking profoundly uncomfortable.

"Sorry," she mumbles, setting them down.

I watch her, waiting for her to look at me or smile, the way that she used to, but she just finishes quickly and hurries away. I tell myself it doesn't hurt.

"You ordered without me?!" a loud voice squeals from the doorway.

Charlie cannonballs in, a force of energy and sound.

"I didn't even know if you were coming! You didn't s-" I begin, but she cuts me off.

47

"Quality time with mum" she explains, rolling her eyes and casting herself down theatrically into the chair she's just dragged over.

She tries to act as though it's no big deal but I know that she's revelling in the attention Wendy's able to give her now. There's child-support coming in and Wendy has been able to reduce her hours at the garden centre down to just full-time, rather than full-time-plus-every-extra-hour-available in order to keep their little family of two afloat.

"I got my fleece though!" she adds, holding up a bag in triumph.

"Super, we'll be incognito in no time," I say with a smile.

"We most certainly will! Never underestimate the power of being correctly dressed!"

I give a thumbs up but my mouth is full of toastie and Charlie's eyes are riveted.

"Alright, tell me everything you've got. I need to order the exact same thing or I will get total food envy!"

I relay my order and Charlie scoots over to join the queue.

"She seems to be doing well," Luke comments in an undertone.

I nod vaguely. After all, she does seem to be doing well. She's as loud and smiley as ever, but there's something under the surface. There's some current of energy that I can't quite identify. I know she's still not sleeping brilliantly, and I can't help but notice that even without the fleece, Charlie's dress sense is a little more sedate than it used to be. I don't know what it all adds up to, but I'm keeping an eye on her, especially once school starts.

One eye on Charlie, one on Dan Cosford- I need to be careful where I'm going.

Chapter 3

"So, what do you need from me?" Charlie asks, sitting on the end of my bed.

"I need to know more about the car."

"Silver," she says instantly.

"Yes, thank you, that's the bit I already know."

"That's all I know too," she counters.

I frown at her but resist the urge to snap.

"Lie back. Relax. Breathe in through your nose and out through your mouth. Think about that morning. You were in trouble. What did your mum say before she left for work?"

Charlie does as I instruct, lying back on the bed and breathing. She's quiet for a long time and I'm just starting to wonder if she's pretending to have fallen asleep when-

"It was a bit like a sports car. Low, and no back seat. But not fancy, it was more boxy, the corners squared off. It might have been a convertible but the old kind. I sort of remember black fabric. It looked sort of... crappy. But like it might be someone's idea of cool. And silver."

She sits up as she speaks the last words and all I can do is stare at her.

"That was great!" I tell her sincerely.

"No make or model," Luke points out.

"It was amazing!" I reiterate.

"A license plate would have been nice," he adds.

"Luke Burrows! Don't make me come over there! That was brilliant!"

Charlie is flushed with pleasure and I'm about to tackle her back onto the bed in the bear hug to end all bear hugs but Luke holds up a hand.

"One question."

He's thoughtful now, his expression serious and pensive.

"Shoot."

"You said it was crappy. By today's standards? Or did it seem crappy even then? I mean, we are talking ten years ago. Cars have come a long way."

It's a very good point and I take a half step back, watching Charlie consider the question.

"You know, I think it seemed a bit crappy even then. I don't think it was the style so much... I've always liked convertibles, but it looked like it was old already and not in very good condition. It wasn't vintage or anything, just a bit of a clunker."

That's all I need. I tackle her, squealing with glee. I'm going to do this. I'm going to find the car. And if there was a witness or a killer in that car, I'm going to find them too!

My mood of elation lasts until the following day just

after lunch, when my anxiety about the impending start of school is compounded by another unwanted event. The ringing of the phone doesn't even register until Coop calls upstairs to me. I haven't used the landline in an age, not since I got my mobile for my ninth birthday.

I head downstairs a little warily, not sure what awaits me. If it was a reporter Coop would have just hung up. He looks pale and uncertain as he holds out the phone but his expression doesn't give me any kind of real clue. I put the phone to my ear.

"This call is from an inmate at Frankland Prison, Shane Owens, do you accept the call?"

A tinny, automated voice is speaking the words in a loop, my dad's voice cutting in and out as he inputs his own name. Coop is staring at me wordlessly but as I watch him, frozen by my indecision, his eyes dart to the kitchen. Mum is sat at the centre island. Her eyes are unfocused and I can see an empty mug clasped in her hand and a dry teabag beside it on the counter. I realise in an instant that she doesn't know who's on the phone.

I move swiftly up the stairs, putting distance between the call and my fragile-as-glass mother.

I close my bedroom door behind me and press the button without giving myself time to think about it.

"Penny?"

My breath catches in my throat. I manage a small rasping noise but nothing else.

"Penny?"

I try again but my throat is suddenly bone dry. I force myself to swallow, then again until it feels almost natural.

"Plead guilty," I croak in a small voice.

He sighs but I don't know if it's relief or disappointment.

"There you are."

"Plead guilty," I repeat.

"How are you?" he asks politely, as though this is just another infrequent check-in and not a call from prison.

Anger sears through me.

"How am I?!"

"Pen-"

"How am I?!" I hiss.

"Look-"

"Thirty two stitches in my arm from breaking the window of the room you locked me in after you drugged me! It'll be scarred for the rest of my life! The smell of coffee gives me panic attacks! Mum's practically catatonic on her bad days and there have been a lot of bad days! The papers are saying that we're monsters! Our whole family!"

He's quiet and I hope fiercely that I've wounded him. I want to hear sobs or the drip of tears. I want him to *feel it*!

"Look, I'm sorry I-"

His tone is light. His apology performative and I can't bear to hear it.

"Save it. I don't care what you have to say, just plead guilty so we don't have to suffer through a trial!"

"But Penny, a trial might mean a new investigation! A real one this time! They gave up last time, they didn't really try! They need to look for Rose!"

"This isn't about Rose! This is about you! It's about what *you* did! You abducted a teenage girl! *Two* actually! If there's a trial they're going to tear you apart, but they're going to tear us apart too! They're going to say that it was all Charlie's own fault, and that I brought it on myself and that our families let us down and that I inherited your crazy genes! We'll be freaks!" I insist.

"But if it helps find Rose-"

"*Why would it?!* Why on earth would you think it'll help find Rose?!"

"But if people hear, that she's the only reason I did this, the only reason I got into this mess, to save my little girl, they'll understand!" he whines.

"No one will understand. You went off the rails dad. So far off the rails. No one is going to understand. What you did is unforgivable. You abducted Charlie. You drugged her. You almost killed her! You gave my photo to the newspapers! You broke into the house!"

"Actually, *you* broke into the house. I couldn't get

though the bloody window! If I had... maybe I could have found something," he counters.

"No dad, not that house. *My* house! *Our* house! You broke in and left that rose on my pillow! Do you have any idea how scared I was! How alone and afraid I felt?!"

My voice has risen and a sob catches, dropping me to the bed and burying my face in my free hand.

"What?"

His voice is small and quiet, I can barely make it out.

"Penny, no, no I didn't. I was never in your house. What rose?! *What rose?!*"

Words fail me and the silence swells to fill the room.

"You have used your allotted time for this call," the tinny voice cuts in.

The dial tone follows.

He's gone.

My thoughts are spinning around the room so fast that I can barely make them out.

Dad didn't leave the rose. Dad didn't leave the rose.

Dad didn't leave the rose.

I want desperately to just not believe him, god knows he's lied enough! But he sounded so sincere, so confused and then so excited that I can't just dismiss his words. He realised immediately what it meant. Someone left a rose in my room when I started asking questions.

The person who took my sister is still here- they're close.

They knew that I suspected them of taking Charlie, and they warned me to stay away.

I need to find them. More than that, I need to find them soon, before my dad drags us all through the courts in his desperation to find the truth at any cost.

I push back from my desk, stumbling to my feet. I can't bear to just sit here, a flood of adrenaline won't allow my eyes to focus. I want to be moving.

I go quickly down the stairs, not worrying about Coop or mum or Olly. I just want to get out of the house.

"Penny?"

Coop finds me digging through the shoe bucket in the front entryway, looking for my trainers. I wish, possibly for the first time, that we hadn't sealed off the back porch after Rose went missing. It would be nice to have a back door to sneak out of.

"Penny?" he tries again.

I throw him a quick look but not much more.

"Are you alright?" he asks uncertainly.

My shoulders tense as I brace myself against the urge to tell him everything. I want to unload all of my concerns and fears onto his adult shoulders, but I just don't know whether or not I can trust him. The fact sears my skin, burning deep down to the very heart of me, but it can't be changed. I need to know the truth, no matter what it is.

"I'm fine, just need a walk," I mutter.

"Your mum's having a good day," he tells me.

I think of her hollow stare and the still dry teabag on the counter and I feel the wild urge to laugh.

"Good, I'm glad," I say instead. "We all need more good days."

He nods sadly and I think he's going to say something else but Olly's call from the lounge draws his attention away.

"I'll be back later," I tell the back of his head, slipping out the door before there's time for anything else.

My feet pounding on the pavement is a salve. I feel each impact through my body, carrying me forward. I don't have a destination in mind, I just move, slowing my breathing down in time with my steps. In for four steps, out for six steps. I let my feet carry me where they want to go, down one street and up another, looping and circling round but ultimately taking me back to just a few streets away from my starting point. Chestnut Drive.

I consider texting Luke but I'm not ready for another debate about creepy lurking and besides, Dan Cosford hasn't lived here in years.

I'm entering the street from the wrong end, walking

the whole length of it with the trees up ahead, just visible between the two houses at the end, only one of which matters. It looks just like it did last time, only this time there's already someone creepily lurking outside it- a small figure with dark hair and a round, protruding belly.

I slow my steps, as though frightened of startling some wild animal. As I get closer and I can make out her expression, I feel the urge to turn and run. I'm clearly intruding on something personal. Her face has a sort of raw wistfulness and her eyes are bright with tears. I force myself to keep going; my steps slow but audible. She should at least have warning that I'm coming. Still, despite my good intentions, I'm almost upon her before she snaps back to herself and hears me. She jumps out of her skin, both hands coming up before her and then wrapping around her middle.

"Tina?" I say tentatively, stopping a couple of steps away.

It takes her a moment, scanning my face, but I see it the second she places me. Her eyes widen in shock and dismay before her brow lowers and her face settles in a frown.

"My name is Penny," I tell her.

A silence follows. Her arms shift up to cross stubbornly over her chest. It's not an inviting pose.

"You remember me," I try again.

"It's not every day someone breaks into my house," she agrees, dripping sarcasm and sass.

I can't help but smirk, though her expression doesn't soften at all.

"Thank you for helping me."

She rolls her eyes slightly and she doesn't say anything but she doesn't leave either.

"Did you get the key back alright?" I ask, referencing the back door key that she illicitly gave me to enable my escape.

She nods and for the first time her face smooths a little. I've ranged up on the same side and she feels a little more comfortable.

"I hope I didn't get you into trouble," I say, but I

know immediately that I've pushed it too far.

Her expression hardens and she looks wary but in a sharp, defensive way.

"I don't know what you're talking about," she snaps.

"I think you do."

"Who even are you?" she demands, turning to face me, her eyes flashing.

"I told you, I'm Penny-"

"Well *Penny*, what were you doing in my house?! What are you doing here?!"

I don't know what to say. I think your husband is a psycho who killed my sister?

"I wanted to know more about your husband," I begin, saying the words carefully to see how they land.

"Are you from the school?! Another one of his students?! Typical! Girls are always wanting to know about Dan, but you can just clear off! You hear me?! He's *married to me*! We're having a baby!"

"No!" I counter quickly, "I promise you, it's not like that, I don't want anything to do with him! Not like that!"

She scoffs in evident disbelief.

"I don't know what your game is, but you just stay away from my husband, alright?!"

She looks more tearful than fierce now and I just nod dumbly and let her walk away.

I want to tell her to stop- to not go home. I want to warn her that she isn't safe with him, but something tells me she already knows.

With no better ideas coming to mind, I keep walking. I wander the streets in a meandering swirl of a route, taking turnings at random. I try to push aside all the thoughts crowding in on my mind like locusts but the incessant trill of them persists. Eventually I stop, bent double, my head pressed down towards my knees as I take great gulping breaths. When I stand back up a woman is hurrying her child to the other side of the street in evident fear. I spare them a quick glance before I straighten my spine and head for home.

"Penny, hello sweetheart," mum calls with a smile and a nod from the kitchen doorway.

"Hi mum."

"I'm about to start dinner, do you want to help?"

She could almost seem normal. If she'd sagged suddenly from the rushing loss of anxiety she felt at the sight of me, she would seem pretty much like herself. Her eyes are a little glassy and she's thinner, but her voice sounds normal and she's moving around alright.

"Sure," I tell her, slipping off my shoes and chucking them into the shoe bin as always. We are a no-shoes-in-the-house household.

"What are we having?" I ask as I follow her.

"I found a new recipe, a baked risotto. I thought we could give it a try."

Wow, a new recipe? It really is a good day.

"Great!" I enthuse, wanting to lend all the support I can muster.

"Are you ready for school tomorrow?" she queries as we gather the right vegetables and group them on the counter.

"Yep. I've got my clothes laid out and I've packed my bag."

"Good, good."

"How about you?" I ask gently, "Are you ready to go back to work?"

Mr Danes, the headmaster, is infinitely patient and solicitous. He gave mum the job when she was at her lowest after losing Rose and he allows her as much time and flexibility as she needs, even now. I suspect he has a bit of a crush on her but I try not to dwell on it. It's one of the hazards of having attractive parents, I've been dealing with it on both sides my whole life.

"I'll be fine," she tells me nodding to herself.

She sounds confident but I'm uneasy.

"I went back to the doctor a few days ago. I'm on some different medication now, and some different sleeping pills. I know things have been a bit rocky, but part of that was just getting used to the new meds and finding the right dosage. I'm feeling better all the time," she explains.

I still. We've never really talked like this. I know mum struggles, I know she takes pills to sleep, I know that she has her 'phases', but we've never talked openly about the situation before. I assumed that it was in part that she was shielding me and in part that she felt ashamed. I've never known how to broach the topic or what I would even say if I did.

"The new meds..." I begin awkwardly.

"Anti-depressants," she supplies.

"If these are new ones, does that mean you were on some before?" I ask.

"I was, though a different kind, and not consistently. I haven't always needed them, just sometimes. "And I have some anti-anxiety medication too." she adds.

I mull this over. Sleeping pills, anti-anxiety meds, anti-depressants. It sounds like a lot, but she does sound like she's feeling better and I definitely don't want her to think that she needs to shut me out of all this.

"And you're feeling good?" I ask.

"I am. The anxiety can hit out of nowhere, but in general I am feeling better."

"Good, I'm really glad," I tell her sincerely.

"I want to be stronger for you Penny. I want to do better and I will. I have a lot to make up for."

Just for a moment she looks utterly destroyed, like crumpled paper, but before I can say anything-

"Well that smells good!"

Coop's voice is loud, making me jump and drop the knife I'm holding.

"Penny!" mum takes my hands quickly, turning them over and examining my fingers, looking for cuts.

She sighs when she doesn't find any and clasps my hands in hers.

"You be careful!" she tells me, raising my hands up to kiss them.

"I will, sorry," I assure her, carefully not looking at Coop.

How much did he hear? I can't help but feel that he interrupted on purpose, startling us out of our conversation.

"And you!" my mum says, playfully rounding on him, "indoor voice!"

He chuckles and kisses her before turning to me.

"All ready for school?" he asks.

"Yep, all set," I say, still focusing on the cooking so that I don't need to turn around.

"Penny and I can drop Olly off at school and then drive in together," mum suggests.

"Are you doing mornings this term?"

"Yes I am, Mr Danes has some more charity commitments this year, so I'll be answering his phone first thing. You should see if he can get you a volunteer position Penny, it would look good for prospective universities," mum tells me.

"That's a really good idea," I say, thinking of Charlie and her master plan. I make a mental note to mention it to her tomorrow.

"St Danes and his charities," Coop says with a laugh and a shake of his head.

I risk a quick glance at him, there was definitely something strange in his tone. I wonder if he's jealous. Coop has always seemed so perfectly cheerful and placid to me, but now I'm wondering if maybe I just never looked deep enough.

Chapter 4

I wake in a haze, not sure for a moment why my alarm is blaring at me. It takes a second for reality to seep in and my memory to piece back together. It wasn't a great night for me sleep-wise and I'm not feeling my best. Finally the recollection of school hits me and I sigh. I fumble with my duvet, struggling my way out of bed, and stagger gracefully to the bathroom.

A shower does much to restore me to myself and by the time I'm dressed in my uniform, with my hair tied up in its traditional knot, I feel almost ready to face the day.

"Penny!" mum calls from downstairs.

I check the time and swear quietly to myself. I must have been moving slower than I realised. I grab my bag and hurry down to join mum and Olly in the hallway.

"No breakfast?" mum asks, eyebrows raised.

"No time," I tell her with a slightly breathless shrug.

"Grab yourself some pop-tarts," she says with a sigh.

"Whaaat?!" Olly cries indignantly as I run to the kitchen and tip a couple of pastries into the toaster. I don't even give them the full minimum time setting before pressing the stop button and grabbing them back out. I can hear the debate between mum and Olly going strong and I'm careful not to be too indiscreet with them as we pile out to the car.

"But you said I *had* to have cereal and banana!" he whines as mum helps him with his seatbelt.

"You did *have to have cereal and banana*, you're a growing boy and you need energy for school," she replies.

"Sorry Olly," I tell him, twisting in my seat to look at him in the back.

"It's not fair," he implores, eyes wide to take in the

full injustice of the situation.

"I know it's not. It's my fault. How about I make chocolate goo for pudding tonight?" I suggest.

"Chocolate goo?!" he gasps.

He's trying to look as though he's thinking it over but he can't help bouncing in his seat with excitement. Mum and I share a small smile.

"That sounds like a lovely idea," she comments.

"Alright deal! Chocolate goo!" he agrees, settling back in his seat with satisfaction.

Chocolate goo is a staple treat in our house. I invented it a few years ago when I tried to make a chocolate cake from memory and had mixed success. When it came out of the oven I was heart-broken at the appearance of the brown mess. Whatever it was, it certainly wasn't a cake. I was so dejected that Coop announced he was going to try it no matter what. He said that looks weren't everything and that the brown goo in the pan smelled delicious. He was as good as his word and went right to the spoons and gave it a try.

When he declared it to be the best thing he'd ever eaten, goo was born.

We drop Olly off first; he's chattering to his friends and bouncing along, and we watch from the car until he goes right through the doors. After a collective deep breath we continue on to our final destination. Mum is trying to look cheerful but her smile is tight.

"Are you... is this going to be alright? Going to work I mean?" I ask her hesitantly.

I don't want to shake whatever confidence she has in herself, but I'd like to know what to expect. More than one of her meltdowns has livened up my school career.

"It should be fine. There are a lot of things here that can be difficult for me, all the noise and the bustle. The bells between classes can shock me sometimes. But I'm ready. I've thought through it all, and I'm feeling prepared."

I feel a surge of affection and I lean over and kiss her on the cheek. She throws me a quick smile before shifting her focus right back to the road.

"Thank you for talking to me about this stuff mum."

"I didn't know if I should, I wanted to protect you from it all, but my therapist pointed out that that hasn't really worked so well. I need to trust you, you've earned it."

I feel a swoop of guilt that takes my heart down to my knees and I just count my blessings that mum doesn't know about the breaking and entering or my continued sleuthing plans.

"It's good to be in the loop," I say in a small voice.

She gives me another smile and then we're quiet, both steeling ourselves as the sprawling mass of Benedict Secondary School comes into view. It was previously named St Benedict after a venerated theologian monk, but then it shrugged off its religious affiliations and dropped the first two letters. Now it's mostly referred to as Cumberbatch- by the students, anyway. We pull into the staff car-park and I grab my backpack from the boot, swinging it up onto my shoulder.

"You should work mornings more often, it's nice getting a lift," I tell mum cheerfully.

She just laughs and gives herself a last check, straightening her shirt and attempting to tuck her mass of dark chocolate curls behind her ears.

I kiss her again before I go inside, keen to prolong this new intimacy we've found. She heads one way and I head the other, aiming for the front doors. I fight my normal urge to hunch my shoulders and keep my head down, instead looking up, trying to get a glimpse of Charlie or Luke. The crowd thickens as I get closer to the main entrance as more people are arriving, ready to start the new school year. After a few minutes however, my efforts are rewarded by a flash of blonde curls. I quickly make my way over, wending between groups of people talking and jostling against each other.

"Charlie!" I gasp in relief as I reach her.

"Penny! Thank goodness! I thought I was never going to find you!"

"Mum drove me in so I was coming from the car-park round the back of the building," I explain.

"Ooh! Is she working mornings? That's cool. You'll still get lifts with me when I get my car though, right?"

"How are things looking on the car front? You could probably get a lift with us until you have one," I suggest.

"Hmmm, I think it's best if I keep slogging it on the bus. The genetic donor is all for giving me a guilt car, but mum isn't convinced. If I get lifts with you she's less likely to change her mind."

"Good reasoning, very sneaky," I laugh.

It's at this point that I notice it. Eyes are turning towards us and people are actually shuffling to get a better view, as though we're a car crash that they desperately want to catch a glimpse of. There's a steady murmur of voices as people mutter to their neighbours but I can't make out their words. I can feel myself flush to the roots of my already red hair, and even Charlie is colouring.

"Maybe we should head inside," she suggests in an undertone.

"Good plan," I say, keeping my voice steady and bright, "I need to go to the sports hall anyway."

Without giving myself time to overthink it, I take Charlie's hand and move determinedly through the group around us. It's actually not hard, they leap back as we approach and I wonder if they're afraid. Once we're through the main doors, the echoing silence peculiar to school buildings surrounds us. All the students are outside, reluctant to step in until the last possible minute, so it's just the two of us and the sounds of our footsteps bouncing back to us off the walls.

"Are we really going to the sports hall?" Charlie asks.

"Yep, I'm signing up for cross country," I tell her.

"Cross country? You? Doing an organised activity? Alongside other people?"

"Well that's the key element, it's *alongside* other people, not actually *with* them."

"An important distinction."

"Absolutely. Besides, Coach Dan teaches cross country," I remind her.

"Ah! So this is less of an impulse to join in with your peers, and more of an impulse to snoop and sleuth."

"Exactly."

"Well, it's good to see you staying true to yourself."

The sign-up sheet for all teams and sporting activities is pinned to the wall of the corridor outside the sports hall and the changing rooms. I write my name carefully, since I never got the hang of writing on anything that isn't laid flat. Mine is the first name there but hopefully more will be added as the day goes on. I feel confident about signing up, but I wouldn't be thrilled for it to be just me and Dan Cosford.

"Is he going to be happy you've signed up do you think?" Charlie asks mock-thoughtfully, once she's put her own name down for netball, studiously ignoring my glare.

"I would guess not happy at all, but what's he going to do about it?" I respond, linking my arm through hers as we meander the empty corridors waiting for the first bell to ring.

As the harsh sound cuts the air, I spare a thought for mum. I hope she has a good day.

Form session is up first. This isn't a real class, we just have attendance taken and get any announcements or reminders from our form teacher. We have Mr Harvey, a no-nonsense educator with zero patience for anything besides his subject - history. As soon as we walk in, Charlie scoots up to him and starts asking about extra-curriculars and practical work that she might be able to get involved in. I move over to two seats at the front, slipping into one myself and putting my bag on the other to reserve it for Charlie.

The hum of speculation from outside is here too, like a low pitched vibration that I can feel through my feet as much as I can hear it with my ears. It makes the hairs on the back of my neck stand up and I don't have to turn around to see that eyes are fixed on me. People are watching Charlie too, but her attention is on Mr Harvey and although I keep an eye on her, she doesn't look concerned. She tips herself into the seat beside me as attendance is called and shows me a list of suggestions for volunteer work she could do or trips she could go on. Her eyes are bright with excitement and I feel a thrill for her. I have absolutely no aptitude for history, with its endless dates and near identical names, but I derive a unique enjoyment from Charlie's enthusiasm for it. She finds it all fascinating, from the ancient Egyptians to the Romans. I prefer science and maths, which are both less about knowing something already, and more about having the tools to work it out.

"I have history first, Charlie tells me excitedly, scanning her new timetable,"

"I have maths with Mr Stines."

"Meet for lunch?" she asks, "And then it's English this afternoon so we'll be together."

We agree a meeting spot, back here in Mr Harvey's room, so that we can venture out into the unknown together, and with that decided I pull my bag onto my back and bid her goodbye.

The hum quietened while everyone answered their

names and confirmed their presence for the day, but out in the corridor it's back. It's mixed in with the general chatter and shouts of the crowd as people make their way to classes, but it's still there. It follows me up two flights of stairs and along three corridors. I suppose this is what happens when you make the national news.

I breathe a sigh of relief when I reach my classroom and I take a seat at the back. I thought that this would save me from the feel of many pairs of eyes combing over my back, but it turns out to be worse. People keep turning in their seats to risk quick glances at me, their plastic chairs creaking with the movement. Mr Stines sets us 'silent work', meaning a lengthy booklet of problems to solve independently. The idea is to get us back in the groove and re-familiarise us with everything we covered last year. It's a good notion, but the silence is interspersed with creaks every few moments as yet another person turns towards me. I don't know what they're expecting to see. Am I supposed to grow horns? To suddenly go mad and attack the class? To break down in the same manner they've seen my mother do?

Whatever it is they're waiting for, I'm not planning to indulge them.

At the end of the session, Mr Stines asks us to close our workbooks and we all shift our attention back to where he stands at the front of the room. He gives us his prepared speech about exam preparedness and dedication to our futures and then sends us on our way. Despite the persistent itch of people's evident curiosity, I feel better for the time spent doing something I'm good at. Working through the questions on Mr Stines' paper, I felt just a little more balanced and capable. I manage to keep my head up again as I walk out into the corridor and I'm rewarded by the sight of dark hair and long limbs moving my way. I almost step back into the classroom but I work to keep my feet rooted to the floor.

Personal growth.

"Penny!" Luke exclaims in pleasure, fitting his hand into mine with ease.

I don't know how he does it, he just seems so calm

about everything all the time. I've been angsting over what this moment will be like, wondering how the school environment will change things, wondering whether he'll even speak to me here or if we'll only exist as a couple outside of these walls. I've lost sleep over it. Even with everything else I have to think about, it has consumed an unhealthy portion of my mind. But Luke? He just walks up and takes my hand, like it's no big deal. He was talking to one of his friends, Chris Tate, and he doesn't even seem to register the way Chris' eyes are fixed on me with alarm and suspicion.

"Penny, you know Chris?" he asks evenly.

"Not really."

"We're just heading to lunch, are you coming?"

Chris' eyes widen at Luke's words but when he sees me looking he flushes and hastens to add his own entreaties.

"I'm going to meet Charlie from history," I tell them uncertainly, reluctant to relinquish the safety of Luke's hand now I have it.

"We'll come with you."

It's nice walking through the school with the feel of Luke's hand entwined with mine. As the hum rises and falls, undulating as we pass, I can tell myself that some small part of it is due not to my psycho kidnapping dad, but due to this good thing. This boy.

It might be a lie, but it's a nice lie so I'm happy to believe in it. I let myself feel bolstered until a familiar face comes through the crowd. I almost turn and run, purely on instinct, but Luke squeezes my hand gently and I remember just in time to act natural. Dan Cosford it appears, didn't get the memo. He glares openly at me as he approaches and turns his head to follow me as he passes just in case I somehow missed his overt display of hostility.

I let out a breath once he's out of view and hurry a little to reach the door of Charlie's classroom. I half expect her to be alone, but Mr Harvey has clearly stayed behind to talk more history. From the glance he gives us when we enter and the small light of relief in his eyes, I suspect that it wasn't solely history that motivated him, but a need to stand guard over one of his students. Charlie's reaction confirms the suspicion. She smiles and waves but she looks tired already, as though the day is already weighing heavy on her shoulders.

"Bad class?" I ask quietly, taking her hand as we all make our way towards the lunch hall.

"A few too many people," she responds meditatively.

"Ah yes. A definite hazard with school," I reply philosophically.

"With lots of places really," Luke chimes in, "people have a tendency to ruin even the nicest of social gatherings."

Chris snorts but Charlie's brow creases.

"That sounds like something Penny would say," she comments.

"It *is* something I said," I admit with a sigh.

"Oh good! Much as I love you Pen, we only need one of you. For a moment I was worried that Luke was embarking on a full-on metamorphosis as the ultimate act of devotion!"

Chris lets out a burst of laughter and then reddens again, as though surprised by his own reaction. I chuckle gently but Luke just sticks his tongue out at Charlie and carries on walking with immense dignity.

People are still looking at us, but I feel less unwelcome with the buffer of our relaxed and happy banter around me. We head along the corridor towards the dining hall but as we pass the changing rooms I nip over to check the sign-in sheets and see who else has put their name down for cross-country so far.

I stop and take a half step back causing one or two people to collide with me before they can alter course.

"Penny?"

Charlie has waded through the crowd to reach my side.

"Where's my name?" I ask in a flat voice.

"Is this some sort of philosophical thing? Like, if a tree falls in the woods-" Luke begins but I cut him off.

"I wrote my name right here!" I state fiercely,

stabbing the top of the page with my finger.

"Where did it go?" Luke asks in a small voice.

"There aren't any pencil or rubber marks, it looks like someone printed out a new sign up sheet," Charlie comments, examining the paper closely.

"Well that doesn't leave many options, does it?" Luke notes brightly.

I think of Dan Cosford's glare. I didn't really need a lot of guesses anyway.

I go to pick up the pencil on a string that dangles beside the sheet, but I stop with my hand still in mid-air.

"Someone give me a pen!" I demand.

Charlie hops to it and hands me a pen with a smart salute.

"As ordered, Sir!"

I write my name in in clear, block capitals and smile to myself with satisfaction. I'm now the fifth name from the top so Dan won't be able to just take the sheet down and start again. He must have seen my name before the first bell and swapped the sheet before anyone else had signed up.

I march on towards lunch with a new energy in my step. I expected Dan not to want me on the cross country team, but actually removing my name?! It feels juvenile and petty and fills me with a righteous indignation and a comforting sense of superiority.

"What was that all about?" I hear Chris ask Luke in a whisper.

"Its a bit difficult to explain," he murmurs.

I allow myself a small smile. It definitely is difficult to explain and I'm not sure the story would sound believable even if I were prepared to tell it. The smile falls from my face the moment we enter the dining hall. I hate it here. I have hated it here since my very first day at this school. It's loud and crowded and smells strongly of cooking oil, no matter what's on the menu. There's no assigned seating, obviously, and the uncertainty leaves me in a panic. Most days Charlie is with me for lunch, but if she's not I either have to find one of my other friends and cling desperately to them, or go hungry. It's bad enough having to have someone random on one side, the idea of sitting alone is unthinkable. With Charlie, Luke and Chris, it's not so bad. This is a reasonable group and if we all sit together I should be able to focus on just us, but the general din and chaos is still almost overwhelming. We shuffle through the mass of people to join the queue and as we edge closer to the front Charlie begins her usual routine, now multiplied by three.

"What are you going to get?" she asks insistently to each of us in turn.

Luke and I are prepared for this at this point, but Chris is flustered and can't understand why she needs to know.

"Charlie has food envy," I explain to him, rolling my eyes.

"Food envy?"

"Yep, it doesn't matter what she's got, she's always jealous of what everyone else has."

"I could get the spaghetti like Luke, but you can't get fries with that! Penny is getting fries!" she wails in dismay.

"Well, I think I'm going to get fries. So, you could get the spaghetti and I'll share my fries with you," Chris suggests tentatively.

Charlie turns upon him with a beaming smile.

"That sounds like a fabulous plan!" she exclaims.

Luke and I exchange a quick look but save any comments we may have for later, when both Chris and Charlie are out of earshot.

Once we've claimed our food, we begin the awkward hunt for a table. Admittedly, the others don't seem to find it particularly awkward, but I'm sure they're just putting on a good show. Luke is the one who finds us seats, a table for ten has half emptied and we group ourselves around the free end, slipping into chairs and depositing our bags on the floor.

We make it half way through the meal before someone chooses to take advantage of the lack of supervision. Trisha Chambers sidles up to our table and slinks into a seat across from Charlie.

"So, Charlie Hople, in all the newspapers! Exciting!" she comments brightly.

Trisha Chambers lives for gossip. She takes great pride in knowing everything there is to know about everyone and delights in sharing her insights with others.

"I'm not sure exciting is the right word," Luke responds doubtfully.

Trisha fixes him with unnervingly blank eyes.

"What do you mean?"

"Well, it wasn't exactly '*exciting*' was it? More like *harrowing*, or *traumatising* maybe," he suggests.

"Is that what you would say Charlie?" she asks quickly, swivelling her focus back round the table.

"Um, well, I-" she stammers, not sure what to say.

I've heard her screaming from nightmares. I saw that house and felt how cold she was. It *was* traumatising, but that doesn't make it any easier to say.

"And you Penny? I mean, he was your dad, did that make it less scary?" she asks, her eyes on me now.

"Less scary than what?" I ask, confused.

"Less scary than if it was a real kidnapper," she explains, as though its obvious what she meant.

"A real kidnapper? What the hell does that mean? I was *really* kidnapped!" Charlie counters.

"How did it happen?" Trisha asks quickly, leaping on what she perceives to be an opening.

There's a drawn out silence. Trisha has already lured us into engaging but we're not really keen to elaborate more than we have to.

"I was drugged," Charlie supplies eventually.

"The whole time?" Trisha asks quickly.

"Not the whole time."

Charlie's voice is small and hollow and I feel the desperate, overwhelming urge to bring this whole exchange to a screaming halt, but Trisha is leaning forward eagerly.

"What did he do to you?" She asks.

Charlie's face closes off and I reach for her hand, clasping it under the table.

"I don't think she wants to think about this," Luke snaps, angling his chair towards Trisha in a vaguely threatening manner.

"Luke Burrows. It was your party," she says thoughtfully.

"Barely!" A loud voice scoffs from behind me.

Charlie and I turn in our chairs to find Marcus Kain standing behind us with Claire Netherhall hanging off his arm.

"*I* planned that party," he announces, puffing out his chest.

"You sure did," Luke agrees in a flat voice.

"Great night, right?" Marcus asks, looking between Luke, Chris and Trisha with a grin.

"Yeah, not for everyone," I mutter grimly.

"I watched some good Star Trek," Luke comments brightly.

"I met Luke," I add, blushing slightly but keeping my head high.

"I got abducted," Charlie points out.

"I was in France," Chris hastily adds.

"It was the *best* night!" Claire pipes up, pressing a hand against Marcus's chest and gazing up at him adoringly.

"Except for the abduction part," Luke counters.

Claire has the nerve to roll her eyes.

"It was just Penny's dad!" she exclaims in exasperation.

"She nearly *died*!" I snap, my voice high with incredulity.

"What, like your dad would actually have killed her," Claire scoffs in obvious disbelief.

"Claire, what the hell do you think was actually happening?!" I demand.

"Like we've said before, we're not getting involved with her drama," she spits, giving Charlie a disgusted look.

"And yet here you are," I mutter.

"What was that Penny Owens?" Marcus murmurs, bending over to bring his face close to my ear. My skin crawls but I force myself not to flinch.

"Do you have something to say Penny Owens? Do you have something to add? About your psycho dad maybe? Would he have killed her Penny Owens? Would he have killed you? Did he kill your sister?"

He whispers the words almost tenderly, so close that I can feel his breath on my skin. Without even thinking about it I grasp the table in front of me and push back with all my strength. My chair strikes him in the midsection and sends him flying. Claire very sensibly saves herself, relinquishing her grip on Marcus's hand and leaping back as he collapses into a neighbouring table. I stand and turn in one fluid movement, looking down at Marcus lying in the chaos of fallen chairs and scattered dinner trays.

"My name is Penny Cooper now actually," I tell him in a shaking voice.

"You bitch!" he screams.

"WHAT IS HAPPENING HERE?!" I turn slowly, my heart already sinking fast.

Mr Danes is frozen behind me, surveying the scene before him in horror.

"She attacked me! She's a psycho! Her whole family are psychos and kid killers!" Marcus roars.

There's a heavy silence in the dining hall as everyone lets the words settle on their shoulders. I'm just thinking that this situation can't get any worse when I see the drained, pale face over Mr Danes shoulder. Mum.

"I forgot to bring lunch," she mutters in a small, breaking voice.

Then her legs give way.

Charlie and I know the signs, I stepped forward and Charlie was out of her seat immediately beside me. We catch mum before she's half way to the floor and I clasp her slender form against me.

She'd been doing so well.

"MARCUS KAIN! You go to my office RIGHT NOW! If you EVER speak like that again you will be OUT of this school!"

I let the sound of Mr Danes voice follow me as I help my mother stumble from the room and along the corridor. I can still hear him as we reach the front door.

The sound of footsteps echoing on hard tiles makes me turn, adrenaline pulsing, but its just Charlie, Luke and even Chris.

"Let me help," Luke offers, putting an arm around mum and shifting her weight into his grip, lifting some of my burden.

"Do you want me to drive her home? If I'm allowed to drive your car that is..." Charlie suggests doubtfully.

"That's alright, Coop's working from home today. I'll call him to pick her up."

I pull out my phone and dial Coop who answers on the first ring. He was half waiting for this. He must be out the door in seconds, I bet he already had his shoes on when I called. We only have to wait for ten minutes of awkward silence as my mother focuses on slow breathing and I focus on why it would be a bad idea to murder Marcus Kain.

"Hello folks!" Coop calls cheerfully as he clambers from the car and jogs up to us.

"Did you speed the whole way here?" I ask in a low voice as he pulls mum into his arms and strokes her hair.

His only answer is a sad smile.

"We should get back inside, it's not long until the bell," Charlie tells me, taking my hand in hers.

She can feel my reluctance to let mum go. I want to go home with them and see her safe and settled.

"It's the first day of school," she reminds me.

"That's right Pen, you go back in, I've got this," Coop agrees, buckling mum into the passenger seat while she sits, limp and vacant, just breathing with her whole self.

I just stand there. I can't make myself move one way or the other.

"I'll text you as soon as we're settled," Coop assures

me.

Luke slips his hand into my free one, adding his entreaties to Charlie's. Gently, they turn me away and we walk back towards the school building. I spare a thought for Chris, who really doesn't know me or Charlie and was just exposed to a tidal-wave of awful and unexpected on his first day back, but before I can think of anything to say he actually pipes up-

"I think maybe we should just eat outside tomorrow."

His tone is bright and I feel myself smile.

"*That* sounds like a great plan!"

We're just in time for the afternoon bell and Charlie, Luke and I all have to hurry to English. It feels nice having them posted on either side of me, especially now that no one is troubling to keep their speculations to a murmuring hum. The scene at lunch has broken the damn and now everyone wants to discuss the topic, apparently feeling that it's fair game after the public outburst.

"Hey, Penny! Penny! Have you heard from your dad in prison?" Lucy Pall whispers from two rows in front.

I can't remember the last time I spoke to Lucy Pall! We've never been friends so I have no idea why she's asking this now.

"Why?" I hiss back in tones of puzzled incredulity.

"Is there going to be a big trial?" she replies.

Other people are turning to look, wanting to hear my answer. It is the big question isn't it. Is there going to be a trial? Not if I can help it.

I have no response for Lucy Pall or anyone else but it seems that that isn't going to stop them from asking. Charlie is getting her fair share of attention too. People want to know exactly what happened. They want details. They want to know the truth that the newspapers have been so unclear on.

"Charlie, is it true you had to spend three weeks in hospital?! Why?!" Someone asks, just as Ms Gittings enters and calls for attention.

Once again we get the talk about exams and focus and planning for our futures. Charlie sits beside me, rigid with attention and even taking notes. She is totally serious about her commitment to her education this year and I suspect that the constant barrage of questions is only strengthening her resolve. She is going to be amazing and get into an amazing university. She is going to get away from this town.

Ms Gittings is small and birdlike, but not in an attractive way. Her eyes are magnified by strong prescription lenses in round, thin-rimmed glasses that perch on a sharp, protruding nose. Her mouth is small and almost always pursed in disapproval. She's never taken much notice of me, but it seems that even she isn't immune to the rumours and speculation circling. Her eyes dart to me more often than is normal or strictly necessary and when it comes time to hand out worksheets, she drops mine onto the table and backs away quickly as though afraid that I might grab her exposed wrist if the opportunity presented. This exchange isn't missed by anyone and it sets off a small flurry of whispered mutterings that she makes no effort to quell. Frankly, I'm stunned. I gape at her in shock but Luke and Charlie both narrow their eyes and Luke's hand grips into a fist on the desk.

The rest of the lesson is passed in silence, though I can practically hear Charlie's thoughts raging in my defence. She keeps trying to focus on her work, but her eyes are drawn up to find our teacher and every time Ms Gittings eyes are fixed on me, Charlie edges a little closer to boiling point. I reach for her hand beside me and give it a squeeze. She looks at me, her eyes flashing and I smile.

I feel so incredibly grateful for her anger. Her rage on my behalf means the world to me. I try to tell her with my eyes that all the moronic Ms Gittingses in the world mean nothing compared to the fact that she's here, standing by me.

I doubt she comprehends the full and complete meaning of my significant glance, but she understands enough to take a couple of deep breaths and keep her eyes down. We make it through to the end of the lesson without any outbursts of retaliation from us, or any further dramatics from Ms Gittings but as soon as we're out in the corridor again the flood gates open.

"That hag!" Charlie rages.

"She did that intentionally! She wanted everyone else to see that she's *terrified* of you," Luke declares in tones of bewilderment and scorn.

"What is she afraid of though? Does she think I actually *did* something? She can't be one of the people who think that I abducted Charlie and dad is just taking the blame, not when the Charlie in question is sitting right next to me!"

"The Charlie in question is going to go back and deck her!" she announces.

"That's not exactly in keeping with our determination to be perfect students," I point out, giving her a brief side-on hug as we make our way through the crowd of students flowing in every direction.

"It would be totally justified though," Luke tells her.

"She better not make things difficult for you this year Penny," Charlie tells me, shaking her head.

"Speaking of making things difficult, I want to go and check my name on the Cross country sign-up sheet," I tell them.

We turn our feet towards the sports corridor but the rant continues.

"If she makes trouble, maybe you could go to Mr Danes," Luke suggests.

"Good point! He's clearly on your side! You pushed someone into a table and didn't even get in trouble for it! In fact Marcus is the one in trouble!" Charlie agrees cheerfully, a beautific smile on her face at the recollection.

It's a good suggestion but I just nod and murmur vaguely in response as I'm already thinking about more important things - like the fact that my name has been removed from the sign-up sheet again.

"That's not even subtle!" I complain hotly.

"No, not particularly," Luke agrees, surveying the damage.

My name has been scribbled out with Sharpie, leaving an ugly black mark that draws the eye. There are two more names beneath it and I write my name again beneath them.

"Are you just going to keep writing your name back in?" Charlie asks.

"Yes. Yes I am. I am going to keep writing my name back in, in a petty battle of wills! Unless something better occurs to me," I finish with a sigh.

Luke heads off to his last lesson of the day but Charlie and I both have a free period. We decide to spend it outside somewhere, rather than risking the sixth form common room with its lack of supervision and guaranteed run-ins with classmates.

"I hope this all blows over by the time it gets really cold," she comments, settling into a corner where the art block meets the rest of the school.

I know what she means. It's already getting a bit

chilly to be sitting on the floor outside. Summer seems to have passed in an intense but brief burst this year, leaving us with an increasingly cold and grey September.

"I don't know, how long do you think things like this take to blow over?" I sigh, leaning back against the wall beside her.

She looks at me out of the corner of her eye.

"I'm sorry we're freaks," she says after a moment.

"I was already a freak remember," I shrug.

"Yeah, but now the whole country knows it."

Her brow furrows as she thinks about what she just said and I laugh as I see her open her mouth to try to back-pedal.

"It's fine Charlie, I know what you mean. It's alright though, I can handle this, I'm just worried about mum. And anyway, this isn't your fault. It's my dad who's the psycho."

"At least he cares enough to be a psycho. My so-called dad didn't even want to *email* with me when I first reached out," she points out.

It's true. My dad, for all his poor judgement and totally insane behaviour, is motivated by love for his daughter. Just not me.

"Never mind all that!" I cry brightly, "we have a whole hour in which to be devastatingly productive! What notes shall we go over? Or maybe we can make study plans?"

Charlie beams delightedly, her focus drawn back to our grand plans for academic success.

We settle on making notes based on what teachers told us about exam preparation. We set a date to start our revision and circle it in our planners. By the time the final bell rings I'm feeling dizzyingly organised. I swing back through the sports corridor and I'm pleased to see that my name still adorns the sign-in sheet. All in all, it's been a better day than I expected.

Charlie and I get the bus home together and we're able to secure seats right near the back. It's a twenty to twenty-five minute journey with all the stops and varying traffic, but today it takes over half an hour. I suppose the whole world is settling back into the routines of a new school year, not just me.

I wave goodbye to Charlie at the end of my road and she continues on while I turn and trudge along the street towards my house. I'm keen to get home and check on mum but I'm also feeling generally exhausted. Coop was as good as his word and texted me to let me know that mum was settled and comfortable, but it doesn't tell me much about what I'm going to find when I open the door.

What I find is Oliver. My exhaustion recedes in the face of his glowing smile.

"Penny!"

"Did you have a good day Olly?" I ask, drowning him in a hug.

He begins a garbled account of everything he did at school, in no particular order and with the greatest emphasis on lunch.

"Have you had a snack since you got home?" I check.

"Dad gave me toast and an apple," he nods, "he's

working."

I don't ask him about mum. Although he lives in the same house and is obviously aware of what goes on, I can't bring myself to address it directly with him while he's still so little. I can't bring him into the team that Coop and I formed to hold mum together.

"Your dad's in his study?" I ask instead.

He nods but looks at me speculatively.

"Why do you do that now?" he asks.

"Do what?"

"Call him *your dad*. You've always said Coop instead of dad, but if you were talking to me you would just say dad, not *your dad*."

He's definitely aware of what goes on.

"I don't know Olly, I didn't realise I was saying it differently from before. Maybe because I've been thinking about *my* dad more," I suggest, not knowing what else to say to the little boy before me.

Because he doesn't feel like my dad any more?

Because I'm not completely sure I can trust him?

Because in disconcerting ways, I feel more like my father's daughter than I have done in years?

"Because your dad is in the newspapers and on the telly?" Olly asks slowly.

"Yes he is. Has anyone mentioned it at school?"

I hold my breath but he shakes his head and I breathe a sigh of relief.

"Nope, I don't think so," he tells me with a shrug.

"Good," I murmur, "That's good. What are you watching?"

"Detective Pikachu!" he tells me excitedly.

"How far in are you? Could we put it back to the beginning?"

"You'll watch with me?" he asks excitedly.

"I sure will! Just let me get changed and I'll be right back."

While he runs back into the lounge to put the movie back to the start, I dash upstairs. I do want to change out of my school clothes, but my first port of call is mum's room. I open the door slowly and peer in.

"Mum?" I whisper.

The room is dark, the blackout blinds pulled all the way down. I can hear her breathing, deep and regular. She's asleep. I close the door softly and continue on to my room to swap my uniform for joggers and sweatshirt.

I flop down on the sofa and Olly curls up beside me. This usually only lasts a few minutes before he's up, whirling around the room looking for something or digging through his Lego supplies, but today he stays settled beside me. He must be tired from his school day too, but I feel grateful for it as he leans against me and I wrap my arms around his soft, warm little form. The movie is almost over when Coop finishes work for the day and comes to find us. He sticks his head around the door and smiles at the sight of us cuddled up together. We're both still awake but Olly's eyes are a little heavy and he's totally relaxed.

"I'll do dinner now," Coop whispers and retreats.

We have spaghetti and meatballs. It's supposed to be a treat meal, it always has been, but now it's connotations feel complicated. We had this meal the day Charlie went missing. We all sat around this food talking about make-up and parties and then a few hours later she was gone. I know that she's back, that she's home and safe but still with every bite I feel a small kernel of fear catching in my chest. I wonder if it will ever fully go away.

"Did you have a good day at school Penny?" Coop asks a little awkwardly.

He knows about mum of course, about her meltdown, though I'm not sure whether he has the details.

"Um, yeah. It was fine for the most part. Lots of talk about final exams and how A-Levels impact the rest of your life," I say, forcing a half smile.

"The rest of your life?" Olly asks, surprised by the concept.

"Yep, big important tests," I say, raising my eyebrows at him playfully.

"Why do they affect your whole life?" he asks.

"Because if I do well in them, I could get into a very

good university, and then I could get a very good job that I enjoy and make lots of money to do fun things," I tell him concisely.

I'm quite happy with this response but Olly looks perturbed.

"A university where?"

It's a great question. One that I've been avoiding. I've been trawling through prospectuses and the teachers last year kept encouraging us to go and visit potential unis, but the thought leaves me cold. I can't imagine living anywhere but here. I can't imagine leaving Olly or mum. I can't imagine feeling comfortable with leaving them alone here without me, especially with my newfound fears about Coop. More than that, in some complex unfathomable way, this little town is where I lived with Rose. I don't know how to envision a life that extends beyond this town. My story is here and it's not over yet.

"Not sure Olly," I tell him quietly.

I can see that there's more he wants to say but I

don't have any answers for him and I'm worried that in the face of his wide, imploring eyes I might make promises that I'll someday regret.

"And how was Charlie? First day back and all..." Coop asks quickly, possibly seeing the look in my eyes.

"She was good," I reply gratefully, "she handled it well. Some people tried to push it, asking questions and speculating, but she was great. She's strong."

"So are you Penny," he tells me, his eyes softening.

I'm surprised and pleased but I don't know what to say. I spent so many years thinking of myself as fragile, and assuming that Coop and mum thought I was too. In hind sight, I think it was mum's way of protecting me. If she kept on saying that I was fragile and quiet and shy, then everyone would treat me as though I were fragile and quiet and shy. They would be careful and gentle with me and keep me safe.

I was happy enough to believe the spiel but I'm pretty sure that fragile, shy people don't break into people's houses and smash windows and carry drugged friends through the woods to safety.

I'm not going to say it out loud of course, but I'm pretty sure I'm strong too.

I give Coop a shrug and a genuine smile. I see it land and crinkle the corners of his eyes and I'm reminded that this man loves me. He would never to anything to hurt us. It must be Dan Cosford. It has to be.

Chapter 5

I wake in the morning already tired. I'd let myself forget how exhausting it is just to be around so many people all day. I drag myself out of bed and to the bathroom but even a shower does little to dispel the fog permeating my mind. It's not until I check my planner that I feel even slightly invigorated. Tuesdays is Cross-country. This is my first opportunity to get close to Dan Cosford; to spend some time with him and hopefully glean something useful. I'm not sure what I'm expecting exactly, I realise that it's unlikely he's going to confess to killing my sister while I work on my running form, but I could at least observe how he interacts with people and see if I can detect anything unusual or maybe catch a glimpse of the monster within.

"Penny?" Coop's voice queries as he taps gently on my door.

"It's alright, I'm up, you can come in," I tell him as I pull my hair up into its customary knot and secure it with a scrunchie.

"Mum won't be going in to work today," he tells me from the doorway.

I'm quiet for a moment, but I'm not entirely surprised.

"I'm going to drive Olly to school but are you alright to get the bus?" he asks.

"Yeah that's fine, I'll go now," I assure him, checking the time on my phone.

"Alright, thank you Penny. One more thing, your mum left her bag under her desk yesterday. If you get the chance do you think you could swing by and grab it for her?"

"Yeah, sure."

That makes it sound as though she won't be in again this week. Charlie really needs to get that car. The bus takes longer than driving independently so I head off straight away, sneaking a couple of pop-tarts without Olly seeing. I made chocolate goo last night as promised, but I'm not prepared to make it a daily occurrence.

"What are you doing here?" Charlie asks as I hustle my way to the back of the bus and slump onto the empty seat beside her.

"Mum's staying home today," I say simply.

Charlie gives my hand a quick squeeze and changes the subject. I let her words wash over me as the bus jolts and lurches along in the way that only an ancient and rigorously maintained double-decker can. Her voice blocks out the incessant noise of a bus-full of overly excited teens, as she tells me about the history project she researched the night before. There are some Roman ruins semi-locally and Mr Harvey might be able to get her a volunteer position at the affiliated mini-museum.

Charlie wants to be totally prepared should this treat indeed come to pass so she's started work on a self-imposed research project on the Romans and their enduring impact in the area.

"What about your extra-curriculars?" she asks as we finally pull up outside the school.

"I'm going to go and check on mine now," I tell her.

She raises an eyebrow in enquiry.

"I'm going to check that my name is still down for cross-country," I explain flatly.

"Alright, I'll come with you. I'm not staying out here with the vultures."

We move quickly through the front doors and along to the sports corridor.

"Damn it!" I exclaim, seeing the unsightly black mark where my name used to be.

"The cut-off for sign up is lunch time today," Charlie reminds me helpfully.

"Do I just camp out here and stop him scribbling my name out?!" I demand.

"You can't. We have double English first period today."

Perfect. Two hours of Ms Gittings and her overwhelming terror of me. Could a morning get any better?

"I guess I'll just have to run back down here after English and write my name back up," I sigh.

"This is a really petty battle," Charlie comments.

"Yeah, it's feeling increasingly ridiculous to me," I admit.

"Are you sure it's even Coach Dan doing it? I mean, he is a grown man."

"A grown man who asks people to call him *Coach Dan*" I remind her.

She laughs but the morning bell interrupts any further debate. We head to registration through the sudden wave of students flooding the halls.

"Mr Harvey?" I ask once he's called everyone's names and they've descended into a gentle babble of conversation.

"Penny?"

I get up and move closer to him, dropping my voice.

"Can I go to the office please? I need to collect my mum's bag. She forgot it yesterday and I don't want to forget."

I see the understanding in his eyes- he must have heard about yesterday. I suppose everyone has by now.

"Of course Penny, let me know if there's anything I can do."

His voice is even but kind and I take the words with me. I go straight to the office, not wanting to be late for Ms Gittings and give her any further opportunity to make a spectacle of me. It's nice to traverse the corridors whilst they're empty like this. My own footsteps echoing back to me are the only ones I can hear and I don't have to duck and weave around a crowd of other people with their own varying destinations and courses crossing my own.

When I reach the office I hesitate briefly, bracing myself to have to encounter Mr Danes after yesterday's incident, but when I knock gently and push the door open the room is empty. My mother's office is actually more like an ante-room before Mr Danes office, and it seems that he's either somewhere else entirely or safely ensconced behind his own closed door. I move forward quietly, barely lifting my feet. If Mr Danes is at his desk I may still be able to avoid seeing him. I gently roll back my mother's chair and settle into it so that I can see beneath her desk, and there on the floor is her handbag abandoned the day before. I reach down to get it but freeze midway through the movement when a sound catches my ears. A booming laugh comes from behind Mr Danes office door. It isn't his laugh, I'm sure of that- Mr Danes isn't ever booming, he's a quiet man. The laugh sounded to me like Dan Cosford.

I grab the bag and settle it on the desk before me, unsure what to do. I might have an opportunity here but time is running out before I need to get to English and I have no way of knowing if I'm right about who it is or how long they might be. I bounce a little in the seat, not sure whether I should just rise and go. I check the time, I still have a few minutes. Four, or five, maybe more if I'm prepared to run to class. I'm watching the time so closely that when Mr Danes' office door suddenly opens I let out an involuntary squeak of surprise. Two sets of eyes turn on me.

"Penny?" Mr Danes asks.

I hold up mum's bag and manage to force a smile to my face.

"Mum forgot her bag yesterday, I said I'd get it for her. I did knock," I finish somewhat feebly.

Dan Cosford's face has closed off, showing no expression at all, presumably because he can't display his true feelings in front of his boss. He turns to go but I call out quickly.

"Coach Dan!"

He freezes but doesn't turn back around.

"I was thinking, I'd really like to sign up for Cross-country this year. I've put my name down. What do you think?" I ask innocently, looking from Dan's back to Mr

Danes' smiling face.

"I think that's a wonderful idea!" Mr Danes chimes in immediately.

"I've never really done many extra-curricular activities like sports or anything, but I'd really like to now," I say, laying it on a little thick just in case.

"Universities do love extra-curriculars!" Mr Danes chuckles softly.

"Coach Dan, when's the first meeting?" I query, watching him intently.

He's still only turned half way back around and he's not looking at me. It seems to take an age for him to respond and right up until he does I'm not at all sure what he's going to say.

"After school today. Probably a bit short notice-" he begins.

"I actually have my running stuff with me!" I say brightly.

"Splendid! I actually have a good view of the sports field from my office window here, I look forward to

seeing you blaze a trail around them later today Penny!"
Mr Danes tells me, smiling simply and honestly.

Dan turns now, a sneer on his face that he barely
tries to disguise.

"I suppose I'll be seeing you later then," he
grudgingly offers, before turning and marching away up
the corridor.

Mr Danes looks speculatively after him.

"Is everything alright Penny?" he asks me gently.

"Sorry?" I reply, sweat beading on my neck.

"Are people treating you well? You can always talk to
me."

I was ridiculous really, to be worried about getting in
trouble for yesterday. I underestimated the impact of Mr
Danes' pity. He works so closely with mum that I
suppose he can never really forget what my family has
been through. I contemplate telling him about Ms
Gittings pulling her hand away as though my skin would
burn her, but really I can't imagine it would help.

"I think some people will just take a little time to get

used to everything," I murmur.

"I'm fine though," I add when he still looks concerned.

"I'll do whatever I can for you Penny, don't hesitate to come to me with anything," he stresses, "Have you got any front-runners for university choices?"

I mumble something incoherent and beat a hasty retreat. The practical part of my mind knows that a letter of recommendation from Mr Danes would look great in my uni application, but I'm not prepared to think about it right now and I definitely don't want to admit to him that I have no idea in the least where I want to go.

I do have to run to English, taking the stairs two at a time, and I arrive gasping. Ms Gittings looks at me suspiciously, no doubt wondering whether I've just come from a fresh bout of axe murdering, but I can't keep the smile off my face.

"What happened to you?" Charlie whispers to me as I settle into my seat between her and Luke.

"I successfully signed up to Cross-country!" I

whisper back.

Luke gives me a quick high-five that he then turns into an unconvincing cough under Ms Gittings critical gaze.

I don't care. She can be as unpleasant as she likes, I have cross-country training with a psychopath to look forward to.

Ms Gittings is *very* unpleasant. She spends the lesson making snide remarks about my future in a manner just subtle enough to keep Charlie from jumping over the desk and attacking her.

"*Some* of you will be looking forward to bright futures, and university is the first step to attaining them!" she sings, sneering slightly across the room at me.

"For those of you deserving of any kind of success," she begins, pausing significantly and throwing me a dark look, "Hard work will be your most important tool."

I wonder if she sat at home last night planning inane statements like these just so that she could make it clear that she doesn't think that they apply to me. I grit my teeth and keep my head down and my eyes fixed on my work. Little does Ms Gittings know, hard work isn't my issue- a complete absence of any kind of plan for my future is. Jokes on her, right?

Charlie is seething again by the time the bell rings and we're all flooding out into the corridors. Luke however looks thoughtful.

"She's an evil old hag, no doubt, but... what do you think she thinks you did?" he asks.

"Sorry?"

"Well, she seems to *really* hate you! But, why? You didn't do anything to her or anyone she cares about-"

"I didn't do anything to anyone!" I cut in, stung.

"You got your dad arrested," Charlie chimes in cheerfully.

"Yes, thanks for that hun, good reminder," I reply bitterly.

"Is Ms Gittings friends with your dad?" Luke asks me.

"What?! No!" I exclaim in surprise, studying his face

to see whether he's joking, but there's no sign of humour in his features.

"It's weird then, right?" he comments, still clearly puzzled.

"I don't know if it is that weird. People vandalise the homes of killers and send hate-mail to their families and stuff after they're arrested," I tell him.

"Really?"

"Yeah, it's like they blame them for what their family member did, even if they had no idea it was happening. Like their lives haven't been completely blown apart by it already," I grumble.

"Wow. People kind of suck."

"Yes Luke darling, they do indeed. Let's get some lunch."

We learn from our mistakes and opt for sandwiches and cardboard trays of fries, taking them with us out of the building and round to the corner outside of the art block where Charlie and I sheltered through free-period yesterday.

"Took my advice I see," a voice says from behind me.

I spin round to find Chris pushing the door from the art block open with his hip, his hands occupied by a sandwich and fries of his own.

"You didn't make yourselves easy to find," he adds, settling on the floor alongside us.

"If you recall, that was sort of the point."

I'm not unhappy to see him, but I'd admit to being surprised. After the drama of the previous day I would have expected Chris to keep as far away from me and Charlie as possible, but here he is. Chris didn't attend the same primary or secondary school as us, he transferred here for sixth form when his family moved to the area. He didn't grow up here, with the story of Rose woven into the fabric of the town. He's only been here for one year and he learned the story only as it related to Charlie's disappearance and subsequent recovery. I wonder if it looks different to him, viewed from the other side- just the prologue to the story in the news. I wonder what he believes about us.

"What sandwich did you get?" Charlie ask, leaning round me.

"Pesto chicken."

"Pesto chicken?! I didn't even see that!"

"They were just bringing them out when I was queuing," he explains.

"I got ham and cheese! I would have got pesto chicken!"

"Go halves?" he suggests, offering one half of his sandwich to her with a smile.

"Yes!"

Charlie is delighted and I can't help but smile at her obvious glee.

"So you have cross country today?" Luke asks me, making an effort to keep his voice even.

"Yep, I sure do," I confirm happily.

"You run?" Chris asks me.

"Yeah, normally just on the treadmill but I've signed up for cross-country this year," I tell him, giving Charlie a brief warning look that she totally ignores.

"She wants to spy on Coach Dan," she tells him through a mouthful of pesto.

"Charlie!" I snap.

"What?!" she asks, eyes wide.

"Don't tell people that!"

"Chris isn't *people*, he shared food with me!" she whines imploringly.

I sigh and give my head a quick shake.

"Coach Dan? Is that the smarmy guy?" Chris asks incredulously.

"Yeah, that's him," Luke agrees.

"I can't believe you like him!" Chris exclaims, clearly more than a little horrified.

"I don't like him!"

"Nooooo, she thinks he's a psycho killer!" Charlie explains before I can dig my elbow into her ribs.

"Ouch!" we cry in unison.

"You used your bad arm didn't you. Serves you right!" she tells me, massaging her side.

I gingerly lift my sleeve to expose the long, jagged

scar that still mars my arm in a ferocious red hue. It serves as a physical reminder of my adventure. I obtained it smashing a window in my efforts to escape captivity with Charlie, and it healed badly. The cut was deep and resulted in impressive blood-loss, but the doctors at the hospital were able to clean it out and stitch it up neatly. That should have been it, but unfortunately the nightmares that I suffered with every night resulted in much thrashing and struggling and I kept tearing the stitches and reopening the wound.

"Geez!" Chris cries, seeing my mutilated arm.

I quickly start to tug my sleeve down, the fabric bunching and catching on itself.

"I have one too!" Charlie declares, pulling up her own sleeve and exposing an inch long scar straight across her arm.

"No!"

I didn't mean to say it. And I didn't mean to grab her arm, wrapping my hand around it to hide the neat red mark. I close my eyes against the wave of nausea and

I feel the immediate heat behind my eyes and wetness on my face.

Charlie leans forward, resting her forehead on mine.

"Sorry," she murmurs.

"It's ok, it's ok, it's ok," I whisper, more to myself than to her.

Charlie was traumatised by what happened, she couldn't not be, but her defence against that pervasive fear is to be matter-of-fact and blasé. I'm trying my best to catch up, to match her beat for beat, but it's a struggle.

"What happened?" Chris asks in a quiet voice.

I don't know if he's asking what happened to our arms, or what happened just now, but I take a steadying breath and try to look calm.

"That's where my dad cut her with a knife."

I push the words out, proud that my voice doesn't shake.

"And Penny smashed a window with her bare hands to get me to safety," Charlie adds, her voice ringing with pride.

I furiously wipe away my tears before making sure that my arm is completely covered by my sleeve once more. That scar on Charlie's arm has a peculiar way of breaking me right down to the ground. Of all the things that my dad did in his mad crusade, that one act is the hardest for me to fathom. He wanted to change the existing narrative, that Charlie had run away, and force the police to consider foul play. His plan was simple, leave one of Charlie's shoes, bloodied and broken, in the same woods where Rose disappeared ten years ago. It was a strong plan, they wouldn't be able to ignore the implications, but for it to work he needed some of Charlie's blood. And he got some.

"Bloody hell," Chris comments, looking between us.

His face is inscrutable and I wonder if this is it, if this is the push too far and we've scared him off.

"You two are going to be able to write some cracking personal statements for your uni applications!"

There's a brief silence as we all digest his words and then suddenly the tension snaps and we're all laughing.

Literally rolling-on-the-floor-laughing. My eyes are streaming and Charlie is clutching a stitch in her side. By the time we hiccup ourselves into silence I feel ten pounds lighter.

"I like you Chris," I say at last, lying on the grass tear-streaked and tired.

Charlie's voice is small but I can hear the gentle melody of her smile in the words.

"Me too."

Chapter 6

First up after lunch I have maths. Feeling it to be a banner day for enlightenment, I decide to utilise the wisdom gleaned from 'Yesterday Penny'. Sitting at the back of the room was clearly a mistake so I return to my usual seat, on the end of the middle row, next to Josh. I feel the awful prickle of uncertainty as I ease myself into the seat, but after all- he did leave it empty.

"Hey Penny," he says briefly, allowing me to let out my anxious breath.

"Hi Josh, good summer?"

"Yeah, not bad. Went to Spain with my mum," he

tells me.

He shows me a few pictures on his phone and I ooh and aah appropriately. It does look amazing.

Mr Stines appears from nowhere, leaning over our shoulders and making me jump half out of my skin.

"Ah! Barcelona!" he cries.

Josh nods quickly and fumbles to put his phone away before it's confiscated.

"Some of the most beautiful architecture in all of Spain! Brilliant inspiration Josh! Lets talk about applicable maths in architecture!"

It's actually an interesting lesson. We spend the hour calculating angles and heights and weights, figuring out which equations we need and which values we can work with. One answer leads to another and another in a pleasing way until the picture is fully built up, populated by all the relevant details needed to build the structure. The time passes so quickly that the bell catches me unawares and I wonder how mum is doing. I have her bag safely zipped inside my backpack while she remains ensconced at home.

As I make my way to science I fire off a quick text message to Coop, letting him know that I have the bag and that I'll be going to cross-country practice after school before coming home. I ask how mum is even though Coop doesn't seem to be on the same 'open and honest communication' page.

"Penny!" Sophie cries, pulling me into a hug as I enter the classroom.

I hug her back, feeling myself flush a little at the sign of affection.

"How are you?" she asks me.

The words are met by the screech of wooden stools on hard, linoleum floor, as everyone within ear shot turns to hear my answer.

"Fine," I say disappointingly, "you?"

She fills me in on her summer as we slip into our seats and I wave for Abed to join us.

Abed is so quiet that his goofy sense of humour seems charming and unexpected, while Sophie is calm, even and capable. I've been sitting with them both in science classes since GCSE year.

It sounds like Sophie's summer was packed with sports. She plays football, netball, tennis and badminton, which tends to keep her pretty busy.

"I see you signed up for cross-country!" she exclaims.

"Yep! First practice today!" I agree, smiling.

"I'll be there too! It's so great that you signed up!" she enthuses.

"What about you Abed? Good summer?" I ask.

It seems that Abed mostly played Fifa this summer, effectively shutting the conversation down. It's fine though, Mrs Haskins enters and all the talking immediately dies down anyway. She's one of those rare teachers who never needs to raise their voice or call for attention, she just stands ready and we all fall in line. I think it's because she seems so genuinely nice.

She starts the class with the now familiar speech about A-Levels and working towards our futures and not letting ourselves down. It's starting to make my chest feel tight. Does everyone else know what they want to do?! When did people stop asking what I want to be when I grow up? How long am I supposed to have had the answer ready?!

"Now, divide into threes and go through the sheet in front of you. I want to start out today with a refresher, just to make sure you're all caught up and remember where we finished off last year. Seven groups of three, read through the set questions and discuss."

I'm with Sophie and Abed of course and we're making fairly good headway when Mrs Haskins drifts over to us.

"Hello you three, good summers?" she asks before colouring furiously as she realises what she said.

Abed blushes right alongside her but Sophie steps into the breach, her speech just a little too hurried to be entirely unconscious.

"I'm on a lot of sports teams," she says.

"Well that sounds lovely!" Mrs Haskins replies gratefully.

We all nod along, pleased with ourselves for navigating a difficult situation that had arisen so unexpectedly.

"I was hoping to ask you three a favour," she says, as though suddenly recollecting why she's here.

"Alright"

"It's the first open evening soon, for prospective students and their parents. I'll have some simple experiments set up in here and I need volunteers to help out for the evening and demonstrate them to people as they look around. Does that sound like something you three would be interested in? It would be something extra to mention in your university applications!"

We all agree quite happily and Mrs Haskins promises to give us the finalised date and all the details as soon as possible. It's nice to see that she doesn't think I'd scare off prospective students. Perhaps it's only Ms Gittings who's taken against me.

Ms Gittings and Dan Cosford. I mustn't forget Dan Cosford, though to be fair to him, he at least has some reason to dislike me. And dislike me he does.

Sophie and I go straight from science to the changing rooms when the bell rings and we swap our uniforms for running gear.

"Won't you be too hot in that? I have a spare vest top if you want to borrow it," Sophie offers, seeing my long sleeves.

I hastily mumble something, pulling the fabric right down to my wrists.

"Ladies?" the shout is followed by a booming knock, then a pause for decorum, before Dan enters.

He's dressed in gym clothes, a cap and whistle and he's clutching a clipboard in his hands with grim determination.

"I'll be putting you all through your paces today. I need to get an idea of where you're all at fitness-wise."

No speeches from him on the importance of our final year of school or university applications. He leads us straight out to the school field and he doesn't look at me once.

"I wonder what's wrong with him?" Sophie mutters under her voice as we do our warm-up stretches.

I raise my eyebrows enquiringly.

"Oh of course, you don't really know him do you? I've been on teams he's coached for years, he's normally fun! Sort of chatty and charming, you know?"

I don't know. Charming is not a word that I would use to describe Dan Cosford.

"Maybe he's just having a bad day," I suggest.

He is having a bad day, thanks to me. I allow myself a small smile but it's quickly wiped from my face.

"Right. You'll be running laps of the field. I'll be timing each of you, so try to keep your pace up. Lets start with ten laps and go from there," he orders.

There are groans and grumblings from some of the other girls, but we all trudge to the starting line and await the whistle. The sound cuts through the air and we surge into motion. My legs are pumping and my lungs sting from the sudden flood of cold air, but I relish the movement. The tussocks of grass and generally uneven terrain is a world apart from my nice flat treadmill at the gym and soon my legs are cramping and sore, my ankles straining to adjust for new angles. I long to stop and massage my calves but I force myself to keep going. The group of us, about eight in all, has drifted as we've progressed, forming more of a panting line than an efficiently working mass.

"You're a good runner!" Sophie calls to me from a couple of metres over. We've roughly kept pace, something I'm very proud of, but she's definitely faring better than I am overall. Whereas she's able to offer praise and encouragement, I feel that if I tried to speak I might just vomit or pass out.

By the time we stagger to a stop my chest is heaving and my lungs are on fire.

"Amazing!" Sophie tells me, holding her hand up for a high-five.

I take one step towards her before giving up and letting myself fall to my knees, my hands on the floor, gripping the grass as I try to slow my breathing. I would feel embarrassed if I was the only one in this state, but actually Sophie is the only girl still standing.

She plonks down beside me on the grass with a laugh and nudges me with her shoulder.

"Penny that was fantastic! I didn't know you were such a good runner."

I give her a withering look but she laughs again.

"It's supposed to be this hard! But you did great! That was such a good finish time!"

She's right. One girl has only just reached the finish line and there's someone still running, while I am slowly starting to get oxygen to my brain again.

"Thank you," I say quickly, feeling unusually precious about the air I'm expending to talk.

"Do you go running in town?" she asks me.

"Gym normally," I say, shaking my head.

"The treadmill? I bet running on grass felt different then."

"Very different. And not better," I agree.

"It gets easier. You'll need different shoes too," she

tells me, looking down at my trainers.

"What? Why?" I ask, protectively observing my purple Asics shoes.

"Trail shoes will be better on this terrain."

I file the information away so that I can do some online browsing later and then I return my attention to my breathing. It's almost back to normal but my chest still stings with each inhale.

"If you're finished, you need to do some warm-down stretches and then head to the showers," Dan barks, his eyes on his clipboard.

I would feel impressed that he's managed to go this entire time without looking at me once, but I just feel annoyed that I haven't learned anything useful. It seems that the usually chatty Coach Dan doesn't want to talk in front of me. Perhaps he's concerned he'll give something away.

I stumble my way through some stretches, my legs screaming out for mercy with every new position, and then I follow Sophie to the showers. This is an aspect that I hadn't considered. I knew that there were showers of course, I'd just never had cause to use them. A standard PE session didn't require a shower and as Luke pointed out, I've never engaged in a group sport in my life. I've never even entered the shower room, let alone used it! My steps slow as we approach. I'm picturing a large, communal space interspersed with shower heads and I'm wondering whether it might not be worth catching the bus drenched in sweat.

"Come on," Sophie says cheerfully, stepping around the wall that separates the showers from the rest of the changing room.

I follow behind her and let out a small sigh of relief. Cubicles. Not exactly perfect, but good enough to allow me to shower. I grab my towel and change of clothes and pick the shower cubicle at the end so that I can tuck myself away in the corner to dress.

I'm glad I took the leap, when the hot water hits my skin it feels like heaven. My sore muscles could sing and the feeling of the sweat clearing my hair is delicious. I step out and wrap myself in my towel, pulling on my bra and pants before I even leave the cubicle. As I pull back the latch and step out, I see Sophie, wrapped in her own towel, sticking her head around the central partition and calling out to the changing room,

"Bye Coach Dan! Great session!"

I hurry to my clothes and start to pull them on, not bothering to dry myself in my haste.

"Penny?" Sophie asks, seeing me in surprise.

"Was that Coach Dan leaving?" I ask quickly.

"Yeah, did you want to talk to him? He's already gone, I think he said he has plans in town," she informs me regretfully.

I stop tugging jeans up my wet legs and try to think. If I can get into town in time, maybe I can see where he's going. I don't have any kind of plan, I just know that so far I've learnt nothing new.

"I wonder when the next bus is?" I ask absently.

It takes me a moment to realise I asked the question aloud and another to realise that Sophie didn't answer it.

I look at her and open my mouth to ask again, but her eyes are on my arm. My skin is red and blotchy from running and my scar is a flaming red gash. It looks ghastly and I blush up to the roots of my hair, pulling my sweatshirt on just over my bra and shoving my t-shirt into my bag.

"Sorry," Sophie mutters, "I didn't mean to-"

She trails off uncomfortably, my wonderfully unflappable friend, definitely flapped.

"It's fine," I tell her, letting out a controlled breath.

It is fine, it's just a scar. It's just something that happened, not like Charlie's that was done *to* her. I push that thought away and focus back on the matter at hand.

"Do you know when the next bus is?" I ask again, checking the time on my phone.

"I have my car, I can give you a lift. Where do you want to go?"

"Into town."

Chapter 7

I'm lucky. Sophie drops me off outside the Co-op since that's where I told her I was going, and I find Dan almost immediately. I round the corner onto the High-street and there he is, in jeans and an Abercrombie and Fitch pullover, moseying along as though he has no reason to hide. I follow along behind him at a distance of about twenty metres, keeping him in sight but not invading his space so much that he would actually notice me. I'm just starting to wonder where he's going when I see her. A small figure is visible hovering by the bus stop. Her dark hair is perfectly styled and her tired face is skilfully made up but I recognise her even at a distance because of the pronounced swell of her belly. He's meeting Tina. I need to get closer. I can't quite pinpoint why, but I'm keen to see them in a public place, to see how they act together. I quicken my pace a little and use the bus stop to block me from view.

"It that really what you're wearing?" I hear him ask her, his expression puzzled.

I can't hear her reply, her voice is too small, too quiet.

"God Tina, you're not stupid, don't pretend you are, you do these things on purpose."

He sighs and presses the bridge of his nose like he's trying to draw on internal reserves of strength.

"I could go home and change!" I hear her offer frantically.

"There's no time now, but you already knew that, didn't you," he says coldly.

"But I don't understand? What's wrong with this? I thought you liked this?" she asks desperately, her voice slightly raised now in her panic.

"Come on Tina, use your brain just a little bit!"

He pauses a beat but her face is a mess of confusion and dismay.

"Look, it doesn't matter. It's fine. I'll just have to try not to think about it. It just sucks because I was really looking forward to this, I never get to see my friends because of you and I thought that this might actually be fun, but whatever."

He starts to walk away, expecting her to just fall in line, which she does, hurrying along beside him. I follow.

"But you saw your friends a few days ago," she reminds him pleadingly.

"Oh I'm sorry Tina, I didn't realise you had a problem with it!" he exclaims bitterly.

"I don't!"

"If you didn't you wouldn't be mentioning it! You always have to pick everything apart, don't you! You can't just let me be happy!"

In contrast with his words, his tone is

conversational, like he's merely puzzled by her behaviour.

"But, I'm not meaning to-"

"Look Tina, I know it's difficult for you because none of these people like you, but you just have to try harder. Actually use your brain a little and think about what you're saying! And a word of advice- these are my friends, so when you act like I'm some monster when they know I'm not, it's obviously not going to do you any favours."

He quickens his pace and she keeps following, desperately trying to stammer apologies that he just isn't listening to. I feel a bit sick but I keep moving, staying behind them as they head into a tapas restaurant. It sounds as though they're meeting other people here so maybe I should just go. I don't want to risk Dan catching me following him, but I'm reluctant to leave Tina. Maybe it's some sort of ingrained feminist solidarity. She's losing a game that I'm not even sure she knows she's playing.

Without giving myself a chance to second guess, I

slip into the restaurant as soon as I see them slide into one of the big booths. I select a booth too, but a small one, backing onto theirs. I'm practically back to back with Dan Cosford and the knowledge sends a chill through me.

"What can I get you?" A cheery voice asks, making me jump.

I quickly point to something on the 'small plates' menu and my server sails off with her notebook to make it happen. I pull out my phone and try to look natural as I actually strain to listen to the conversation behind me. I hurriedly shift my gaze down to my phone screen again as another couple arrives at their table. When Dan Cosford stands to greet them with hugs and air kisses all round, I dip under the table and try to act as though I'm looking for something. When another couple arrives a few minutes later it must look as though I've dropped everything I own under that table.

I rummage in my sports bag, my head down, until I'm sure that no one else is joining them. I can't keep leaping under the table without arousing suspicion.

Stray words catch my attention but it's hard to follow any particular thread with so many conversations going on at once. They're all catching up with each other's news and asking about other friends and acquaintances, but Tina's voice is conspicuously absent, it takes a while for her to relax and start to speak. Once Dan starts talking to one of the other guys about his work as a Personal Trainer, Tina starts a tentative conversation with one of the women. It sounds like she's talking about the pregnancy and I start to hear a smile in her voice.

"Tina," I hear Dan's voice summoning her but the woman she's talking to is speaking and Tina doesn't respond immediately.

"Tina!" his voice is harder now and I feel a small shiver of fear.

"Typical," he booms with a good-natured laugh, "Someone just has to pay her a little bit of attention and you can't drag her away."

The rest of the table laughs along with him and I don't need to turn around to picture Tina's flushed, unhappy face.

I feel my blood bubbling in my veins in sympathy for the casual humiliation.

Tina's voice drops out after that. I wait for it to pick back up again as I eat my salt and pepper chicken wings, but it never does.

"So, shall we head to the bar then?" Dan asks the group in a bright voice once their table has been cleared.

There are general murmurings of assent and they start to stand, shuffling into jackets and heading for the door.

"Tina's too tired, she's going to go home," Dan announces after hesitating a moment by the table.

She mumbles something but I can't make out the words. They all say goodbye to her cheerfully and the two women come back over to give her brief, one armed hugs and kisses.

"Are you sure you're alright?" one of them asks her in

concern.

"I'm fine, just tired," Tina hastens to assure her.

She does sound tired. Her voice is weak and once the group is out the door, she slumps back into her seat.

"Oh Tina! I forgot my scarf!"

I twist in my seat. It's the woman who checked on Tina, hurrying back to the table with a flustered smile. She digs behind her seat and retrieves the scarf. Winding it around her neck.

"Bye then!"

She moves to leave but before she can go, Tina's hand reaches out and clasps her wrist. I shuffle over a little, to get a clear view of what's happening. I can see Tina's face, desperate and sad.

"It's always like that," she whispers plaintively.

"What?" the woman replies, her tone wary.

"It's awful! Couldn't you talk to him? Please!"

She's breathing the words rather than speaking them aloud and I've leaned closer to catch them.

The woman pauses, her body tensed, before she

replies.

"Relationships, even marriages, are a choice Tina. If you were *so* unhappy you would just leave."

Her tone is cold and she pulls her hand out of the slackened grip.

"Dan is such a nice guy, I don't know why you have to make things so difficult."

She marches away and I see Tina crumple. Not on the outside, she just leans back slightly, her arms wrapping around her middle, but on the inside.

Her face barely moves but somehow she is the absolute picture of despair.

And then her eyes meet mine.

I walk home in the twilight, my thoughts running on a loop. I keep replaying every moment of interaction between Tina and Dan, ending with Tina's desperate plea for help.

"Where have you been?!"

Mum's voice is sharp and brittle. Shards embed

them selves in my skin the moment I walk through the door.

"Oh! I- um-"

"Where have you been Penny?! You didn't text, you didn't call, you just didn't come home!" she cries, her eyes wide and frantic.

"I'm sorry mum, I forgot-" I begin feebly.

"You forgot?! I've been terrified! I called you and messaged you and *nothing*! I've been frantic!"

"I'm sorry, I didn't mean to make you worry," I tell her sincerely.

"What did you think would happen then? When you just didn't come home, what did you think the result would be?!" she demands.

Honestly, if I'd thought about it at all, I would have assumed that she wouldn't notice. She's been in bed since her meltdown at school and I would have expected her to stay there for a few more days. Her new meds really are an improvement.

"I was just hanging out with Sophie after cross

country, I must have forgotten to take my phone off silent after school," I tell her, pulling my phone from my pocket and wincing at the sight of all those missed calls.

"I'm so sorry mum," I repeat, stepping tentatively towards her.

With a gasping sob she pulls me into her arms and clings to me, her chest heaving.

"I'm fine mum, I promise," I murmur with my face full of her hair.

"Are you acting out because of my scene at school?" she asks, pulling back and studying my face.

"What? No!"

"Is that what this is? I would understand, I really would. I am so sorry about that Penny. I'm sorry I keep embarrassing you."

Her tone is so sad and earnest tears sting my eyes.

"No! Mum! It was just an accident! I'm wasn't *punishing* you!" I tell her desperately.

"I've made you an appointment with Janet for tomorrow afternoon."

"What?! Why?! I'm fine!" I insist.

"I should have made the appointment as soon as the incident happened on your first day back," she says, shaking her head, presumably at her own inefficient parenting.

"I don't need to see Janet!"

"You'll have to miss your afternoon classes, but your mental health is more important. *That* is my priority. I am so sorry Penny," she says again, pulling me back into her arms.

I want to argue, to tell her again that I don't need a session with my therapist, I just had my phone on silent, but Coop is standing in the kitchen doorway and his eyes clearly ask me to give in.

"Alright mum," I murmur with a sigh, "Thank you for setting it up for me."

I'm rewarded with a bright, genuine smile. There's a light in her eyes that was inconspicuous in it's absence but now that it's back I don't know how I didn't miss it all this time.

Sleep is an elusive creature. I lie in bed, slowing my breathing, counting my inhales and exhales and willing myself to fall asleep. My body is exhausted, my legs heavy, but my mind is racing. Dan's friends obviously love him, but to me he seemed like a monster. I play back every word he said to Tina and I wonder if I'm reading too deep into it. Am I listening to his words or am I looking for my own meaning in them? Am I just searching for confirmation of my own preconceived notions? It's a trap that police fall into all the time. They find their suspect and from that moment on they see everything through blinkers, blocking out any other possibility. Is that what I'm doing here?

No.

Tina's face when she asked the other woman for help- that wasn't in my head. Tina Cosford is afraid. She's terrified. I want to know why.

I finally drift off as light starts to filter through the gap around the curtains and my alarm wakes me before

I've even started to dream.

"You look ghastly!" Charlie exclaims when she sees me.

"Well thanks for that, good to know."

"Was cross-country really that bad?!"

"No, I just couldn't sleep last night," I explain.

She raises her eyebrows in enquiry and I sigh.

"I forgot to take my phone off silent. Mum was calling me in a panic and I didn't answer. She was... upset."

"She was calling you? When you were at cross-country?"

"No, after that."

"After that? Surely you were at home after that," Charlie says slowly, nudging me step by step to a full explanation.

"No, I was following Coach Dan while he went out to dinner with his wife and friends."

"Penny!" she exclaims.

"What?"

"Did you let Luke know? You must have, right? Because you didn't let *me* know!"

My silence is answer enough.

"Penny Cooper! We had a deal! We will stop you going off the mental deep end but you have to tell us when you're sleuthing so that we can keep you safe!"

"Well, I'm getting my comeuppance for breaking the rules, I have an appointment with Janet this afternoon. First one my mum could book."

Charlie lets out a low whistle.

"Your mum works quickly!"

"It would appear so."

"And she drove you in today?"

"Yep, she's back at work. Back on track providing me with consistency and a reliable structure to my day."

"And a lift to school."

"Yes that too," I agree.

"Apart from Monday, she seems better," Charlie suggests tentatively. It's a fragile concept and she doesn't want to break it with clumsy handling.

"She's much better," I agree, my tone light.

We leave it at that, neither of us quite confident enough to take the conversation further.

"You know I'm going to tell Luke on you, right?" she says after a moment.

I should have expected no less.

Chapter 8

It's one of those odd quirks of life, that the passing of time is so heavily impacted by one's occupation. If say, you're occupied by dreading a session with your therapist in the afternoon, the morning will pass by in a flash. I barely have time to pull out my pen in science class before the bell is ringing to signify my free period has begun. Neither Luke nor Charlie have a free now, so I just wander around outside avoiding anyone I see. I consider trying to find someone else, maybe Sophie or Josh or even Chris, but I don't know their timetables yet and I don't want to risk going to to the common room when for all I know they're sat learning about German verbs or rock formation.

Instead, I go on doing solitary loops until five minutes before the lunch bell, then I station myself outside Charlie's French class and wait for her to appear.

"Shame you weren't taken to France when you were kidnapped really, isn't it!" a sing-song voice calls out, over the initial babble of people stepping into the corridor.

I tense, straining to see what's happening, and find Claire Netherhall looking impossibly smug. Charlie is a few people ahead of her, keeping her head down and speeding through the crowd in silence. I see the elation on Claire's face when she realises that Charlie isn't going to fight back. But what could she say? Any argument that she could make, any detail that she could reveal, would hurt me and my family. She isn't going to do that.

Claire's books are stacked in her arms because her bag is some ridiculous patent leather purse that none of them could possibly fit inside. I don't think, I just move forward through the crowd and directly into Claire, my elbow flicking up and sending the books spinning out of her grip. Thanks to the force of my arm they go in every direction and she lets out a small screech of anger and alarm. I force myself to stand still and look at her with a level gaze.

"Oh, I'm so sorry Claire. It was an accident," I shrug.

I'm making no effort at all to sound sincere and she glares at me with open hostility.

"Penny! You are such a-"

I don't wait to hear it, I just walk away. I hurry a little to catch up with Charlie, linking my arm through hers.

"Hello you."

"Penny! Shall we get some lunch? You're going to need your energy for your battle with Janet- Gosh, what happened there?" she wonders, seeing the commotion behind us as Claire hastily tries to gather all of her books before they can be trampled by the mass of students traversing the corridor.

"Karma," I say in a playful voice.

Charlie studies me intently.

"*You* wouldn't be karma in this particular instance, would you?"

"What can I say? Sometimes the forces of justice and equality need a helping hand."

"You didn't attack her, did you?" Charlie asks quickly, practically walking backwards in her efforts to get a clear view.

"Just her books," I admit grudgingly.

"Ha! Well that karma could just be for her ridiculous school bag!"

"Very true, she got what she deserved."

The moment I say it I pull up short, my hand pressed to my mouth. I know those words. Those are the words that the Facebook user named Nomatter said about Charlie when she was missing. Those words filled me with fear. I feel a little sick at using them myself and I wonder what that says about me, but I'm not sure I care. I'm pretty certain that it was Claire behind that account anyway. Claire slowed me down finding Charlie.

Claire kept information and even photos to herself that would have told the police that Charlie was really in trouble. Maybe I should have attacked her after all.

"Well thank you karma," Charlie tells me, bumping my hip with hers.

"She's giving you a hard time?"

"She's the only person outright *saying* that she thinks the whole thing was some kind of prank, but the more she says it, the more I can see other people doubting."

"Maybe it should go to trial," I suggest with a sigh.

"No way! I meant it Penny, I will get *torn apart* at trial! Claire bloody Netherhall saying it is bad enough, but a lawyer saying it and all the papers saying it?! Everyone will know how much my fault it all was! Call me a coward if you like, but I really don't want that."

"Charlie, it was *not* your fault," I tell her firmly, keeping my voice low.

She rolls her eyes but gives me a small smile and unexpectedly kisses me on the cheek. Charlie's always been a touchy-feely person but more so than ever after everything that happened.

"Oi! Penny is mine thank you very much!" a voice cuts in a moment before Luke leans between us and puts an arm around each of our shoulders.

"*Yours*?!" I demand, drawing the word out, my eyebrows practically swallowed up by my hairline.

"The thousand closest feminists just started rolling up their sleeves for battle," Charlie tells him.

"Alright, alright, point taken," he demurs, carefully withdrawing his arms.

"Those were very foolish words, mate," Chris chimes in, shaking his head in disappointment.

Charlie unhooks her arm from mine as we soften from a knot of two to a group of four.

"We doing sandwiches and chips again?"

We do indeed do sandwiches and chips, though Charlie also treats me to a cookie.

"Penny needs a little comfort food in preparation for

her uncomfortable afternoon," she explains.

"Why? What lessons do you have?" Luke asks, puzzled because he has my timetable noted down in the front of his day-planner.

"My mum has signed me out for the afternoon. I have an appointment with Janet," I grumble.

"Her therapist," Charlie explains to Chris in a stage whisper.

"She has a therapist?" he asks, clearly shocked for a moment.

"You don't?" she asks in tones of surprise.

"Charlie has one too," I say, as though it's the ultimate accessory that no teenaged girl should be without.

"Mine is called Claudia. She believes in *positive thinking* and *emotional honesty*."

"Janet's keen on those too, but she also likes *appreciating the world how someone else sees it*."

I think that this might be because Janet wants to repair my relationships with my many parents through practised empathy. She's asked in every session whether or not I've been trying to appreciate how my mother sees the world. She even asked the same about dad but I wasn't particularly patient with that one.

"Why the sudden visit with Janet?" Luke asks.

I glance quickly at Charlie but she just frowns and rolls her eyes.

"No reason?" I try hopefully.

"I'll explain later. You can scold her tomorrow when she's feeling emotionally regulated," Charlie tells him brightly.

"Emotionally regulated? From two hours talking about myself?!"

Chris grimaces in sympathy, Luke smiles and Charlie laughs, but I know that therapy is helping her. She gets something from her talks with Claudia that she doesn't get anywhere else. She always seems lighter and calmer after her sessions- not like a weight has been lifted exactly, but maybe like she has a better hold on it.

Janet's office tries too hard. It has comfy chairs and beanbags on the floor and shelves full of books. It's a lie. It's not like I could actually spend the session sitting in an armchair, reading- it's a deceit designed to lower your guard. All the chairs just give you the illusion of choice. Would you like to sit on a sofa and talk about yourself? Or sit in a beanbag and talk about yourself? Or lay on the floor and talk about yourself?

It's safe to say I haven't warmed to Janet.

Today I choose the regal looking armchair in slightly faded red brocade. If I'm going to be asked invasive questions, I at least want to feel like Sherlock Holmes when it happens.

"What would you like to talk about today Penny?"

Excellent hostage negotiation tactics. Use the subject's name. Humanise them. Make them feel that you have a connection, that you understand them.

The silence drags out.

"Your mother mentioned that there was an incident. That you dropped out of communication for an extended period of time."

Typical. The *incident* isn't her public meltdown in front of half the people I attend school with, it was me forgetting to take my phone off silent mode.

"Talk to me about that Penny. Do you think you were hoping for a reaction?"

I roll my eyes. Janet is a moron. You could argue that I've given her very little to work with since I do my best not to tell her anything or talk about anything of any real importance, but she's a therapist! She should be able to work some things out for herself, shouldn't she?!

"Dad called," I say unexpectedly.

I'm not sure where that came from but I watch Janet closely for her reaction. I expect her to start scribbling furiously in her notebook, but she just looks at me, her gaze steady and calm.

"From prison," I add, waiting for her flinch.

She just gazes back at me through clear, hazel eyes.

"I think he might plead not guilty. That would mean a trial."

Saying the words out-loud is freeing somehow. Putting the fear into words, breaking it down into syllables and letters. Vowels and consonants.

"How would you feel about a trial?" Janet asks, her voice even.

I sigh, pushing the air out through my teeth.

"I don't want a trial!"

She doesn't say anything, just continues to look at me.

"We're already a spectacle. People are talking about us all the time. People are hassling Charlie at school!" I tell her hotly.

She still doesn't respond and I feel a tension, bubbling beneath the surface of my skin.

"People think we're freaks and psychos! They think that I'm dangerous! They think that Dad killed Rose!"

I come to a screeching halt.

"And would a trial make that worse?"

Janet's voice is light but I know that she sees it.

"No, a trial would probably prove he didn't kill

Rose," I admit quietly.

"Probably?"

"He didn't do it!" I need her to understand this. I need her to know that he would never have hurt my sister.

"Every crazy thing he did, was because he wants to find Rose! He's desperate to know what happened to her!" I explain.

This is about as much as I've ever spoken to Janet about what happened in the summer. I expect her fingers are itching to make notes on my tone and inflection.

"Do you think that was his only motivation?" she asks me, taking me by surprise.

"Well, I think drugs played a part in his reasoning..."

"Not his reasoning, his motivation."

I don't know what she means. Dad wanted to know what Charlie saw the day Rose went missing. Then he saw an opportunity to bring fresh attention to the case and get it reopened, and he took it.

"This is what I've been talking about Penny.

Appreciating how other people see things, how they experience the world and how that experience shapes their actions. What do you think motivated your father?"

"I don't know! I don't care! If you think it's important why don't you just tell me?!" I demand, impatient with games.

"I think that your father was motivated by guilt."

"He didn't kill Rose!"

"I'm not saying that he did," she replies calmly.

I take a couple of breaths, thinking it through.

"He wasn't there to save her. He wasn't there,"

This thought tugs at the corner of my mind but I push it away.

"Does that matter? Does his motivation matter?" I demand.

"I think that one day it might matter very much."

I snort and cross my arms over my chest. I don't think I ll ever stop being angry enough that I'll actually care about dad's side of things.

"What do you think motivates your mother?" Janet

asks.

"What? Well- she wants to protect me. Dad wanted to find Rose and mum wanted to focus on keeping me safe."

Again Janet doesn't answer me, she just sits there looking at me in my big wing-back armchair.

"Fear," I mutter finally, "and guilt."

Because isn't that present in every moment too? Hasn't mum been desperately trying to protect her remaining daughter as some kind of penance?

"Does it matter?" I ask again, wearily.

"Doesn't it?"

I sigh but it's a sad, tired sound.

"What motivates you Penny?"

Her voice is still calm, like she hasn't just asked me a crushing question, heavy with the weight of my very existence.

"I- I don't know," I stammer, looking around the room as though I might find inspiration here.

"Break it down. What do you want?"

I pause. These are absolutely the type of question that I've been dodging from Janet since our very first session. These are topics that I've worked hard to stay away from.

"I want to know what happened to Rose," I breathe.

"Why?"

I do not feel better. I don't feel that a weight has been lifted or that I have a better hold on things. I feel twisted up and bitter. I want to run or shout or hit something. A defiant rage is bubbling within the heart of me and I want to let it out.

I didn't have an answer for Janet.

I don't know why, but I couldn't for the life of me think of anything to explain why I want the truth about Rose. The truth! What's wrong with wanting the truth?!

She never explicitly said that I should just *let it go*, but the idea was there. By posing the question she attacked the foundation of my certainty in my own actions. Just because I can't put together some eloquent explanation of my *motivations* doesn't mean I'm wrong to want to know who took my sister from me, does it?!

I considered telling her about Dan and Tina Cosford. I might have been able to make her understand that I see a monster when I look at him. I'm certain that he could hurt someone again. But would that be an acceptable motivation? And what might she do with that information? Who might she tell?

And then there's Coop and the seed of doubt that my dad planted. What would Janet have had to say about that?

I pace up and down in the street outside her office building, waiting for my bus to come. I wish I could run home but it's too far and most of the way there aren't even pavements. I breathe deeply, trying to slow my heart and steady my thoughts. By the time the bus pulls up I've regained some semblance of calm. I don't need Janet's infuriating introspection, I need to *do* something. I need to be proactive.

I let the bus take me past my house. I've not ridden

this particular bus this far before and I overshoot by a stop, watching my goal flash past me. I ring the bell and hover anxiously by the doors waiting for them to open. When we finally judder to a halt I leap down, my legs jarring against the pavement on impact and I start walking back the way I came. It's not far but it's already almost three and every minute passing feels like a minute wasted. School ends at three and I won't have long after that.

The house looks just as bland and innocuous as it did last time I saw it but I'm more sure than ever that it's not a happy place. I approach from the right, careful to keep close to the building and stay out of view of the front window from next-door. I'd rather that Dan didn't hear about my visit. I knock and ring the bell, not wanting to waste any more time, but it still takes Tina a few minutes to come to the door. She looks tired, pale and far younger without her make-up on and her hair styled. Fragile. Vulnerable.

"Tina?"

Her eyes are wide with alarm and they dart quickly up and down the street before she steps back quickly, ushering me inside.

"Who *are* you?" she demands.

"Penny Cooper," I remind her feebly.

"That's not what I meant. What are you doing here?!"

She's whispering and I feel my heart rate ramp up.

"Is he here?!" I hiss.

"What? No- no, he's not. But he will be soon. You can't be here! I'm not allowed to have people at the house!"

She's stopped whispering but she's still speaking in a hushed voice, as though she can't bring herself to risk a normal volume.

"I'll be quick," I assure her.

"Why are you here?!"

"There's something I need to see."

I lead the way upstairs and into the main bedroom. There are still no signs of Tina in here, not a hair tie or a single piece of clothing, this is Dan's domain.

I drop to the floor before the wardrobe and pull the doors open, shuffling inside. So many boxes, but I remember with perfect clarity the one I'm looking for. I hunt for the plain, unassuming box, perfectly free from dust. I remember the exact size and hue.

It isn't here.

"There was another box in this wardrobe," I say frantically, turning to Tina.

She's hovering in the doorway, afraid to come all the way into the room. All she can do is shrug helplessly, her arms wrapped around herself for comfort.

"I don't know! I don't come in here! I clean once a week in this room and he watches me the whole time! This is his space!"

With a muttered curse I shift to the bed, lying flat on the floor to get a good view beneath it.

"You need to be quick!" she pleads, "why is this box so important? What is it you want with us?!"

She has no idea why I'm here. Some strange girl has

stormed into her life without giving a reason. I broke into her house, I followed her and her husband, and here I am again, going through their home. All that and she's just letting it happen because whatever I do, I am less of a threat than the one she already faces.

"I think that the box contains proof that Dan is dangerous," I tell her.

She moans softly, her arms wrapping tighter around her middle.

"Why don't you run?" I ask.

She's shifting nervously from foot to foot, like she could take off at any moment but she doesn't.

"You should run Tina, you're not safe here!"

"I know."

Her voice is so low I almost miss it.

"So run!"

"Run where?! I have no friends. I have no money. I don't have a bank card, I never have. There's no phone, I don't have a mobile or a computer. He has a laptop but I'm not allowed to touch it! Even if I managed to use his phone without him knowing, my family is in Devon! They're seven hours away! He would know I called them before they could ever reach me! What am I supposed to do?! I've been with Dan for ten years! *Ten years of my life*! I don't have anything else left! There's no way I could make it alone!"

Ten years.

I try desperately to focus on the terror in Tina's voice. I try to prioritise the fact that she is clearly afraid for her life. But I can't.

Ten years.

Tina looks so young with her tiny petite form and her big, sad eyes that it never occurred to me that she could have been in Dan's life that long. She must be older than she looks. I can't believe that I never even wondered- I never thought to ask.

"Tina, ten years ago, did Dan-"

A lock clicks downstairs, like gunfire in the quiet of the house.

"Tina!"

It's a summons. She takes a breath and tries to look natural. I see the effort in every step as she makes her way across the landing. She throws me one last agonised look before her face disappears from view.

"Hi Dan!" I hear her say, her voice soft but filled with a terrible false brightness.

"Why were you upstairs?"

"I was just lying down for a moment in my room."

I hastily make sure that everything looks just as it did when I arrived and then I tread softly onto the landing. I strain to hear but they've moved their conversation to the lounge. I risk moving down a step, and then another. I go slowly despite my every muscle screaming at me to run. How can I be back in this situation?! I think fleetingly of the key in Dan's dresser, but I discard the notion. I'm not going back for it and leaving Tina to try to hide it again, I'm going to keep moving slowly down the stairs and get to the front door. Each step is agony and the closer I get to the bottom the more clearly I can hear their voices.

"How was work? Good day?" Tina asks.

"It was a long day Tina. I just want to have a moment to relax before I have to face your inquisition, is that seriously too much to ask?"

His voice sounds so close that I break out in a sweat.

"I'm sorry Dan, I-"

"I just want to sit down in my own house and have a few minutes to rest. I've been at work all day. Can I just sit down please?"

"I'm sorry, of course you can! Sit down-"

"I have your permission, do I? You really are unbelievable. What gives you the right to talk like that? What do you actually contribute? I thought that our lives were going to be so amazing Tina. I thought we were going to be so happy, you were so wonderful, but it was all an act wasn't it. As soon as you had me trapped, you dropped everything I ever liked about you."

"I didn't mean to, I don't know what-"

"Tina can you just get a drink? Is that too much to ask after a day at work? I shouldn't even have to ask.

You're not stupid Tina, you knew I'd want a drink, you could have got me one but no. You have to put me in the position of asking, right? Just so that you can have something over me?"

"Dan, I didn't mean to- I'll just go get it, I'll get it now."

I'm at the door now, my hand on the latch but I can't bring myself to turn it. I can't leave her here.

As I hesitate she steps out into the hall. How can she be even paler? Soon she'll disappear entirely into the magnolia wall behind her.

"Go!" she mouths silently.

"Come with me."

I breathe the words as quietly as I can and hold out my hand to her. She takes a step towards me and then another. I turn the latch and gently ease the door open. I reach a little further for her hand and she takes one more step towards the door.

A cough makes her head swivel round. She turns back and pushes me through the door, shutting it behind me as softly as she can but it still gives a click that makes my heart stutter. I hear Dan's voice, muffled through the door.

"What the fuck are you doing?"

"The door wasn't closed properly, I'm just-"

I run.

It feels sickening and cowardly and awful, but something tells me that Dan finding me here won't do Tina any favours. When I'm halfway down the street I risk a glance back and my chest constricts. Dan is standing in the road looking along it in my direction.

Did he see me?

I run home, as though it's not already too late. If he saw me he saw me. But did he?

I have to fight the urge to turn back. I want to burst into the house and drag Tina away with me. I remember with perfect clarity the look in her eyes when I held my hand out to her. She wanted to leave, I could see it. That woman wants to run.

Ten years. I keep turning the fact over in my mind, that Tina has been with Dan for *ten years*. My sister went missing ten years ago and I'm sure that Dan is responsible but I never even thought to ask Tina about it.

"Penny? Are you alright sweetheart?"

My head snaps up. Mum is looking anxiously at me across the dining table.

"Sorry?"

"Are you alright?" she repeats.

I look back at my food. I don't even remember how I got here. I don't remember the run home or the time in between then and now, it's all lost in a haze of my own anxious internal monologue and fears for Tina Cosford.

"I'm fine, just thinking," I tell her, summoning up a smile to soothe her worries.

"Did you have a good session with Janet?" she asks.

My smile falters.

"It was fine. How was work?"

"Good! I had a really good day!"

"Me too!" Olly pipes up with a beaming grin.

"Oh really? What did you get up to?" I ask him.

"I had pizza for lunch!"

We all laugh and Oliver looks affronted.

"What?" he demands.

"Nothing Olly Wally, it's just not exactly an expansive description of your day," I explain.

"Oh. But- lunch was the best part," he tells me with a shrug.

"Pizza isn't exactly healthy for a school dinner. I thought you'd been learning all about healthy food choices," Coop comments.

"There were lots of vegetables on it. That makes it healthy."

"Vegetables?! I exclaim in tones of horror that earn me a glare from mum.

"It's alright though, I just picked those off."

I laugh again but this time I'm alone.

"Vegetables are good for you," mum says pleadingly.

"And delicious!" Coop adds brightly.

Olly looks unconvinced.

"You like some veggies Olly," I remind him.

"Not pizza ones," he replies firmly.

"Maybe we should have a pizza night soon," I suggest, eyeing mum discretely.

"A pizza night?" Olly queries suspiciously.

"Yeah. A pizza night. We'll make our own pizzas, with just the good veggies, but *lots* of them!"

"*Make our own pizza*?!"

He's already starting to bounce in his seat.

"Yep, we can talk in Italian accents and make pizzas."

He's now moving so fast that it's walking the line between bouncing and vibrating.

Mum and Coop are both beaming at me and I can't help the smile that tugs at my own mouth.

"Pizza night!" Olly cries, throwing both hands into the air in glee.

"We'll do it soon Olly, so you better get thinking about all the great veggies we can use," I say.

I keep up the golden child routine through the rest of dinner and I even offer to wash up. I don't want mum sending me for any more appointments with Janet, and if I'm going to keep sleuthing and investigating I may need some favour that I can trade on down the line. Besides, standing at the sink, my hands tingling from the hot water, I can let my mind wander. I need to check on Tina and make sure that she's alright, but how do you check on someone who has no phone and no access to emails or any other form of communication? I can't imagine being so isolated. I've always been introverted, but at least I've had a choice. Tina is trapped, with no one but Dan Cosford in her life, controlling her every move.

I wish I knew for sure whether or not he saw me.

I sleep badly, tossing and turning, tangling my limbs in the bedsheets so tightly that they begin to feel like ropes.

"Penny! We're going to be late!"

Mum's voice is bright but there's an edge to it that

sends me down the stairs two at a time.

"Sorry," I pant as I reach the hall.

"No breakfast again?" she asks, hand on hip.

"Not hungry," I tell her, bowing to Olly's suspicious gaze.

It's true. I'm not hungry at all. My stomach is churning, thinking about Tina and wondering what kind of monster I've left her alone with.

Mum sighs but doesn't put up a fight.

We drop Oliver off at school and again we wait until he's through the doors before we pull away.

"Olly doesn't seem to be getting questions or anything at school," I say, my gaze still fixed out the window.

"Are you getting questions?" mum asks quickly.

"And Charlie," I tell her, giving a vague shrug.

"I'm sorry," she says in a low voice.

"It's not your fault."

"This is *all* my fault," she sighs.

Even from here I can see tears filling her eyes and I

don't know what to say.

"We should do pizza night tonight," I suggest, turning back to the window.

Perhaps guilt is my motivation, or maybe fear, but whatever the reason I decide to walk with mum to her office before going to morning registration.

"Chivalry," I say casually when she asks.

"Well it's much appreciated," she responds with a small smile.

I give a fake bow as she unlocks the office door.

"We're here before Mr Danes?" I ask.

"All his charity work remember. Thursdays he drops off supplies with the food-bank."

"Blimey, the man's a saint."

"You need to ask about volunteering," mum reminds me.

I do. She's right, it would look great on a university application, if I ever decide where I want to go.

"Do you know Dan Cosford at all?" I ask suddenly.

"Dan Cosford?"

"My new cross-country coach," I explain.

"Oh! Of course! You have another practice today, don't you?"

"Yep, just while we're getting in shape after the summer, then it drops down to one session a week," I confirm.

"You're enjoying it?" she asks me as she settles behind her desk.

"Yeah, running is good. Coach Dan though..."

"You don't like him?"

"How long has he worked here?" I ask, side stepping the question as best I can.

"I'm not sure, longer than me I think," she replies vaguely.

"Did he work here ten years ago then?"

Mum's attention has shifted to her computer and she just 'umms' in response but a voice comes from behind me.

"He did work here ten years ago, yes. He'd worked here a year or two by then."

I flush and spin around to see Mr Danes smiling from the office doorway.

"Oh! Mr Danes! Sorry, I didn't know you were-"

He holds up a hand to quiet me.

"It's alright Penny, you can't expect to like *every* teacher. Your secret is safe with me," he chuckles.

My flush deepens and I cast around for something to say.

"I was just talking to Penny about volunteering," mum mercifully supplies.

"Yes! I'm looking to do some volunteering! For charity!" I agree eagerly.

"That's brilliant news! There are so many worthy causes out there! I'd be happy to help you set something up!" Mr Danes beams at me.

"Brilliant! Well, anything I can do to help save the world," I offer awkwardly.

"I'll find some options for you, but in the meantime, how about you start with heading to class," he suggests.

I gratefully agree and hasten into the corridor,

counting my blessings that it was Mr Danes who overheard my questions about Dan, rather than the man himself. It's interesting to know that Dan Cosford was already working here at the school when Rose disappeared. I'm not sure it really moves me further forward, but I'm sure that my dad would have something to say about him working around young girls for so many years. Even his wife looks far younger than her age.

I do my best to push these thoughts aside as I walk into registration and tumble into the seat beside Charlie.

"Have you even heard of sleep?!" she demands, taking in my dark eyes and wan face.

"Maybe briefly, but I guess I kind of thought it was just a myth," I reply, resting my head on my arms on top of the desk.

"It's not. Have you been sleuthing again? You better not have been following anyone or doing any breaking and entering!"

I sigh.

"Not exactly."

"Not exactly?! *Penny*! We both have second period free today. You have to tell me absolutely everything you've been up to so that I can decide how mad I am."

To start with, very mad.

Luckily this initial rage doesn't last and by the time I'm finished she's chewing a curl of blonde hair, her eyes so wide that she's reminding me of Tina.

"What are we going to do?" she asks.

Six words. Just six words but I absolutely love her for them.

"Well, first things first, I need to check on Tina."

"You're not *sure* he saw you?"

"Nope, but he definitely could have," I tell her grimly.

"Bugger."

"Indeed."

"You have cross-country after school today, right?" she asks.

"Yep. Two practices this week and next, then it drops

down to one."

"So he won't be home until gone four-thirty?"

"He won't, but I'll be at cross-country. If he *did* see me and I don't show up at training, he might be suspicious. What if he realises I've gone to Tina and he goes straight home? I could make things even worse," I say.

"So I'll go. You go to cross country, and I'll go check on Tina."

I pull her into a tight hug before scribbling down Dan's address on a loose bit of paper and watching as she stows it safely in her bag.

We lunch with Luke and Chris again, but the weather really is getting too cold for sitting outside on the grass. We'll need to find somewhere else soon or brave the canteen again. For now the cold is bearable and it gives me an excuse not to talk. I sit beside Luke, curled up into him to steal his warmth and I shiver quietly in a ladylike fashion.

"How was Janet?" he asks when I've been quiet too long for it to go unnoticed.

"Oh you know, she just tore my life apart for the hell of it," I shrug nonchalantly.

"Yeah... Claudia doesn't do that to me," Charlie remarks.

"Maybe you need a new therapist. Is that a thing? Can you just trade her in?" Luke queries.

"Not really. There aren't a huge number of therapists locally and Charlie has one and my mum has another." "You can't share?"

"It's not a good idea apparently. You're too aware that the other patient might have been talking about you. You don't want your therapist to know secrets you haven't told them," I explain.

"That makes sense. Still, I don't like the idea of Janet tearing your life apart."

"No, I'm not keen on it either," I mumble.

Reading my tone, Luke moves the conversation on and the three of them chatter away happily. I do my best to dial in to their frequency but my mind keeps drifting back to Dan Cosford. Did he see me?

I have a solitary free period after lunch so I stay where I am on the grass, uncomfortably aware of Luke's absence beside me. My whole right side feels cold beyond belief and my attempts to distract myself with my maths homework are futile. The numbers keep slipping away across the page as my eyes lose focus. Eventually I give up and spend the rest of the hour walking around outside. It feels good to keep moving and it's easier to let my thoughts run their course. As my limbs thaw out a little, I finalise my plans. I message Charlie because I won't necessarily see her again before the final bell, and I tell her to message when she gets to Dan Cosford's house and then to keep messaging so that I'm aware of what's happening. I in turn will message her as soon as cross country practice ends so that she can get the hell out of there. We don't want to risk anyone else potentially being seen lurking outside Dan's house.

I feel better by the time I head to my science class.

It's good to have a fixed plan, and when Charlie messages me back with a thumbs up at my instructions, I can almost concentrate on what Mrs Haskins is saying.

"Is that alright Penny?"

My head snaps up and I force a quick smile.

"Yes! Absolutely! Sounds good!" I hasten to agree, wondering what on earth we're talking about.

Mrs Haskins is fixing me with one of her kindest smiles and I suspect that she's noticed that I'm not really 'with it' today.

"Are you alright Penny?" Sophie asks me under her breath, leaning in close.

"I'm just really tired. I've not been sleeping well," I tell her, figuring that a half truth is better than no truth at all.

I've barely spoken to Sophie or Abed all lesson and they're both shooting me furtive looks of concern.

"Are you coming to cross-country? I can tell Coach Dan if you need to go straight home," she offers.

"No! No, I'm definitely coming. Running will do me

some good, it'll help tire me out."

Sophie looks at me doubtfully, and it's no wonder since I look absolutely exhausted already, but she doesn't call me on it and when the final bell rings she waits for me so that we can walk to the changing rooms together. I keep my phone in my hand, waiting for my first message from Charlie confirming that she's reached the Cosford house. It doesn't come until I'm already on the field, my phone slipped into the pocket of my leggings.

I try to steady my breathing. She's there. She can check on Tina. It's going to be fine.

"You ready?" Sophie asks me eagerly.

She's bouncing on the balls of her toes, raring to go, and I quickly start stretching, trying to match her energy despite my depleted resources. We all line up and I look back over my shoulder at Dan Cosford and I freeze. He's looking at me. For once he's not ignoring my presence, he's looking right at me. A small smile hovers over his mouth and I could swear that the look in his eyes is amusement. My stomach clenches.

He saw me. He must have seen me.

Fear for Tina cuts through me at the same time as the starting whistle sounds and I tear off down the field. We're doing ten laps again, our muscles still sore and aching from Tuesday's session, but we all move off. Sometimes running feels like flying. Sometimes my gait is just right and the ground seems to barely exist and the world just streams by. This is not one of those days.

My legs are screaming out to stop and my lungs are heaving as my stomach rolls, but the look on Dan's face pushes me on. I keep moving, faster than I thought possible, scared to look back because I can't quite believe that he's not behind me, closing in.

Adrenaline is coursing through me and by the time I reach the finish I collapse straight to my knees and dry retch. I flush to the roots of my hair, my face going from red to burgundy, but there's no one there to see it. I've left the other runners behind.

I push myself up to sitting, looking around in a fresh wave of panic. Where is he?!

I sigh and flop backward. He's still here, he's at the finish line behind me, noting everyone's times as they reach him.

"Oh my God Penny! That was incredible!" Sophie gasps as she tumbles to the ground beside me.

"Where did that come from?!" asks Molly, a girl I remember hazily from long ago French lessons.

"Faster you run, sooner you stop," I gasp.

They both laugh and I smile but I keep my eyes fixed on Dan. He hurried out of here last time, but that was because of his dinner plans. Will he take longer today? Or if he saw me in his street, will he be rushing home to guard Tina? Maybe I should be messaging Charlie now to tell her to flee. I pull out my sweaty phone to check for any updates and my stomach sinks. I have half a dozen messages from Charlie, all saying basically the same thing.

There are no signs of life at the Cosford house.

Chapter 9

No signs of life. No signs of life. No signs of life.

The words are on repeat in my head. Every time the bus stops I feel like I'm going to scream. People are moving so slowly that I start to wonder if it's on purpose. What if there's some huge conspiracy trying to slow me down when Tina is in trouble.

No signs of life. No signs of life. No signs of life.

Am I already too late?

Charlie's remark, probably made unthinkingly, is blocking out all other thought from my mind. By the time the bus finally crawls to a stop at the end of my street I can barely breathe. I'm out of the doors before they even have time to fully open and I race down the street on legs that still shake with exhaustion.

"Penny! You look awful!" Charlie exclaims.

She's waiting outside my house just like she said she would be and I fall gratefully into her embrace.

"I didn't stay to shower, I just went straight to the bus stop," I tell her breathlessly.

"I can see that."

"So what happened?" I ask, searching her face.

"Nothing. Like I said, I didn't see anything at all. The blinds are down and there was no movement at all. No lights were on, no sound of the TV, nothing to show anyone was there," she explains with a small shrug.

"But Tina should be there!"

"Maybe she's gone away? Maybe she's staying with friends?" Charlie suggests vaguely.

"She doesn't have any friends! Her family is hours away! She's alone!"

Charlie's trying to absorb this, I can practically see

the wheels turning, but she still can't quite comprehend it.

"Maybe she ran?"

Her words are hesitant but I grasp them gratefully.

"Maybe. Maybe she ran!" I agree.

I start to think it through. She was definitely ready. She was ready to leave him, I could see it in her face. She was terrified but she would have gone with me if he hadn't started to come towards the door just then. Maybe she really did it, maybe she saw an opportunity and she ran.

"No. I don't think so," I say thoughtfully, "Dan looked so... smug. He was smiling at me like he'd won, like he'd defeated me."

"Penny, do you really think he'd actually hurt her?" Charlie asks, disbelief still ringing in her voice.

"Yes."

She tries to find the right words but she doesn't see Dan the way I do, she hasn't met Tina or been inside their house. To her this is all hazy what-ifs rather than the concrete certainty that I feel. She's saved by my front door opening behind her.

"Hello you two, I'm off to get some pizza bases. Charlie? Are you staying for dinner?"

Coop's voice is bright and cheery and jars uncomfortably against my panic. I try to take a slow breath and find my footing.

Charlie looks a question at me and I press my face into a smile.

"How's your Italian accent?" I ask.

Charlie's accent is horrendous, but so are the rest of ours. Mine is so awkward and stilted that I have to keep repeating myself over and over until a phrase sounds bearable. Charlie clearly learned hers from watching the Godfather and she's not afraid to go big with it.

"Ai Maloney I wanna the pepperoni!" she cries theatrically, gesturing wildly with one hand.

"Maloney?" I query in an undertone.

"Maloney rhymesa witha alla the good Italian

wordsa!"

"Such as? I mean, um- sucha asa?"

She considers this for a moment in some confusion.

"Pepperoni!" she cries eventually.

Olly is delighted. He goes into whoops and treats us to shouts of 'Oi Maloney I wanna the pepperoni!' for the rest of the evening.

We create a small pizza each, selecting our toppings with care. Charlie makes a picture with hers, turning her pizza into a work of art. Oliver of course wants to do the same and we're able to guide him towards a colourful, though admittedly unrecognisable, picture of a Pokemon, incorporating more veggies into his meal than mum could have imagined, in even her wildest daydreams.

Once they're all in the oven we start the important task of selecting something to watch.

"Why aren't we eating at the table?" mum asks in despair.

"Because it's Italian night!"

"What does that have to do with the table?"

"Everyone knows Italians don't eat at the *dining table*!" Charlie announces shamelessly.

Mum rolls her eyes but gives in, knowing it was a fight she was never going to win.

"Ratatouille!" Olly insists.

"Isn't that set in Paris?" Coop asks.

"That's closer to Italy than we are here," Charlie shrugs.

We decide that food and funny accents is enough for Ratatouille to fit our theme and I make a mental note to find some more Italian films before we do this again.

The pizzas are surprisingly good and Olly eats every single vegetable on his, even the yellow pepper.

"I love Italian night!" Olly exclaims.

His eyes are bright and his cheeks are a little flushed, both sure signs that he's tired and about to crash.

"It was brilliant! So brilliant that I need an early night," I tell him.

"Very Italian," Charlie adds, nodding sagely.

"Really?" Olly queries, eyeing us both suspiciously.

"Oh definitely! Italians go to sleep really early because it gets dark so much earlier."

Charlie is fabulous at lying to Olly. She can tell him the most ridiculous and outlandish falsehoods with a perfectly straight face.

"Why does it get dark earlier in Italy?" he asks immediately.

Charlie grimaces at me and I glare back at her. She made this bed, there is no way I'm going to be the one to lie in it.

"Err-" she starts feebly.

"Dad! Why does it get dark so much earlier in Italy?" Olly demands as Coop comes in to collect our empty plates.

"What's that Buddy?" he asks, confused.

"In Italy! It gets dark earlier than here."

"That's why they go to bed earlier," Charlie adds hopefully.

Coop sighs.

"That one might not be quite worth it Charlie," he suggests.

Charlie sighs back, but then does embark upon a complicated explanation to Olly that despite what she said, it does not in fact get dark earlier in Italy than in England.

"Unless you count the time difference, but I'm not sure if that goes forward or back" she finishes eventually.

"Time difference?" Olly asks.

My heart sinks.

"It's super boring Olly, don't worry about it. Charlie and I are going to help clean up in the kitchen."

I drag Charlie to her feet and out the door before Olly can protest.

"You need to be more careful," I tell her.

"What?"

"Did you want to spend the next hour explaining time difference and looking up the time in different countries? Because that's what was about to happen!"

"Oh!" she laughs, "Yeah, I'm glad we escaped!"

Charlie and I do help clean up, though really mum and Coop had already done most of the work.

"Well Italian night was certainly a success!" Coop declares happily.

"It certainly was! Thank you for this girls, it was brilliant. We'll have to do it again soon!" Mum adds.

"Would this be a good time to ask for a favour then?" Charlie asks hopefully.

"Favour?" I enquire suspiciously. Why it this the first I'm hearing of it?

"Mum wants to have her friend Marion to stay overnight soon. She's the one who lives in Cornwall and she hasn't visited in a couple of years. Problem is, she's scared of dogs..." Charlie trails off.

Mum and Coop's faces have been transformed by expressions of absolute panic.

"The dog?" mum mutters in accents of horror.

"Overnight?!" Coop asks.

"Probably just the one night! Or maybe two," Charlie admits.

"How's the house training coming along?" Coop asks.

"Um... better," Charlie replies uncertainly. I can't help it, I snort in amusement.

Charlie looks daggers at me and I quickly try to turn the sound into a cough and think of a way to backtrack and lend my support.

"I'll walk him! Loads! And Olly would love it! And... I'll clean up the pee! And maybe he could sleep in the bathroom so it's easier to clean up! Or we could open the back porch-"

I stop abruptly. Where did that come from? We locked up the porch when Rose went missing and haven't used it since. We got a new back door that only provided access to our securely fenced off garden and left the back porch to rot. My eyes search mum's face for any sign of panic or distress but she just looks thoughtful.

"Alright. Penny, so long as you accept full responsibility for all dog duties and clean-up. I suppose a night or two with that terror might cure Olly of any dreams of getting a dog of our own."

Charlie looks affronted but she's too sensible to push it.

"You let us know dates and we'll give the porch a good clean. You're right Penny, the tiles will make it much easier to deal with any... accidents."

Her voice is light but I can see the slight strain in her face. I feel an immense swell of pride for the progress she's making and a faint shiver of uncertainty about what I've suggested.

"Sounds good!" I say brightly.

Charlie flings her arms around mum, gratitude tumbling from her lips. It's only then that I see Coop's face. His expression is inscrutable but for some reason it makes the hairs lift on the back of my neck. I open my mouth to ask him what's wrong but no words come.

Charlie eventually has to go home. Mum offers her a lift but Charlie insists on calling her own mother to pick her up, just one more move in her battle to get a car.

With my friend gone my mind reverts back to its steady loop of one question after another until I feel ground down with uncertainty.

Did Dan see me outside his house? Where's Tina? Is she safe? Did she run? Did Dan see me?

No answers come before I finally fall asleep, gratefully allowing the darkness to smother my thoughts.

In fact, no answers come until I arrive at school the next morning and go to my locker to get my science text-book. Resting atop the jumble of books and loose papers is a single, perfect, blood red rose.

He saw me.

"Penny?"

Charlie's voice sounds muffled, as though it's coming from impossibly far away.

"Penny? Are you alright?"

I can just about hear her but I can't make myself turn and look at her. I can't force my mouth to move and form a response.

"Penny?"

A different voice this time, deeper and more sure of itself. Luke folds his arms around me, guiding me gently one step to the left, breaking my line of sight with the rose. I spin round, the spell broken, searching the corridor frantically but it's filled with the usual mass of swarming babbling students.

"Why is that there?" Charlie asks, her voice high and strained, like a violin wire pulled too tight.

"He must have seen me," I murmur, my voice sounding foreign and harsh.

"He must have seen me in the street, he knew I was there, he knows I've been talking to Tina, oh God! Tina!" I end anguished and wild.

Luke pulls me back into his arms, his grip tight.

"I need to go!" I say frantically, trying and failing to push him away.

"But we have school," Charlie replies feebly.

"School?" I laugh.

It's a bitter, crumpled sound. Distorted out of any semblance of amusement.

"If he realises you're not here, he might know where you've gone. It might be worse for her," Luke tells me reasonably.

"She could be dead already!" I hiss, trying to keep my voice low in the crush of the crowd.

"She could not."

His voice is so calm and I stare into his eyes, trying with all my might to seep out a little of his peace for myself. He's right. If Tina is dead then- what? What's to be gained by running off half cocked to her house? I need to operate under the assumption that she's alive, in which case I could do more harm than good by running off there now.

"I have netball today," Charlie tells me, obviously forcing herself to rally.

"Netball?"

"Until five. He'll be home at five fifteen at the earliest," she adds.

"Ok," I murmur, willing myself to calm, "Ok, five fifteen."

Hopefully that'll give me enough time for whatever it is I need to do.

The day crawls by at an agonising pace. Each breath seems to last an age and I find myself watching the second hand on the clock tick round in every class. The final bell is a starting pistol, sending me hurtling outside, ricocheting off of small collisions but refusing to slow down. It's ridiculous, I know it is, the bus won't leave early just because I'm on it, but I can't bring myself to ease my pace.

"Penny!"

The shout brings me up short and I nearly stumble when I grind to a sudden halt.

"Penny! Here!"

I spin round and find Luke over to the side of the bus-park, waving his hands in the air. I hesitate uncertainly, looking back and forth from the buses that aren't due to leave for at least another fifteen minutes.

"We'll give you a lift!" he calls in some exasperation.

My eyes actually fill as I jog over to him but I can

read the doubt and incredulity in his face even though the teary blur.

"I asked mum to pick us up today after what happened this morning. She's parked a bit up the road so we don't get stuck behind any of the buses," he tells me as he takes my hand.

I start to jog and as he hurries to keep up he gives my hand a reassuring squeeze.

"You really think something's happened to Tina Cosford?" he murmurs under his breath.

I don't know what to say. Luke and Charlie just aren't quite on the same page as me on this issue and I know it. If I tell him that I'm worried Tina is already dead, that I'm being haunted by visions of her wide eyes turning glazed and milky, he might think I'm going crazy.

How unhinged would I need to seem for him and Charlie to decide it's time to rein me back in?

I just nod.

"Hello Penny!" Mary calls in her sing song voice as

we approach the car.

She's warmed to me in recent weeks, though occasionally I still get the impression that she and Richard do wish their son wasn't dating the girl from the news.

"Hi Mary!" I reply, trying to keep my voice natural.

"What's the plan then my lovelies?" She asks as she waits for us to finish buckling ourselves securely into the back seats.

"Penny's house please mum," Luke tells her immediately.

He throws me a quick look but it's unnecessary. I know we can't ask his mother to drive us to Dan Cosford's house. That would absolutely result in questions that I wouldn't be able to answer.

"Rightio!"

She makes conversation with me for a few minutes but I'm so distracted that eventually Luke has to take pity on me. He claims that there's a new album he wants me to listen to and he plays it over the Land Rovers audio system. After a few seconds of panicked scrolling he closes his eyes and stabs the screen of his phone with one finger.

"Ohhh... I didn't know you liked Taylor Swift Luke," his mother comments slowly.

"Oh! Um, well, this one album is... I mean this is a new one and..." he begins blithering.

I just smile and watch him go.

"Well, you two have fun!" Mary calls, waving goodbye as she pulls away and drives down the street.

We wait a full minute, waving goodbye and then just counting down, making sure she's gone before I set off at a sprint, a panting Luke beside me. I have to drop down to a walk after a few minutes since it's apparent that Luke isn't going to keep up otherwise.

"Taylor Swift? Really? You?" I ask.

"I just went to New Releases and clicked something!" he gasps, clutching his side.

I laugh and slow even more at the sight of his red face.

"I'm never going to live this down!"

"She'll probably be buying you Taylor Swift merch for every birthday and Christmas for the rest of your life," I agree brightly.

"The sacrifices I make for you," he murmurs.

"My hero."

I take his sweaty hand in mine with a smile but it slips from my face almost immediately.

"This is their street." he mutters to himself.

I nod even though I know he's not looking at me. We're both looking along the road towards Dan and Tina Cosford's house.

My steps slow as we approach until I can't be sure if I'm moving at all. My head starts to swim and I force myself to exhale and fill my lungs with fresh air.

Charlie was right- the house is completely silent and it feels abandoned. There are no lights on upstairs or down. The blinds cover all the windows but I can still see that it's dark inside. I go to the front door, my feet dragging, and I knock.

"Tina?" I call in a whisper.

I bend to the letterbox and lift the flap but there's no gap. Someone has nailed a piece of wood over it from inside, sealing the opening. I don't know if this is a new development, but surely it must be? How would they get post otherwise? There's no box attached to the wall or anything else that could be used. For some reason Dan has sealed off the house. I go to the side gate but it's locked tight and when I reach over the top my fingertips brush what feels like a padlock. I suppose I won't be checking the back of the house then.

"Penny?" Luke's voice is gentle but I ignore him. I need to be sure, I need to know what's happened.

"It doesn't look like there's anyone here," he tries again.

I knock on the door again and press my ear to it but I don't hear anything. I move to the front window, trying to peer between the blinds to the darkness within. I get as close as I can and cup my hands around my eyes to block out the light that lets me see nothing past my own reflection.

There!

I tumble backwards, landing on my rear, as a face comes into focus. It's distorted and broken, but it's there!

I let out a dry sob and clamber back to my feet, rushing as quickly back to the window as possible.

"Tina!" I hiss.

The double glazing works against me, she can't hear me and I can't hear her, but she knows I'm here.

I press my face back to the glass and I see her huddled form beside the dark sofa. She shuffles closer again and pushes the blind aside. I hear a sound between a gasp and a retch behind me and I'm aware of Luke doubling over and backing away.

I force myself not to react, to stay right where I am, where Tina can see me through her bloodied and swollen eyes.

Her face is a deep purple with caverns of red running through it where skin has ruptured and burst on impact. I hold her bloodshot gaze and will her to understand everything that I'm thinking and feeling right now, through my look alone.

"He saw me," I say, more to myself than to her.

She sees my lips move and bows her head in confirmation.

"The door?" I mouth, pointing.

She mouths something through the scabbed mass of her lips but it takes a couple of goes before I can make it out. Locked. She's locked in.

"What should I do?" I mouth to her.

She moves away from the window and I rest my head against the glass, my breath misting in front of me. My stomach churns but I push the feeling down and take a breath, reminding myself that she's alive. Tina is still alive.

She shuffles back to the window, her movements awkward, one hand wrapped around her belly, and she places a piece of paper against the glass. Written upon it is a number and I hastily copy it into my phone. As soon as she sees I'm finished, Tina casts an anxious look into the street and moves back, allowing the blind to swing back into place as though she were never there.

I wait but she doesn't come back. The house is dark and still again.

"We should call the police," Luke says behind me. His voice is shaky and when I turn to him he looks pale and slightly clammy.

"No," I say slowly, shaking my head.

"Penny he could have killed her! Her face!"

He stops there, not knowing how to go on. I know exactly what he means anyway- I'm sure that Tina's broken face will stay with me for the rest of my life.

"No, she could have asked me to call nine nine nine, but she didn't. She asked me to call this number," I tell him, holding up my phone.

"B-but-" he stammers ineffectually.

"Luke, I have listened to endless true crime stories that started as domestic violence. If I call the police now, they *might* be able to break down the door and get Tina out, but then what? She has to argue that he's a clear and present danger and press charges right away, and even then he might be released waiting for trial. And what's she supposed to do? What's the plan for her? She gave me this number. This must be her plan to escape."

I speak forcefully and hope that he can't hear how afraid I am. Maybe we should be calling the police. Maybe we should be forcing our way into that house with all the help that we can get. I really don't know, I've never been in this position before! What it comes down to, is trusting Tina's decision. I just hope it's the right one.

We cross over the street and sit behind some parked cars. Dan shouldn't be back yet but it makes sense to be careful. I dial the number and each ring is an earthquake, a typhoon, a tsunami, until a voice cuts in, smooth and efficient.

"PC Chalmers speaking."

"Um," I begin haltingly, "Do you know a Tina?"

"Tina? My sister Tina?"

I could almost cry. A wild and heady hysteria is

clawing up my throat.

"You're police?" I choke out the words.

"For almost two years now."

I take a deep breath.

"Tina needs your help."

"What? What are you talking about? Who is this?" she demands.

"My name is Penny, I know Tina. Could you come and get her? She's not safe. You need to get her out of that house."

"If Tina needs me why isn't she calling me herself?! She cut us off! She hasn't spoken to any of us in years! She didn't even invite us to her wedding!"

She's silent for a moment as she processes her own words within the new context of my call for help.

"Fuck," she says at last.

"Yeah."

"How bad is it?"

"How soon can you be here?"

Current traffic conditions indicate that it's seven

and a half hours. Seven and a half hours to come up with a plan to get Tina out of that house alive.

Chapter 10

"What's happening?"

Luke asks me frantically when I hang up the phone.

"Well you got your wish, that was the police," I tell him.

"It was?"

"Yeah, it turns out Tina's sister is a PC. I doubt Tina even knows, she said they haven't spoken in years and Tina said she's not allowed a phone or computer access."

"So she's coming?"

"She's getting in her car right now," I assure him.

"You said seven and a half hours, right?" he asks.

"Yep. Seven and a half hours, and Dan needs to have no idea that anything is going on in that time."

"So what do we do?"

"We need to get Tina out of that house, but we need to do it at the very last moment and without Dan being aware of it. What we need is a distraction."

He follows my line of sight back across the street to the house next-door to Dan and Tina's.

"The nosy neighbour?" he asks.

"The nosy neighbour."

We surreptitiously make our way back across the street to knock on Deb's door and she answers so fast that I suspect she may have been watching us from her front window.

"Penny, wasn't it?" she asks me with a bright smile.

"Yes, Penny. And this is Luke. Hi Deb," I smile back.

"Are you looking for my neighbours again? I'm afraid Dan's still at work and Tina's away at the moment."

"Away?" I ask quickly.

"Yes, she went day before yesterday to visit family. She'll just be gone a week or two though," she explains.

Long enough for her face to heal up a bit, I bet.

"How long have they lived there?" I ask, trying to make the question sound casual.

"Five years," she answers promptly, "Almost as long as they've been together."

"You mean almost as long as they've been married," I correct.

"No, as long at they've been together. Six years. They've only been married four. They got together when she was just nineteen, he swept her off her feet," Deb recounts happily.

That's not right, the dates don't match up. I am absolutely certain that Tina told me that she and Dan had been together ten years. Ten years of her life, I remember her saying those words exactly. That would mean that she was fifteen when she and Dan first got together. I feel a sinking in my stomach as an idea starts to form there, but I don't allow myself to analyse it. I don't have time right now.

I take a deep breath and leap.

"Deb, I need your help. Tina and the baby need your help."

Deb starts off hard to convince. She has a picture in her head of what life is going to be like for her neighbours with their new baby, and she's reluctant to let it go. Once I've successfully torn it from her grip, forcing the truth into the cracks and crevices until she can't hold on any longer, she's transformed. The challenge shifts from trying to make her believe us, to trying to keep her from storming round there now and screaming for Tina to be let out.

"She's locked in. We can't get to her just by shouting. We can't break down the door, Deb. We need a plan, we need to be organised."

I keep repeating the words until they sink into her skin and become a mantra, flooding through her veins as they flow through mine.

"Alright, what do we do?" she asks at last.

I explain about Tina's sister and how long it's going to take her to get here.

"That means, what? Just before midnight?" Deb asks me, looking at the clock.

"Yep. Just before midnight."

"And then we storm the house?" she asks simply.

I can't help but smile. We'd be an unexpected assault party, we'd definitely have the element of surprise, but somehow I don't think that would be enough for us to get into the house without Tina getting hurt. No, what we need to do is get Dan out.

"You're going to provide a distraction." I tell her.

"If you want to," Luke adds in, making me flinch.

"Of course! Only if you want to Deb! You don't have to do anything you're not comfortable with," I tell her quickly.

"I want to help!" Deb insists without hesitation.

"Thank you. In that case, I'm going to give you a mobile phone," I say.

"I have a mobile phone!" she cuts in proudly.

"I'm going to give you a different one though. I want to be sure that you don't get into any trouble for anything that happens. I don't want Dan to know you had anything to do with this."

She nods briefly and squares her shoulders.

"I'll put it through your letterbox this evening. When I call it, you start the diversion."

We have to sneak out of Deb's house thanks to a message from Charlie telling me that Dan's on his way home. Deb smuggles us over the end of her garden fence onto a narrow footpath favoured by dog-walkers. From there we head away from the Cosford's street, trying to look casual and unconcerned whilst still moving as quickly as possible. I don't think we get the balance quite right, but we don't see any sign of Dan.

"What do we do now?" Luke asks me

"We buy some burner phones," I tell him.

We get a few of the cheap blocks of plastic with limited functionality that my dad favoured. I look down at them in the carrier bag and fight the exhaustion that washes over me. He made his calls to Charlie on a phone like this.

"These phones run on credit, not a contract, so there's nothing linking us to them," I explain.

"Is that important?" Luke queries.

"Hopefully not," I sigh.

I don't want to admit to Luke or anyone else how nervous I am about this. By helping Tina to disappear, you could say that I'm following in my father's footsteps. The fact that that's where the similarity ends wouldn't save me in the media if all this came out. I can practically read the scandalous and dramatic headlines now. *Another girl vanishes in Owens family's wake!*

I don't doubt that I'm doing the right thing, I'd just rather that no-one ever found out about it.

I insert a pay-as-you-go chip into each of the phones and make a note of the numbers, but with that done I'm left adrift. More than six hours until the plan gets put into action and I have nothing to occupy my time.

"I really need to get home," Luke tells me regretfully.

"Of course, yeah, that's fine," I tell him absently.

"I'll sneak out though, I'll come and help with the actual plan, but I need to put in an appearance at dinner before that."

"You don't have to help," I tell him quickly.

"Yes, I definitely do."

I give him one of the phones with strict instructions to use it for all communication about tonight's plans, and kiss him goodbye, letting myself sink into the moment.

"I'll see you later," he tells me, stressing the words like a promise.

He doesn't need to. I know he won't let me down.

I turn and start walking aimlessly, meandering around town. I want desperately to go back to Tina and watch over the house, as though by doing so I could keep her safe. She's in there with Dan. What could be happening to her?

I push the thoughts aside. We have a plan. It's not a

perfect plan, just the best I could do with such a close deadline, but it's a plan all the same.

I message Charlie to tell her that we got away from Dan's house alright and that Tina is alive. I don't know if I should say more than that, I can imagine the thought of Tina alone and captive inside her house might be difficult for Charlie to process alongside her own recent trauma. My reticence backfires however, as Charlie immediately demands that I meet her at her house and fill her in on everything that's happened. I fire off a quick message to Mum to let her know where I'm going, then I head towards Charlie's wondering how best to downplay Tina's situation.

"I'm coming with you!" she cries.

I did a rubbish job of downplaying the situation.

"Charlie, you can't-" I begin.

"To hell with that! I absolutely can!"

"Charlie, I'm going to have to sneak out! At night! You can't do that! What happens if your mum comes to check on you and finds your bed empty?!"

It feels like a low blow, using Wendy's fear, but it's true. She lost her daughter. For days she didn't know whether Charlie was dead or alive and the wounds of that experience are still raw, just starting to knit back together. Charlie sags. She knows I'm right but that doesn't for one moment mean that she has to like it.

"I *fancied* him!" she moans, her voice catching and turning into a sob as she bends double, her head between her knees.

"You didn't know," I tell her soothingly.

"You can sleep over here," she says straightening up, her tone suddenly business-like.

"Sorry?"

"Your mum can't find you missing either. You can sleep over here, I'll cover for you and I'll help you sneak back in. It'll be easier to get into my house than yours, my bedroom is ground floor."

It's a good plan and I let out a slow breath, the air whistling through my teeth.

"Thank you," I say, reaching for her hand and giving it a squeeze.

"This is crazy," she says, dropping onto the edge of her bed beside me.

"I know."

"You realise this is going to be your second daring rescue within two months?" she points out.

"I'd been thinking of it more as an abduction. You know, following in my dad's footsteps."

I try to keep my voice light but Charlie gives me a knowing look and raises her eyebrows.

"No, Penny. Definitely a daring rescue."

"Hopefully not as daring as yours," I sigh, flopping backwards to lie down.

"No, that's a good point," she agrees, wrapping her hands around my arm, her fingers splaying to try to cover the full length of my scar, but it's too long.

I call mum but she doesn't pick up so I call the house phone. Coop answers and agrees that I can sleep at Charlie's house. Apparently a sleepover sounds like 'a great way to celebrate the end of the first week of school'. I agree with him, actively ignoring the sense of unreality that's creeping in. One week. One week back at school. How can I be here, in this situation?

Wendy agrees too, though she gives me a few concerned and doubtful looks.

"What was that about?" I ask Charlie as she sifts through a stack of take-out menus

"What was what?"

"Your mum, does she not want me staying over?"

Charlie sighs and hands me the menu for Pizza Town.

"She's just worried you're going to be disturbed by my nightmares."

"Are they still bad?" I ask gently.

Her voice was flat but her eyes are bright and defiant so I know that she's feeling vulnerable.

"A bit worse again since school," she admits.

I teeter on the edge of asking her about them but as always I take a step back instead. I know it's cowardly, but I just don't want to know. I don't want the details of her experience with dad. I don't want to know what parts have her so afraid that she's waking up at night screaming. Every night I spent with her at the hospital, holding her when she woke thrashing and calling out for help, I still didn't ask a single question. It's a good thing she has Claudia the super-shrink.

"How about Hawaiian?" I say instead.

She grins.

"You *hate* pineapple on pizza!" she reminds me.

"Yeah, but I love you."

The estimated delivery time is forty minutes so we decide to wake up the dog and take him for a walk. All Charlie has to do is jingle his leash quietly and the pup is up, flipping dramatically and not so gracefully into a standing position. He's raring to go so we pull on our shoes and our delightfully ugly fleeces and set off, sharing the strain of holding the leash as he jumps and gambols ahead of us.

"Any closer to a name?" I query.

"I'm thinking maybe *Stallion*. It sounds powerful and majestic."

I gaze at the powerful and majestic creature as he snaps at a falling leaf and falls flat on his back.

"I'm not sure it suits him," I murmur.

"No," she sighs, "that is a bit of a problem."

We stroll without direction at first, but soon I start fingering an object in my fleece pocket and I start walking with a little more purpose.

"What is it?" Charlie asks me suspiciously after a few minutes and one too many specific turnings.

"Would you do me a favour?" I ask uncertainly.

"Depends what it is, but yeah probably," she says with a shrug.

"Would you post something through a letterbox for me?"

"A specific letterbox? Or would any do?"

I crouch behind a parked car at the very end of the street and watch through the merest sliver of space as Charlie and her unnamed dog walk casually along the pavement on the other side. She looks totally natural and at ease and I barely even see it when she slips the phone through Deb's door: the movement was so quick and disguised by her pretending to lose control of the dog for a moment. She's absolutely perfect.

I rest my hands on the floor, feeling myself tremble. I try to focus on the sensation of the tarmac pressing into my palms. The chill of the air. The faint buzz of the street-lights, already coming to life.

I'm still kneeling on the floor when Charlie reaches me. She went all the way down to the end of the street and then back up the next road that runs parallel, before coming to get me.

"Penny?"

Her voice is uncertain and I have to force myself up onto my knees so that I can scramble backwards and away. I brush my hands off against my legs and try to look calm and measured as we walk away.

"Everything alright?" Charlie asks nervously.

"Sure," I manage after a moment.

Of course not. I'm terrified.

Charlie doesn't ask again and we walk on in silence until my heart-rate slows and I stop looking for Dan Cosford in every shadow.

"Maybe something historical?" I suggest when we're almost back on Charlie's street.

"Oooh! That's a good idea! Historical dogs or historical people?"

"Either I guess. I don't know many historical dogs," I admit.

"I think we may need to do some research!"

We manage to pass the next hour eating pizza and looking for historical figures to name the dog after, but by nine o'clock I'm incapable of concentrating. I obsessively search traffic conditions and estimate where exactly Tina's sister should be at each moment. It's the only thing keeping me from imagining what might be happening to Tina if Dan realises that something's up. I pick up my phone to call the police a hundred times without ever actually doing it. I keep reminding myself-

We have a plan. We have a plan. We have a plan.

There's also a small, selfish part of my brain that's ticking over questions that shouldn't be my first priority right now. How long has Tina been with Dan? Does she know what happened to Rose?

A nagging suspicion started when I was talking to Deb but I can't even let the thought take form in my mind, there's too much at stake for me to admit that I could be wrong.

"Penny?" Charlie whispers from her bed.

"Hm?"

"Just checking you haven't fallen asleep."

There's no risk of that. We've changed into pyjamas and put on a show of going to bed for the night for Wendy's benefit, but I feel more awake than I have in my entire life.

"Not asleep," I whisper back."

I check the time and shuffle out of my pyjamas and into jeans and a jumper, zipping my fleece up to my chin. Dark colours. I remember my ninja outfit when dad and

I first went to investigate the Cosford house, and again I feel a pang at the parallels.

"Are you ready?" Charlie whispers, her voice catching on her own anxiety.

"Yeah, yeah I think so. It should be about half an hour until Tina's sister arrives but I want to be ready in case."

I don't say that I can't just wait any more. I need to start, to get moving and feel that I'm doing something, anything at all.

Charlie hugs me goodbye and helps me to climb out of the window, allowing a blast of cold air into her room in the process. I give her a last look before I walk away. I saved her. I saved Charlie and I'm going to save Tina.

I start walking, shooting off a quick text to Luke and one to Deb, telling them that we're getting close to time. I try waiting in a nearby street, crouched behind a row of parked cars, but it's too cold. The air is frigid, my breath misting with each exhale. I feel the wild urge to breathe out a great gust of 'dragon breath' like Rose and

I used to when we were little, but instead I get back to my feet and I keep walking. I circle the streets surrounding Dan's, not actually venturing onto his road, and my heart stops with every security light that flashes on as I pass. *This is supposed to be a safe town* I think to myself. I wonder if there is such a thing.

At seven minutes past twelve my phone chimes.

Tina's sister is almost here. It's time.

I silence my phone and the burner I bought myself, then send a message to Luke. He's in position, across the road from Dan Cosford's house so that he can act as a scout. I turn onto the street and walk slowly along it, my feet feeling impossibly heavy. This could all go wrong.

When I reach the house I creep up to it, keeping low to the ground and close in to the walls. There's a hedge that starts beside the front door and then reaches round the side of the driveway to provide some privacy for the front windows. I quietly tuck myself into it, concealed in the darkness, the branches pressing against me. I place a call to Deb and then wait, perfectly still.

One breath.

Two.

Should I have gone next-door and made sure that she was awake? Maybe she changed her mind?

I'm just considering trying to get out of the hedge and going to Deb's when the sound of glass breaking makes me freeze.

The sound came from Deb's house.

A moment later I hear her door open and the shuffle of slippered feet hurrying the few steps down her driveway. I press myself flat against the wall and try not to breathe as Deb approaches the Cosford's' door and hammers against it.

She knocks for almost a minute before the door swings open and I flinch as the light from the hallway spills out across the path.

"Dan! Thank goodness!" Deb exclaims in a panicked stage whisper, "There's someone in my house!"

"What? Deb, what do you-"

"QUICK! Please! You have to help me! Someone

broke in! I think he's still there!" Deb insists, dragging Dan along the path with her.

"Did you call the police?" he asks, still slightly bleary with sleep.

"I didn't even think of that! I just came to *you*! I knew you'd help me," Deb tells him.

That does the trick. Any reluctance is gone. Without a backward glance, Dan goes with Deb back towards her house and in a swift movement I step sideways out of the hedge and catch the door just before it clicks shut. My heart is pounding but I ease the door open and pull the roll of tape from my pocket. I rip off a short length of it and press it over the latch so that the door won't lock as soon as it closes. That done, I hurry to the stairs. We might only have seconds, I can't afford to waste even one.

"Tina!" I hiss.

A small sound comes from the bedroom that I know she sleeps in. I push the door open and there she is- sat up in bed clutching the covers to her chest like a shield.

She lets out a small sob at the sight of me and scrambles out of the bed. I look around quickly, grabbing a thick dressing-gown from a hook on the back of the door and motioning for her to follow me. She bends with some difficulty and slides a duffel bag and a pair of shoes from the wardrobe but even that movement is difficult. I help her with the shoes, manoeuvring them onto her feet and tying the laces quickly. It feels strange, like she's a child rather than a woman a few years older than me. I sling the bag over my shoulder as she pulls on the robe over her thin cotton nightgown, and we're away. We start slowly, moving with care but once the front-door comes into view we speed up, I don't think either of us can help it. We rush down the stairs and I pull the door wide, ushering Tina through. She chokes on another sob as she steps out into the cold night air, free but not yet safe.

Her body is broken and her belly is cumbersome, keeping her steps slow. Too slow. I take her hand and pull her along, lending her speed that she doesn't have alone. I know I'm hurting her, I can hear it in her wincing breaths, but we need to move. Not until we're in the next street do I allow her to slow down, and even then only slightly. I'm scanning the street ahead of us, but everything is dark. We keep moving. She doesn't even know where we're going but she follows without question, her thin hand tightly clasping mine. Then, just as her step falters, I see them - headlights.

I pray that she won't sound the horn, but she's too smart for that. The car pulls up alongside us and a moment later she's out of the door, sobbing and clutching Tina's small form in her arms. Tina is crying and shaking as her sister tenderly cups her swollen bloodied face.

"*I've got you,*" she says, over and over again.

"*I've got you now.*"

The duffel bag is taken from me and while it's being stowed in the boot I clasp Tina's hands. It's now or never.

"I need to ask you something," I whisper quickly.

She nods, her eyes wild and bright.

"Ten years ago- Ten years ago my sister went missing. Was it Dan?" I mutter, urgently, desperately.

Her eyes widen and she scans my hair, my face, with fresh recognition.

"Were you with him that day?" I press.

I can see that it hurts her to speak, a small droplet of blood blossoms on her lip as a split reopens.

"We were together all weekend," she murmurs thickly.

"It was the first time we were together, just before I tuned sixteen. He was supposed to be at some work training course with another teacher but my parents were away so he stayed home to be with me. His boss never even noticed he didn't go, he just pretended he'd been there. When we saw the news that a little girl was missing he helped with the searches, I thought he was such an amazing guy," she tells me, tears coursing down purple cheeks, running along crevices carved by his fists.

My heart has stopped beating.

A car door slams a few streets away and Tina swings

round like a rabbit caught in headlights.

"Alright, into the car Tina!" her sister tells her, gently guiding her into the passenger seat.

She turns to me, looking me up and down in surprise and dismay.

"You're just a kid," she mutters.

"PC Chalmers I presume," I respond with a small smile.

"Becca," she tells me.

I nod.

"You should go. I don't know how long you have," I tell her.

She looks uncertain, not sure if she can leave me here, but her eyes are drawn back to the car.

"I've got this," I insist.

She inclines her head slightly, allowing herself to be reassured. With a last nod of thanks she climbs back into the car and disappears into the night, ferrying her sister to safety.

At least someone can.

I call the police with the burner phone, reporting a break-in at Deb's. Luke hasn't messaged or called yet, which means that Dan is still inside with her, looking for the phantom intruder or possibly surveying the damage. It sounded from the noise of glass breaking as though Deb set the scene, but I'm not going to risk her being alone with Dan when he discovers his wife missing. I message Luke and then take a moment to breathe deeply and savour the cold night air against my skin before I start moving again. By the time we meet at the end of the road, the flashing of red and blue approaching from the opposite end signals that the police have the situation well in hand.

"Did it work?" Luke asks me in an undertone as we hurry away.

"It did. She's gone."

I leave it at that.

We split up at the end of the next street, me hurrying back to Charlie's and Luke heading home.

"What happened?" Charlie asks in a hurried whisper as she helps to hoist me back through the window.

For some reason I'm feeling incredibly tired now. I suppose the fading adrenalin has something to do with it. I hold up a hand to hush her, glancing significantly at her bedroom door. Not until I'm changed back into my pyjamas and settled on the mattress on the floor do I speak again.

"The plan worked," I say simply.

Charlie lets out a gentle sigh of relief.

"Thank God for that. I've been sat here thinking about all the ways it could have gone wrong!" she whispers back.

"I know. Dan could have refused to help Deb. He could have waited to close the door behind him. He could have gone back to his house before we had time to get away."

The more suggestions I make the more nauseous I feel. I can't believe we actually pulled it off, that Tina is safely away where Dan can't get to her.

"You met the sister?" Charlie asks.

"Becca. She'll look after Tina now, I'm sure of that."

I fall asleep thinking about the look on Becca's face when she held her sister in her arms. Would Rose have looked at me like that? If she'd lived?

"Gosh you two! This is a waste of a Saturday, isn't it?!" Wendy calls from the hallway.

Charlie just grumbles and rolls over, not ready to return to the waking world.

"I let the dog out but I'm not walking him!" Wendy's voice comes again.

Charlie sits up, a mass of wild blonde curls and disgruntled expression, as the magic word 'walk' sends the dog into a frenzy.

"That was just mean!" Charlie shouts back, her voice thick.

"He's not going to stop, is he?" I sigh from under my duvet.

"Nope."

We drag ourselves out of bed and prepare for the day with all possible haste, but our canine companion is clearly indignant at what he perceives to be a crawling pace.

"We're here! We're here!" Charlie grumbles as she clips the leash to his collar.

I stifle a yawn as we step out into the chill air. The world feels damp, in a way that tends to signal that rain is on the way.

"We need to walk him somewhere with hot drinks," Charlie mutters, throwing a dark glance at the sky.

We walk into town and Charlie's so tired that she only hesitates for a brief moment about being seen in public in her ugly fleece.

"Needs must!" she announces with determination, squaring her shoulders and marching in the direction of the cafe.

I text Luke to check how he's feeling after the night's adventure and he responds immediately. I suspect that he was waiting to hear from me, not wanting to risk waking me with a message or call of his own.

"Luke's going to meet us," I tell Charlie as we join the queue.

"Well he can buy his own bloody coffee, I'm not ordering a caramel latte however good they smell! Ridiculously pretentious drink," she mutters, ordering us infinitely more dignified hot-chocolates with marshmallows.

I order Luke a caramel latte and order three pastries too, sensing that Charlie would be the better for a little extra sugar and carbs. We collect the dog from his position tied up outside, unsuccessfully attacking passing pigeons, and head for the woods so that he can get some running in without being an absolute menace to society.

"Give me the pastry," Charlie demands, holding out a hand.

I quickly oblige, smiling at her scowl and hostile pose.

"Pain au chocolate?" she asks, peering into the paper bag.

"Yep," I confirm, chuckling as her shoulders instantly relax a fraction.

"What's with the mood?" Luke asks, sauntering over to join us with his long, easy steps.

"She's tired-" I begin before Charlie cuts me off.

"And for no good reason! At least *you two* are tired because you were having adventures and saving damsels in distress! I'm tired from being sat at home waiting!"

She finds relief in taking a vicious bite of pastry, sending crumbs flying.

"That's all I was doing too, really. I was just crouched in the street in the freezing cold doing it instead of being at home in the warm like you," Luke tells her.

Her expression softens as she processes this statement. Charlie doesn't like being cold and I can see her enthusiasm for being involved wavering.

"Honestly, I don't think any of it was as exciting as you're imagining," I add.

"Tell me then. Spare no details, I want the whole

story. That way I can *pretend* I was there," she insists.

I sigh but I relay the night's events right up to Becca's car meeting us a few streets away.

"How did she find you?" Luke asks curiously.

"I shared my location on Googlemaps on my phone. She just drove straight to us."

"And she took Tina away?" Charlie asks tentatively.

I can hear the question she doesn't want to voice and I know I won't be able to deflect it.

"I asked about Rose," I admit.

"And?!"

"It wasn't him."

There's a ringing silence as they both digest this statement and then-

"But he lied! He lied about being involved in the searches!" Charlie cries.

"He almost *killed* Tina!" Luke adds in a hushed voice.

"But he didn't kill Rose. He lied for a stupid, mundane reason and because he's a total creep!" I snap, crushing my pastry in my hand.

"Ta ta ta ta!" Charlie exclaims, lifting my hot chocolate out of my hand before it can suffer a similar fate.

I take a deep breath and then reach for my drink back.

"Are you calm? Is this drink safe with you?" she demands.

I chuckle and nod, assuring her that I'll be very careful.

"Tell us everything."

I repeat what Tina told me about the weekend that Rose disappeared. The words grate in my throat but I force them out.

"So he lied to you because he was supposed to be at some stupid training event for work?" Charlie asks incredulously.

"Not just that, he couldn't exactly say that he was here in town defiling his fifteen year old student girlfriend! So he stuck to the lie he'd already gotten away with," I say, forcing down another sip of hot chocolate though it feels pasty and foreign in my mouth.

"So he is a monster who likes little girls, but he still didn't do it?" Luke exclaims in despair.

"I think Tina's age was more about control," I reply thoughtfully.

"Well that's no less horrifying."

"No, it's not."

We walk on in silence, the only sound the crunching of twigs and scuffle of dirt and leaves as the dog continues to run on ahead.

"So what next?" Charlie asks after an age.

"Next I'm going to eat this squashed pain au chocolate," I say.

For now that'll have to do.

The trouble is of course, that I *do* have a plan. It's just not a plan that Charlie and Luke are going to like. It's not a plan that *I* like. I need to speak to my dad.

Charlie would say that I shouldn't engage with him

and his madness and Luke would be worried about him upsetting me or sending my thoughts spiralling, but for me the biggest problem is *how*. Unsurprisingly I've never contacted someone in prison before. I don't even know if it's possible for me to phone him up, maybe I just have to wait for him to phone me. The thought is excruciating. After our last conversation I have no doubt that he'll call me again eventually, but I can't just sit here and wait.

A call from Coop summons me home after lunch and I'm half considering asking him or mum to help me contact dad, but the idea is fleeting, driven away by mums pale face and anxious eyes.

"Are you alright?" I ask quickly.

"Just a bad day," she murmurs back, her voice low and her gaze tired.

"What happened?"

"Nothing, nothing, just tired," she tells me, unable to meet my gaze.

My heart sinks. I want to tell her that whatever the truth is, I can handle it. I want to beg her to trust me, to talk to me, to not tear down the fragile lines of communication that we've been constructing.

"Alright! We'll only be gone a few hours, we'll be back in plenty of time for dinner! Just look after Olly and don't burn the house down!" Coop calls cheerfully as he makes his way downstairs.

He helps mum to put her jacket on and ushers her towards the front door.

"Where are you going?" I ask, looking from him to mum.

"Just for a nice walk. Some fresh air," he tells me brightly, his eyes fixed on mum.

"What happened? I thought she was better," I mutter, keeping my words quiet but infusing them with urgency.

He doesn't respond, just gives me a swift look and leads my mother out of the house. I watch them go with fear prickling beneath my skin. She'd been so much better. Except for the one incident at school, she's seemed like herself again. Even after the scene at school she'd gotten better so quickly! I'd let myself believe that things were going to be different now and I didn't realise how committed I'd become to that dream.

"Penny?"

I swivel round to find Olly hanging off the door-frame to the lounge.

"Is mum sick?" he asks me, his face creased in worry.

"No Olly, she's just... sad."

The word doesn't feel like enough.

"Do you want to watch one of your movies?" I ask him, guiding him back into the lounge.

"Yeah?" he replies eagerly.

"Definitely."

I set him up with a film and some pop-tarts. He's thrilled with the unprecedented treat of breakfast in the afternoon and I'm able to go to my room and start googling. My research tells me that I can't call dad directly, but he can call me. The best bet seems to be his lawyer. If I speak to his lawyer, I can ask him to speak to dad and have him call me.

I recognise that this is supposed to be difficult, that removal from society is a part of the penal system and the loss of freedoms like this is intentional, but I can't help feeling that it's inconvenient. *I* didn't abduct Charlie! *I* didn't drug anyone! Does the law really have to make things so difficult for *me*?

With a sigh I set about finding out which lawyer is representing dad. I know I've been told, but the name sounded so bland and anonymous that I didn't retain it. It takes half an hour for me to source the information. The firm of Davis and Brown. No wonder I forgot.

I spare a thought for whether or not it's appropriate to call them on a Saturday, but ultimately I know I'm going to, so I try not to let it trouble me. I needn't have worried of course, the partners of a law firm aren't the ones who answer the phone. My call is answered by a secretary who sounds almost as though she doesn't mind working on a Saturday afternoon. She tries to make me an appointment with one of my fathers lawyers to discuss any concerns that I may have, but I cut her off.

"I just want to talk to my dad," I tell her firmly.

There are sympathetic crooning noises from her side of the call.

"I can't call him in prison, but could one of the lawyers talk to him and ask him to call me?" I ask.

She doesn't commit herself either way but promises to pass the request on.

"Now?" I press.

She's quiet, clearly weighing up the importance of my request. I consider saying that it could impact his defence or even his plea, but I suspect that that would bring a whole lot of trouble and attention that I don't want.

"I just want to talk to my daddy, I need to hear his voice," I say instead, forcing my words to tremble slightly.

I hope that my discomfort will come across as emotion and apparently it does because she sighs and agrees to contact one of the lawyers immediately. I thank her and end the call before I can say or do anything to ruin it.

Now I just have to wait.

I help Olly build a Lego tower, read through my school notes for the week and make good headway on an essay for English. Apparently this year will involve lots of practice essays and poetry analysis to get us ready for our final exams. We're writing about Lord Of The Flies at the moment, and I wish we weren't. The slow devolution into bestiality and self destruction is all feeling a little too relevant in my life at the moment. I wonder if I would get marked down for using dad as an example of real-world application. Ms Gittings would probably have a fit. I'm immersed in an exploration of the dehumanising effects of face-paint when the phone rings, sending my pen skittering across the page, leaving a blue blemish in its wake.

"I'll get it," I say hastily, leaping up and heading for the phone in the kitchen, leaving Olly still entranced by the TV.

"Hello?" I ask uncertainly, my fingers crossed so

tightly that it's painful.

"This call is from an inmate at Frankland Prison, Shane Owens, do you accept the call?"

The sound of that tinny voice sets my heart racing and I can feel sweat beading on my back as I press the button.

"Dad?"

"Penny! What's happened?! Have you found something?"

I want to feel proud that he thinks I'm capable of some kind of discovery, but I'm not. I see it for what it is now. It's not about me, none of this is about me, it's all about Rose.

"It's not Dan Cosford," I snap.

"You're sure? You're completely sure?" he asks eagerly.

"He has an alibi, for definite. A sleazy, disgusting alibi, but he definitely wasn't involved in what happened to Rose. It wasn't him."

I hear him breathe slowly as he realises that our best

suspect has just dissolved from the mix. I wonder if he thinks of it as a step forward or a step back. I wonder if he trusts me to know for sure.

"There were other people on the list, other people you'd heard of. The police won't let me see it, they're claiming they don't have it but I know they're lying! The list was in the house somewhere! They must have-"

"I have the list," I admit with a sigh, "I have everything. All your notes. All your insane ramblings."

He chuckles. He actually chuckles, as though this is a fantastic turn of events and he can't believe his luck. I feel heat rising in my chest.

"You need to look at the other names then! You need to keep going!" he tells me.

"And if one of them is dangerous? If one of them is a killer?" I ask.

"You need to find out which!"

"A sacrifice to the cause," I murmur, my eyes stinging.

"You need to look at Coop," he presses on, ignoring

my words or maybe not able to let himself hear them at all.

"Coop?"

"I never trusted him. He wouldn't say where he was that day."

"It can't be Coop," I say resolutely.

"Of course it can! He makes the most sense!"

"You thought mum was having an affair with him? Why?" I ask.

"She was acting secretive. She was sneaking around and hiding things and... she stopped acting so jealous. I don't know if you know- if she ever told you- but I made a mistake or two. Your mother was livid. She screamed and cried and kept throwing it in my face, but then she stopped. I thought that maybe she-"

Maybe she lost the moral high-ground. He doesn't need to say it.

I grip the kitchen counter to keep the world from spinning but it doesn't help. How could I have thought that they were happy? How could I have thought that they were a team?

"And you think it was Coop," I say through clenched teeth.

"They got together the moment I was gone! It was too fast! I think he was already in the picture, looking for a way in," he explains.

"And the women you slept with? The ones you cheated on mum with? Did you look at them as potential suspects?"

I want him to flinch. I want my words to make impact, to hurt him, to carve deep into his skin, but I don't stand a chance.

"Connie and Ruth? I- Ruth had already moved away by then. She left the company and moved up north with her husband."

I almost ask if it was because of him but I don't want to know. I don't want to add Ruth and her husband to the tally of lives that my father tore apart.

"And Connie?" I ask.

"It wasn't like that, she didn't have any animosity,"

he tells me feebly.

"Might she have wanted to get your family out of the way?" I press.

"I know it wasn't Connie."

His tone is firm but I can't help pushing.

"How can you be sure? Does she have an alibi? Did you check it?"

"Penny, it wasn't her."

"How do you know?! *You cheated on your wife with her*! How do you know she wasn't involved?!"

"Because I was with her! I was with her when my little girl was taken! That's why I wasn't there, that's why I missed your mother's calls!" he cries.

My heart stops beating. Just for a moment, but it does stop. Some small voice in my head sighs with relief at a puzzle being solved, but I'm hardly aware of it.

"You were working-" I mutter lamely.

He lets out a sound between a sigh and a sob but doesn't answer me.

"Does mum know?" I ask after a pause.

"No, I-"

"Do the police?"

He pauses again.

"Yes, I had to tell them, they had to verify where I was that day. Your mother was home with you girls, but I wasn't there and I wasn't at a conference. They had to know."

"But mum wasn't home alone," I say slowly, dragging my thoughts forward out of the quagmire.

"She always said she was but-" he falters.

"But Charlie saw a car. Charlie saw an old, beat-up, silver convertible with a fabric top. You think it belonged to Coop?" I ask in a flattened voice.

"I don't know. A beat-up convertible? Not a rental car then. That's a good description, you got more details than me."

"Well it probably helps that *I* didn't drug and traumatise her. *I* didn't nearly kill her. *I* don't do that! *I* don't destroy people's lives! I DON'T HURT PEOPLE! I'M NOT LIKE YOU!"

My voice has risen until I'm shouting and choking down sobs, with tears streaming down my face.

I look up when I hear a small shuffle and I notice the kitchen door is now slightly ajar. I know that I shut it behind me so I cross quickly over to it and ease the door open. Olly is standing there, frozen in the hall, his expression torn between guilt and concern. He looks impossibly small. I don't even think about it, I just hang up the phone and pull my brother into my arms. I'm sobbing but I don't care and he clings tightly to me as I rest my face on the top of his head.

"I'm sorry, I wasn't snooping," he murmurs, his arms still holding tight to me.

"You absolutely *were* snooping, but that's alright, I was being pretty loud."

"Were you fighting with someone?" he asks me, pulling back to look at my tear-stained face through wet and glistening eyes.

"Yes I was, but it's alright," I tell him slowly, trying to remember everything I said.

When did he start listening? Before or after I started talking about infidelity? I look closely at his troubled face and his wide, sad eyes.

"You listened to all of it, didn't you," I say with a sigh.

He shrinks slightly but doesn't say anything.

"Don't worry, I was talking about some people who aren't together any more," I say reassuringly.

"Not mum and dad?"

"Not your mum and dad, no."

He takes a moment to digest this, his thoughtful expression making my heart ache.

"And you were talking about Rose?" he asks.

"Yes. I still want to know what happened to her."

"What *did* happen?"

His voice is low and his bottom lip trembles threateningly but I don't know what to say to him. I really don't know how much he knows. It all happened before he was born and I don't know what mum and Coop have told him, if anything. What I do know, is that

I can't tell him the story of his older sister vanishing in the woods while we were playing and never being seen again. He must have the broad strokes at least, but I can't bring myself to admit that that's all there is, after all these years. Broad strokes. A loose framework for people to drape their theories over and see how they fit. A frame to hang a suspect on. But who?

"She went missing. And she stayed missing," I say, shaking my head helplessly.

"But what happened to her?" he presses.

"That's not the important bit," I tell him.

"What's the important bit?" he asks.

"She is."

I hold out my hand and he clasps it with his small fingers. I lead him upstairs and into the the slightly musty room across the hall from my own. I sit him on the bed and tell him how happy Rose was to get this floral duvet cover.

"She loved anything to do with flowers," I tell him, "she wanted to be a florist, or a vet. She thought that

Rose was the perfect name for a florist and she wanted a shop called Rose's Roses. But she loved animals too so vet was her other choice. She couldn't decide. Any animal she saw, she was sure it was her friend. Mice, cats, dogs, birds, foxes. She loved them all. And she did great drawings of them! She loved drawing flowers and animals!"

I drop to the floor beside the bed and pull out a drawer. It's full of sheets of paper, covered with her drawings. There are foxes surrounded by sunflowers and cats with daisies and birds carrying bluebells.

"She loved pairing up animals and flowers for a new picture, and she would work on it until the whole page was filled."

I hand him page after page and he takes them reverently, his fingers gentle with the paper that feels crisp with age.

"She was always making up fantastic games too, she would create whole worlds full of pirates and mermaids and we would run together having adventures all day."

I talk and talk, loosening memories that I thought had been lost. I can almost smell her and feel her hand in mine, so sure and bold as her fingers laced with mine. The words come rushing out and Olly drinks them in, gulping down details about the sister he would never know.

"She was so bright. She was quick and clever and funny and she just seemed to shine," I finish wonderingly.

We're both still, revelling in the fully realised picture of a young girl that my words have conjured up. For a moment, she seems almost real to me, her rich red hair picked out in gold in the sunshine and her eyes blazing with life. But the faint smell of dust creeps in and starts to corrode her crisp edges. The pervasive cold of the bed reminds me firmly that no one sleeps here now.

"You love her," Olly says in a small voice.

I jump, surprised that this is his response. I do of course, I have always loved Rose. Even when we fought, even when I hated her, even when she teased me until I cried, I still loved her. That's what a sister is I suppose. I got so used to missing her and wanting answers and burning with all my unanswered questions, that I forgot where it all started.

"I do, I love her very much" I agree.

"I think I love her too. Is that ok?"

"That's more than ok Olly. She's your sister," I tell him, "she would have loved you too. Wherever she is now, I know she loves you."

We stay there for a few more minutes but the spell has broken. I'm out of words and I can't feel Rose any more, I can't see her. Eventually we move back downstairs and put something on the television but my thoughts are back on my conversation with dad and everything I learned. I want so much to resist the idea, but I just keep thinking that however things seem, you really have no idea what's going on sometimes. I want to believe that I can trust my own judgement, that I know what's going on with my own family, in my own home-

but clearly that isn't always true.

If dad's right and mum was having an affair, that could explain the car that Charlie saw and mum never mentioned. It would place someone else here the day that Rose went missing. Someone else right on the spot. Someone right by the woods where she vanished. Someone who could even have intercepted her on her way home, someone who was perfectly placed to do so.

But could that person really be Coop?

Chapter 11

I make a decision.

Whatever the truth may be, I need to know. I'm aching from the realisation that my happy childhood with my happy family was all a fiction, but the truth is still better than the lie. If there's a killer in my house I need to know about it.

"I thought I'd start clearing out the back porch this morning," I say brightly as I sip my tea and wait for my poptarts to toast.

Mum flinches, a large clumsy motion, and then she swings around to face me.

"Remember? We told Charlie we'd clear it so that we can look after the dog overnight for her."

"Oh- oh yes- of course," she replies vaguely, massaging her eyes.

"Maybe we should hold off," Coop suggests tentatively.

"But then we'll end up with dog pee everywhere! Don't worry, I'll do all the work, just like mum said," I tell him.

I force myself to maintain eye contact, a challenge in my gaze until eventually he shrugs and turns away. I try to feel some satisfaction but I don't. I don't know how to read him, I've never felt that I had to before- he was always just straightforward Coop, nothing to fear under the surface.

I eat my poptarts in front of the television with Olly and I allow myself the time to finish my tea, but then I have to get started.

The back porch. It's just a tiny little room, half filled with shoe buckets thanks to mum's life-long no shoes in the house policy. I remember it so clearly, though I haven't seen inside it in ten years. The shoe buckets are actually wicker baskets that rest upon the white tiled floor. The walls were white too, with a floral border around the top that Rose and I both loved. We declared it a 'transition room' between home and the woods, and those flowers were the woods creeping inside by magic.

I can barely lift my hand to the handle. I've shifted the end table full of pictures and dried lavender to a bare stretch of wall, so the way is free and clear, but I can't bring myself to do it. A small voice in my head is screaming that I don't want to see the horrors behind that door, but I stamp it down.

No more ghosts. No more secrets. No more locked doors.

I'm going to drag everything out into the light until there are no shadows left and the truth can't be hidden any more.

With a last deep breath I turn the handle.

White tiles. White walls. Small blue flowers in the

border. Buckets of shoes left abandoned for ten years.

Was it always *so* small?

I eye the baskets but I can't bring myself to start there. Instead I grab the cleaning supplies from the kitchen and begin by washing the dust from the walls. For a sealed room, a surprising amount has accumulated and my sponge is sweeping it into clots of wet grime. I have to rinse the sponge out every minute or so and change the water twice before the walls look remotely clear and presentable. I'm sweaty and gross, covered in dirt and I don't feel as though I've expelled any ghosts at all. I step back into the hall to find mum, staring vacantly into the porch, her eyes alarmingly glazed and her arms hanging limply at her sides.

"Mum?" I ask hesitantly.

She doesn't respond or react in any way.

"Mum?" I say again, taking a step towards her.

She's still staring into the porch with those empty eyes.

"Mum?" I try again, but it isn't until I firmly shut

the porch door that she shifts.

She gives a small start and looks around as though she can't quite remember where she is.

"Mum."

I take hold of her arms and try to look into her face but she shrugs me away, already shaking off the moment.

"Sorry love, I was miles away! How are you getting on with the- with the cleaning?"

"Yeah, slowly I guess, but it's progress," I tell her, still worried by the look on her face.

"When is the dog coming?"

"Not sure yet. But I'll get it done in time," I assure her.

Suddenly I don't want her in there. I don't know where she was just now, but it was hard- too hard- to call her back.

"Are you alright?" I ask, willing her to look into my eyes instead of just around them.

"I'm fine love, everything's fine."

She slips away and into the kitchen, leaving me

looking after her.

I hesitate, but I don't know how to help her. Perhaps I don't have the right to, after all, if I drag all the secrets out into the light some of them might be hers.

I decide on a shower. I turn the heat up as high as I can bear and stand under the scorching water long after the last traces of dust and grime have washed away. I've only half got my t-shirt on when a knock sounds and my door swings open to reveal Luke.

"Oh! Sorry! Your mum sent me up, she seemed a little out of it," he tells me, blushing furiously.

The air is thick from the inadvertent intrusion and I can't bear any more awkward tension, so I step towards Luke and wind my arms around his waist, pulling him close. My lips meet his softly and his hands settle on my heated skin. We remain that way for a minute or two or maybe twenty, until a sound in the house recalls me to the fact that we're not alone.

"I'm glad you're here," I tell him sincerely as I step away and push my arms into my sleeves, tugging my top down over my stomach.

"Really?" he asks, one eyebrow slightly raised in a hopeful way that makes something inside of me squirm pleasantly.

"Yes, I need your help."

My tone has become business-like and he shifts neatly into practical mode.

"Sure, what is it?"

"You're not going to like it."

I was right, he didn't like it.

"It's not going to seem natural!" he's still hissing an hour later when we're called for lunch.

"Just try to seem normal!" I mutter back.

"But *normally* I wouldn't do it!"

I shoot him a look somewhere between warning and pleading as I push open the door to the dining room and he gives an exasperated sigh in response.

"This looks great!" I say brightly, seeing the food already laid out on the table.

"Yeah, thank you for having me, it looks amazing," Luke agrees, already blushing slightly.

"No problem at all Luke! Good to have you with us!" Coop tells him happily as he sets a tray of crispy roast potatoes on a trivet.

Mum is already sat down, staring slightly absently at a wine glass half filled with water.

"Are you alright mum?" I ask lightly.

"Hm?" she responds, looking up with a smile, "oh I'm fine! I just didn't sleep very well. I'm tired but a delicious roast should sort me out!"

She does look tired, but I don't think that's all it is. She was so strange earlier and even Luke commented on it when he first arrived. Maybe her meds aren't working any more.

"Potatoes!" Olly cries in delight as he hurtles into the room and collides with Luke.

"That's right little man, lots of them!" Luke agrees, peeling my brother off him and holding one hand up for a fist-bump that Olly solemnly provides.

We all shuffle into our seats and I help Olly and myself to food as everyone digs in.

"I want more potatoes than that!" he insists confidently.

"You know the drill, eat everything on your plate and if you still have room you can have more potatoes," I tell him.

Olly's love of potatoes needs to be reigned in. If he had his way he would eat nothing but a mountain of roasties generously coated with gravy.

He grumbles and mutters under his breath but he gets to work on his broccoli and carrots so I let any mumbled complaints slide.

"Thank you," mum mouths across the table and I feel a small pang. She seems to be right on the edge, hovering between 'OK' and desolation and I can't help but feel afraid that my pushing and prying is going to tip her over.

"This is all brilliant!" Luke announces through a mouthful of chicken.

"Why thank you," Coop replies, giving a small bow.

His roasts are absolutely superb. Mum's cooking can be great, but she's a bit more hit and miss. Coop only makes a few things, but he is absolutely consistent. His roasts are a testament to his perfectly calculated timings and years of practice. They are always just right. Reliable.

Olly wolfs his food down in an effort to earn extra potatoes but by the time he's cleared his plate he's obviously full. He has the tiniest roast potato he can find in the tray, just a small sign of his determination, and then he asks if he can get down and go back to his Lego.

As soon as his foot touches the floor I start sneaking Luke significant looks. He colours and clears his throat, trying to look unconcerned.

"So," he begins eventually, his voice sounding altogether too practised, "how did you two meet?"

He looks at mum and Coop hopefully and I try not to wince. When I said those words in my room they sounded fine. When I rehearsed them in my head they seemed perfectly natural and normal. Coming from

Luke however, they seem awkward and staged.

"Sorry?" Coop asks, raising an eyebrow.

"You two, you used to work together, right? Is that how you started dating?" Luke presses on valiantly. I love him for it but to be honest I'd quite like to melt into a puddle on the floor right now.

"Yes, at a marketing company. I'm still there actually, as IT Director," Coop agrees uncertainly, waiting for some sort of explanation.

"And you started dating? Ten years ago, right? After the divorce?"

"Of course," Coop agrees, his face smooth.

"Penny, what is this?" mum asks sharply.

I hesitate, but that doesn't mean I'm not committed.

"Dad thought you might have been having an affair... you know, before."

"That's rich!" she cries, her face turning a deep russet.

I incline my head in agreement but I can't let it drop.

"That doesn't mean-" I start but she cuts me off.

"Penny your father is clearly not a saint! I don't know why you would even listen to him after everything he's done! When did he even say this?! Have you been talking to him?!"

Her voice has risen to a shout and she sounds almost hysterical.

"*He's* the one who's crazy!" she cries, "*He's* the one! It's *his* fault! *I'm* trying to protect my family!"

She screeches the words and then breaks down into sobs, struggling to catch her breath.

Without another word Coop leads her from the room, shutting the door behind them.

The silence is deafening.

"I don't think that was such a good idea," Luke whispers after a minute or two, when the quiet has become unbearable.

"No, possibly not."

"I think I should go," he says gently.

I don't want him to leave, but he's right. It's not fair

to make him stay here after what just happened, and Coop and mum would probably prefer he left for now.

I sigh but I nod and lead him to the front door. A slight shuffle as we pass the lounge tells me that Olly may have been listening in again, and I'll need to have another talk with him at some point, but right now I can't face it. I kiss Luke goodbye and then go back to the dining room, dropping into my chair and burying my face in my hands.

"What is it that you want to know, Penny?"

My head snaps up. I didn't hear him approach but Coop is in the doorway holding me in his gaze.

I want so much to tell him that it's nothing, that I don't have any questions at all.

"Where were you the day Rose disappeared?"

"I was at home."

His voice is cool and level and he doesn't look away when I search for some answer in his eyes.

"Alone?" I ask, hearing my voice shake.

"Yes."

"What sort of car did you drive back then?"

He just looks at me for another moment before turning and walking away.

I think I might be sick.

I retreat upstairs and don't reappear until the next morning.

I hover awkwardly in the hall, not sure whether mum is in a fit state to go to work or whether she'd be prepared to drive me even if she is. She storms down the stairs at the last minute, with Olly hurrying in her wake.

"I made you another appointment with Janet. Ten o'clock! You'll have to come to my office and I'll drive you there. I don't know what's wrong with you Penny, but clearly you need to talk to someone!"

I don't argue- I'm too relieved that she's upright and functioning and still talking to me. Besides, I wouldn't mind talking to Janet.

"That's fine, I can get the bus," I say, hurrying after her without a second thought.

"No. I don't want you missing more school than you

have to, I'll drive you. Sean will understand."

I sigh but I still don't fight. I'd rather Mr Danes didn't know that I'm in therapy, but I suppose it's unavoidable considering I keep going during school hours. I bet mum already told him anyway.

We drop Olly off and he hurries out of the car without a word. I feel a sharp pang of regret that I haven't made time to speak to him yet after everything he overheard yesterday. I promise myself I'll talk to him after school and then I try to push the worry aside. My efforts have limited success. Concern for Oliver keeps jostling with anxiety about the future, fear of Coop, anger at my dad and guilt for all the damage I'm doing, all vying for dominance in my thoughts. They are all steamrollered when I catch a glimpse of a dark, seething face through the crowd of the corridor.

I step back into a recess between some lockers and hold my breath as he passes.

"What are you up to?" a cheery voice asks me as Luke steps into view.

"Hiding."

He looks both ways, up and down the corridor.

"Unless you've found a new nemesis since I last saw you, I think you're safe," he reassures me, reaching out for my hand and pulling me back into the corridor from the safety of my alcove.

I allow myself a quick glance around, just to be sure, but there's no sign of him.

"Dan," I mutter by way of explanation.

"Ah. I'd almost forgotten," he admits.

"Yesterday was a little... distracting."

"It certainly was. How are things on that front now?" he enquires.

"Completely awful, but- not too bad."

"Well there's a mixed message for you. And things here? Do you think Dan might make trouble?"

"To be honest, I'm hoping he has no idea I was involved," I say

"You think he suspects though," Luke probes.

"Probably," I admit with a sigh.

"How about, until we know the lie of the land, I walk you to your classes. I'd feel better," he tells me in a plaintive voice.

"Won't that make you late for your own classes?" I point out.

"I'll be very speedy."

I can tell he's serious so I agree and let him know about the impromptu Janet appointment at ten, changing my schedule for the day. He walks me to registration and promises to see me again in a few minutes to escort me to double maths. I smile as I watch him go and I still have a small smile on my face when I settle into my seat beside Charlie.

"Where were you?! I've been texting!" she exclaims, clearly frustrated and in no mood for my cheer.

"What?"

"I texted you!" she repeats.

I dig through my bag to retrieve my phone but it's not there. In fact, not much of anything appears to be there.

"Damn! I curse under my breath.

"No battery?" she guesses.

"No phone! I left it at home! And my purse and my keys and half my books too, it looks like."

She whistles under her breath in a sympathetic way.

"Alright, you're forgiven for making me worry, since karma has clearly already dealt out it's punishment."

"But you were only worried in the first place because I don't have my phone with me! So how can that be my punishment?!" I demand.

"Wow! That's like a modern day version of 'if a tree falls in the woods and there's no one there to hear it, does it make a sound?' my mind is blown right now!"

I stare at her deadpan, wondering how I'm going to get through the whole day without my most crucial possessions.

"Not appreciating philosophy right now?" Charlie asks astutely.

"Not right this second, no."

"Need money for lunch?" she offers.

"I might still be with Janet at lunch anyway," I grumble.

"Another Janet session?! How come?"

"Mum made the appointment after I caused a minor scene at lunch yesterday," I tell her.

"What did this minor scene consist of?" she asks intrigued.

"I accused her of cheating on Dad with Coop before they got divorced."

"*Minor scene?!*"

"Then I asked Coop where he was when Rose went missing and asked what sort of car he drove," I add.

"Penny Cooper! What brought all that on?!" she demands.

"I spoke to Dad."

Her expression flattens, like water washing away a design in the sand.

"I knew you wouldn't like it," I sigh.

"I *don't* like it."

"But I didn't know what else to do!" I say

imploringly.

"Then you should have called a meeting. Rallied your forces. You do not need him Penny."

My heart is pounding and I fumble for her hand, giving it a quick squeeze that she doesn't return.

"I'm sorry. I want to have a meeting! I do! You, me and Luke, as soon as possible. Talking to Dad has left me... confused."

"Which is exactly why you shouldn't have called him."

Her voice is still stern but her fingers apply the slightest pressure to mine and when I continue to watch her hopefully she rolls her eyes.

"Fine! Meeting asap. Consider your forces rallied!"

Chapter 12

My thoughts are a teeming mass. What will I say to Charlie and Luke? How much am I going to tell them about the fear slowly germinating in my chest? If they believe me in the least, they'll both want me to get out of my house as quickly as possible and not go back. But Olly's there. And mum. I can't leave them and I can't bring them with me.

Besides that, I'm not sure I'm ready to admit to them that I suspect Coop. They're my closest friends, a part of my life day to day, sharing my doubts with them would give this horrific situation substance and form.

There'd be no going back.

"Penny?"

My head comes up fast as someone nudges me in the ribs. I turn to see Josh looking at me expectantly, his eyes flicking to the front of the room.

Maths class.

I don't even remember walking here. Luke must have escorted me but I doubt I was a good conversationalist.

"Sorry?" I ask, panicked.

"He asked if you were listening," Josh hisses, nodding his head slightly towards Mr Stines.

"Sorry, I'm not feeling well. Can I go to the office?" I say, running my hands over my face.

"Of course, just make sure you get the notes from today. You don't want to fall behind now and jeopardise the future you've worked so hard for," he tells me.

Was that really necessary? Is the constant fear-selling mandated in the last year of A-Levels? Surely if we've got this far we're already working hard, we already

310

care and we don't need constant reminders of the stakes. I don't even know whether I'm going to need maths! I have no plan!

I grab my bag with its limited contents and hurry out into the hall feeling a wave of nausea. I still have almost half an hour before I need to leave for my appointment with Janet, so I decide the bathroom is as good a place as any to spend the time. At least there'll be no risk of running into Dan Cosford.

I splash cold water on my face again and again until the nausea passes. By the time I've scraped off the last stubborn vestiges of mascara that this process has smeared under my eyes, I feel a little more steady. I just need to figure out a plan. First, a plan to find out what happened to my sister, then a plan for the rest of my life. No problem.

I lower the toilet seat and collapse onto it, locking the stall door and clutching my bag in my arms. I wish I had my phone so that I could be mindlessly scrolling or googling things right now, rather than just mulling over all the things I don't know. I'm considering giving up and going back to maths for the last ten minutes, just to have something to do, when the bathroom door bangs open.

"Oh my gosh, he is so hot!" a voice sing-songs.

"Yeah, but he's a teacher."

The reply came dismissively and I recognise the voice instantly. Claire Netherhall.

"He's not *just* a teacher, he's a personal trainer too."

"Having two jobs is not something to be proud of," Claire counters disdainfully.

"I can't believe you don't like him! He reminds me so much of Marcus!"

"He looks a bit like Marcus, but Marcus is really intelligent. He'll probably go into finance like his dad," Claire says proudly.

It takes a lot of self control not to snort, but I don't want to give myself away.

"Well *I* think he's hot."

"Like it matters. He's *married* Rosemary! And

Marcus has met her a few times when he's been round there for weights sessions. He says she's really pretty, and pregnant."

"Uh! His wife is *so lucky*!" Rosemary laments.

"He's a teacher!" Claire repeats, her words dripping with disgust.

I wonder for a moment what she'd say about Charlie's crush on soft-spoken, corduroy wearing Mr Danes. Again I almost laugh.

"I still think she's lucky," Rosemary insists.

If only they knew.

They finish touching up their hair and make-up and head back out. Aside from their remarkable delusion when it comes to men, I learned that Tina Cosford's departure isn't common knowledge yet. It seems that people don't know that Dan's *lucky* wife is gone. I probably have a few minutes left but I decide to go straight to the office to find mum. I don't want to make things worse by keeping her waiting, and even if Dan is keeping things quiet, I'd still rather not meet him in the halls.

I knock gently on the office door before slowly edging it open and peering through.

"Mum?" I ask hesitantly.

"Penny. You're early."

"Sorry, I wasn't feeling too well so I left maths a bit early," I explain.

She looks at me enquiringly, not ready to let her anger drop but clearly concerned.

"Not well?" she probes.

"I think I'm just anxious, with all the exam talk this year," I tell her.

"Talk to Janet."

With that she seems to brush the issue aside, considering the matter taken care of.

"Good idea. I'll talk to Janet," I mutter.

"Are you going to buy lunch after your appointment or get something at home?" she asks, "you'll need to take the bus back remember, I need to get back to work once I've dropped you off."

"I actually forgot my purse at home," I admit, "and my keys, and my phone."

She looks at me in surprise and exasperation.

"What is going on with you Penny?!" she demands.

I don't even know how to begin to answer that question so I just shrug non-committally and chew my thumb nail.

She sighs and reaches into her bag, rummaging for her purse and pulling a ten pound note from it. Next she opens a desk draw and reaches right to the back for a ring with two keys on. She hands both items to me with a frown.

"These are my spare keys, I'll need them back," she tells me firmly.

I nod my understanding and thank her briefly.

"I can't help with the phone but you won't need it in your appointment anyway. You'll need to focus on Janet."

She drives me to my appointment as promised, but we don't speak at all in the car. I want to tell her that I'm sorry, but I don't think I can apologise when I'm going to keep digging anyway. Instead I let the silence settle around us, thick and stifling. It's a relief to climb out into the fresh air and wave goodbye.

"This is Penny Cooper, I have an appointment with Dr Reeves," I tell the receptionist.

"Of course, take a seat, she'll call you in shortly."

I settle into a seat in the waiting room and begin pondering which chair I should select today. Maybe the beanbag. I've never chosen the beanbag because it's such a ridiculous thing to have on offer in a therapist's office, but perhaps it would make a good impression that Janet could report back to mum.

"Penny Cooper?" Janet's voice sounds.

I slip into the office and hesitate, looking around at the many chairs.

"If I sit in the beanbag will you tell my mum I'm making an effort and giving the therapy thing a chance?" I ask.

"No, sorry," Janet replies, faintly amused.

"Why even have it then?" I mutter as I settle into

the formidable wing-back once more.

"Penny, you do realise that anything you tell me doesn't leave this room? I don't report to your mother, or tell her anything you've said. What you do or don't tell me would never leave this room, unless I head reason to believe from something you said that you or someone else would be in danger."

I stare back at her.

"Anything you tell me is in confidence."

I continue to stare.

"Penny?"

"I don't know what to do."

I blurt the words almost without thinking.

"About?" she queries, her voice level.

"About anything? I want to find out what happened to Rose. I know you think that's crazy, and you probably think I have no chance, but I do. I just don't know how! I thought I was onto something, that I'd figured out who it was, but I was wrong. Now I feel like I'm back to the beginning but with almost nothing to work with, except-"

I falter for a moment, not sure how far I can really go but not able to stop.

"-except I talked to my dad, and he thinks mum was having an affair when Rose disappeared. It turns out he was too. That's why he's motivated by guilt, that's why he can't stop looking for Rose, because he feels so guilty that he wasn't there for her when she needed him because he was off sleeping with some co-worker! But if mum was too, then that could be who took Rose! That could put someone at our house that day!"

I'm panting when I finish, and scanning Janet's face for a reaction. I stopped just short of mentioning Coop, since living in the same house as a killer might bend the confidentiality rule until it breaks. Still, it was an awful lot of information to unload and I'm interested to see what she does with it.

"You spoke to your father?" she asks gently.

"Yes."

I can't help physically tensing at the thought.

"It sounds like he told you an awful lot of things that people tend to hide from their children."

There's no overt criticism in her words or her tone, but it's clear that there's more behind them than just an innocuous comment.

"You think he should have protected me from the truth?" I ask.

"Do you?"

I actually think about it for a moment before responding. I've been angry, furious even, since I spoke to dad, but-

"Yes. I think he should have protected me. Or maybe- I wish he *wanted* to protect me. But I'm glad that he didn't, I'm glad he told me. I want the truth."

I wonder if that sounds dramatic to her, if I look like a stubborn child insisting on being treated like a grown-up.

"I deserve the truth. It's important," I add, almost imploringly.

"Yes you do. Everyone has a right to the truth, even

if that truth may be hard sometimes."

"My sister was ten years old and one day she just...
vanished. The truth about that was never going to be
anything other than hard. I've known that for a very long
time."

"So what's next?" she asks, not missing a beat.

"Next?"

"What do you plan to do now?" she clarifies.

"I plan to keep looking for Rose. I don't think I can
move on or do anything else until I find her."

Again, dramatic.

"Some people are never found Penny. It's a sad truth,
but there it is. What if Rose is never located? What will
that mean for you if you put your life on hold?"

I don't answer. I don't know what to say.

"Why do you think you can't move on until she's
found?" she asks after an agony of silence.

"What's my motivation?" I ask with a wry smile.

"Yes," she smiles in response, "what's your
motivation?"

The truth is, I've been thinking about it. Once the indignation subsided I started to mull it over in the recesses of my mind. I gently probed the desire until it took on a more recognisable shape. When I sat on the floor of her room with Olly, I worked it out.

"Because she's not just my sister. This isn't just something that happened to my family. She wasn't just taken from me," I begin stammering, my voice trembling, "*she* was *taken*! She was this whole, vibrant, amazing person. She could have been anything, she could have gone anywhere, and she never got to find out! She never got to live! She was so little and so alive and someone just... killed her. She's going to be *gone* forever. Just *gone*! It's... unthinkable. Inconceivable. I can't-"

I break off. Word's can't explain it. The horror of it. The injustice.

Someone can make someone else... gone.

My eyes plead with Janet to understand, though she can't.

"Alright, you have your motivation," she says softly,

tipping her head gently to one side as she assesses me.

I just nod dumbly.

"You have recognised the love and the grief that you feel. You recognise the loss. I would just ask that you recognise yourself too. You are more than the tragedy of what happened. You are a whole and vibrant person too."

She allows me a moment to collect myself, wiping my eyes hastily on my sleeve since the tissues are for the sort of people who cry in therapy sessions.

"So, here and now, what do you want? And what do you need to do to get it?"

She's business-like now. Her voice calm and practical, helping me to find my feet.

"Here and now? I want a plan. So, I need to go over what I know and work out my next steps."

Just saying the words brings relief. Street-lights appear along my misty path. It's not clear yet, but I know where I'm going and I can make out shapes ahead.

My brow furrows in concentration and Janet looks at me enquiringly.

"What might guilt look like? Just like my dad? Or might other people react differently?"

I buy a sandwich and a drink from the Tesco Express on the corner so that I'll have change for the bus and I eat them feverishly, feeling suddenly ravenous. I'm just dusting the last crumbs from my fingers when the bus pulls up and I climb on, itching with the inconvenience of paying with cash. A seat by the door is open so I slip into it and settle my bag on my lap, hugging it to me as the world slips by. I feel... different.

If this is what Charlie feels after her sessions with Claudia, I can see why she's happy to keep going. Janet didn't really tell me anything life changing- there were no great wisdoms imparted, but I feel as though the world is less hazy now. My hands have discovered tools they were already holding and my grip feels more sure.

I can do this. I just need a plan.

I exit the bus at the stop near my road and jog to the house, using mum's spare key to let myself in. My phone, purse and half my books are in my room, safely on my desk so that I wouldn't forget them. Best laid plans. I shove them into my bag and check the time. Twenty seven minutes until the next bus back to school. I head downstairs and make myself another sandwich, still feeling famished after the emotional upheaval. I eat it as I walk, eventually catching the bus four stops further along, just for the last leg of the journey.

I disembark outside the school but it's half one now, lunch is over and the next lesson is in full swing. I don't want to enter half way through. Instead I turn my steps to the right and walk along the street a short way, to the separate entrance to the Rose Owens Garden.

Rose never got to attend this school, she was about to start here when she went missing, but the school donated this piece of land and Mr Danes arranged a memorial garden. It sounds macabre, a memorial to a little girl who could potentially still be alive, but I don't think it is. I think it's the perfect tribute. Rose would have absolutely loved it. The whole garden is filled with roses, every size and colour, bordering small walkways and ringing benches.

It's clearly suffering a little from the cold already, but many of the bushes are still in flower. One or two are wrapped in some kind of gauze, to protect them from the early chill. I give silent thanks to Mr Danes for protecting it so well.

I take a moment sitting there in the garden, just to remember my sister.

I head back to the school just before the bell sounds so that I can join the throng of students in the corridors and slip to my next class with the rest of them. I keep a vigilant eye out for Dan Cosford, and that's my mistake.

"Been to therapy Penny?" A sickly, sympathetic voice asks at full volume.

I turn slowly, Claire Netherhall coming into view.

"Yep," I mutter back, forcing myself to hold her gaze for a moment before I turn to continue on my way.

"Because of all the trauma?" she presses, matching me step for step.

Her voice is still raised, clear as a bell and people are falling silent around us to listen and observe.

"Sure," I reply dismissively, still shouldering my way through the crowd.

"Because of what your dad did, right? What *did* he do?"

"Traumatic stuff," I snap, rounding on her, "what do you want Claire?"

"What? I'm just showing an interest! It's polite to be concerned! Didn't your therapist teach you that?" she asks sweetly.

"You're just being polite?! Oh I didn't realise! *No matter*," I tell her, twisting my face into a smile.

I know I've hit my mark. 'No matter' is Claire's mothers dismissive catch phrase. Those are the words she uses again and again to make her daughter feel small, inadequate, unheard.

Did you do your cardio this morning sweetheart? No? No matter, you can double up this evening. You need to stay trim if you want to keep Marcus interested!

Did you pack a salad? No matter, I'll get you one now.
We don't want you snacking if you get hungry later.

I'm sure that Claire created the NoMatter Facebook profile in the summer. The profile that repeatedly suggested that whatever had happened to Charlie, she deserved it.

Claire looks at me, her face a mask over rage and bitterness.

"What does that mean?" she demands in a cold whisper, taking a step closer to me.

"What? You're just being polite, right? So am I," I tell her, forcing myself to hold my ground.

"You bitch," she hisses and suddenly her hands make impact with my chest and I stagger backwards.

I leap forward without thinking, driving my shoulder into her and sending her backwards into a bank of lockers.

"THAT'S ENOUGH!" a voice calls.

People immediately start to shuffle away, their faces turning back, flushed.

My heart sinks but I stay where I am. This is the second time Mr Danes has walked up just as I physically assaulted another student.

"Mr Danes she shoved me!" Claire cries immediately, frantically adjusting her hair and straightening her clothes.

"She shoved me first!" I murmur under my breath.

"She started it! I was just trying to be *nice*!" Claire counters.

"Are you alright Penny?" Mr Danes asks in his gentle voice, turning sad eyes upon me.

I shrug and half nod, not sure what to say. How much has mum told him? He must know that I just got back from another emergency appointment with Janet.

"Is *she* alright?!" Claire shrieks, "she just shoved me! For trying to be nice! But just because you fancy her mum you-"

Mr Danes swivels around and Claire immediately falls silent.

"You were not being *nice* Miss Netherhall, you were

being vicious and cruel and I will not stand for it. If you say one more word to Miss Cooper here you will be suspended. Is that understood?"

He doesn't raise his voice, he doesn't need to. Mr Danes might be a headmaster but he still has that almost magical ability that some teachers possess, to make students fall silent effortlessly. Claire nods sullenly at him and beats a retreat. He watches her go for a moment before turning back to me.

"I'm sorry you're having so many problems Penny. Please do let me know if there's any way that I can help."

"It's fine," I shrug, already feeling like I'm being given more free passes than I expected.

He gives me another sad, sympathetic look and turns to go but at the last moment I call him back.

"Actually sir, there is one thing–"

My request probably confirms his opinion of me as a fragile and broken child, but he does at least smile when he agrees.

Chapter 13

English class is as unpleasant as I could have predicted, but at least I have both Luke and Charlie to see me through it and thanks to therapy it's only a single period instead of a double.

"I'll give you my notes later," Charlie whispers as I settle into the seat reserved beside her.

We spend the remainder of the lesson sighing over Ms Gittings continued dark looks and snide remarks, until the bell sets us free and we hasten from the room.

"Still meeting today?" I ask once we reach the safety of the corridor.

"That's the plan!" Luke agrees.

"At my house, so we can walk Caesar," Charlie adds.

"Caesar? He has a name?"

"A trial name. I'm going to see if he likes it. If he doesn't I'll try something else," she shrugs non-committally.

"Yes of course, a perfectly normal way to name a dog," Luke comments levelly.

Charlie sticks her tongue out but makes no further retort.

We take the bus back to hers together, while Luke and I both text our respective parents to keep them updated.

"My mum says it's fine," Luke announces after his phone chimes at the arrival of a message.

"And mine isn't responding, so I guess that's fine too," I say uncertainly.

Mum's starting to worry me a little. It's just a nagging concern at the back of my mind, and heaven knows her behaviour isn't as bad as it has been in the past, but for some reason it feels more alarming now- she feels less like herself. More erratic.

"Want to go home first and check?" Charlie asks me, studying my face.

"No, no I'm sure it's fine."

I need to focus on making a plan. The sooner we have answers, the sooner we can all start to heal.

Wendy is still at work so we clip a leash onto an ecstatic Caesar and head straight back out once we get to Charlie's. She croons apologies for leaving him alone and praise for his supposed good behaviour as we walk, though we all saw the puddles in the kitchen and the lounge. I really should get back to clearing the porch soon.

Caesar happily gambols along, heedless of his new name being used.

"Do you think he likes it?" Charlie asks thoughtfully.

"He certainly doesn't seem to *mind* it," I tell her.

She sighs but has to settle for this since Luke is stifling laughter and it's threatening to spill over. I hastily change the subject.

"So I had a good chat with Janet."

"Really?" Luke is incredulous.

"Yeah, she told me about confidentiality and I told her... lots of stuff."

"You didn't know it was confidential?" Charlie asks with a frown.

"Well you always hear about doctor-patient confidentiality, but on TV they always seem to just break it anyway," I argue.

"Yeah but that's TV. This is a real doctor."

"But I'm still technically a minor, I thought she might be able to report back to my mum at least."

"Definitely not. Unless you tell her you're going to murder someone or something, she has to keep everything you say a secret," Charlie tells me confidently.

"Are you planning to murder someone?" Luke asks lightly.

"No, but she'd have to tell someone if she thought *I* was about to be murdered too, right?" I counter.

"Are you about to be murdered?" Luke asks, his voice sharpening to a point.

"Almost certainly not."

They both watch me, waiting. I made the decision to talk to them. They're my team and I made the choice to trust them, I'm just not sure how carefully I need to tread.

"I want to look into Coop. I need to."

I decide not to mention dad, there's no need. He may have planted the seed but it's already taken root. Luke nods in understanding though he doesn't look happy. He clearly knew that this was the direction things were headed after the disastrous Sunday lunch. Charlie's expression is inscrutable.

"Charlie?" I press her, needing her thoughts.

"You love Coop."

It's a simple statement that cuts me to the quick. I do love Coop. Even now, with all my doubt and suspicion, the feeling hasn't gone away.

"That doesn't mean he didn't do it," I say with a

sigh.

"What makes you think he did?" she asks.

"I'm not saying that I think it was him," I say quickly, "I just need to know it wasn't."

"Alright, my question still stands though," she says.

I take a moment to put my words in order before I lay them out.

"I've always thought that mum and Coop were a bit like Marianne and Colonel Brandon," I begin.

Charlie nods slowly but Luke looks utterly lost.

"In Sense And Sensibility. He was always in love with her, because she was this lively, exciting, beautiful person, but then when he actually got her, it was because she was broken. I felt kind of sorry for him."

"For Colonel Brandon or for Coop?" Luke queries.

"Both. Coop loved mum for years, it was a bit of a joke because he just couldn't hide it. He was soft and baby-faced and sweet, and mum was way out of his league. Everyone always thought that dad looked like a film star or something, and next to him Coop was... just

Coop. But then everything happened and dad was gone and suddenly Coop was a hero to us and mum married him and it seemed from the outside like he won. He got the girl. But actually, she wasn't really the same girl any more. She was quiet and sad and scared and all of the things that used to make her amazing were different now. He's never seemed unhappy, but I felt a little bit bad for him."

My words are coming faster and faster as I rush to explain thoughts that I've never voiced before.

"So what does that mean?" Luke asks when I fall silent.

"Well, what if I was wrong? What if he didn't only get mum once she was sad and broken? What if they were already seeing each other? What if he's the man she was cheating with?"

There's another question. A darker question. One that I'm not ready to ask.

What if he broke her on purpose? What if he split her life apart so that he could step in and put it back together, with himself at the centre of it?

"Are you sure she was cheating?" Charlie asks.

I think about mum's face when we posed our questions at lunch.

"I think she was," I say slowly.

"If I had to guess, based on her reaction when we brought it up, I'd say so too," Luke adds.

Charlie leaps on this with outrage.

"You sleuthed without me?! Tell me everything!"

We fill her in briefly on Sundays conversation and every ounce of indignation leaves her.

"I've changed my mind. Thank you for not including me in that debacle. You couldn't have paid me to be there! You couldn't think of a more casual way of asking?!" she demands.

"It sounded better in my head!" I tell her defensively.

"Well it seems it couldn't have sounded *worse!*"

"Well what would you suggest?! Give me an example of a tactful way to ask someone if they had an affair!" I challenge, hands on hips.

Charlie lets out a low, slow breath.

"Yeah, I take your point. There probably isn't a good way to go about it. But you think they did have an affair?" she asks again.

"Mum looked really guilty and panicked," I reply grimly.

"Your dad cheated first though," Charlie reminds me in a would-be comforting voice.

"That actually doesn't make me feel any better. I really thought that before Rose went missing, my family was happy. I don't remember them fighting before that. I don't remember shouting or tension or anything, I thought all that came after."

We're all quiet for a moment. I know they don't know what to say. Luke's parents are still together and Charlie's never were in the first place. I realise that there's no such thing as a perfect family setup, but neither of them had to watch their family fall apart in front of their eyes.

"So what next?" Charlie asks, imbuing her voice

with some brightness.

"Next in what?"

"Next in the plan. Is there a plan?"

"The plan now is to make a plan," I tell them with a decisive nod.

"An admirable intention," Luke comments.

"How are you going to go about it?" Charlie asks.

"Well... I'm going to figure out what I need to know, and then work out how to find it out," I say slowly.

"I don't follow," Luke admits.

"I need to know what sort of car Coop drove ten years ago. So I need to figure out how to find out that information."

"You're definitely focusing on Coop then? Just him?"

"He's top of the the suspect list. He's top of dad's suspect list," I admit, "and he doesn't have an alibi for the day Rose went missing; he says he was home alone. Plus, if he was already seeing mum then he could have been the one with the old silver convertible. That would put him right there, right on the spot when and where Rose vanished."

"Alright, he's top of the suspect list. How do you find out what sort of car he owned?" Charlie queries.

"I'm not sure. Google?"

We walk back to Charlie's and settle in her room with a delighted Caesar holding court with frequent scratches and tummy rubs. Charlie hands her laptop over and I get to work.

"Anything?" Luke asks after a quarter of an hour of my frowning and scowling at the screen.

"No," I snap, my eyes not wavering in their focus.

"Anything now?" He asks again when another quarter of an hour passes without me saying a word.

"I don't think it's possible. There's no record or database of car ownership. No official service tracks past car insurance or anything like that. I don't even think I could find out what car someone owns *now* just by googling." I announce, pushing my hair off my face and breathing deep.

"Would the police know?" Charlie asks thoughtfully.

"I doubt it. But even if they were able to find out, they wouldn't tell me."

"True," she admits.

"What about pictures?" Luke suggests.

I look at him in wonder for a moment before launching myself at him.

"No canoodling in my bedroom!" Charlie shrieks, her voice caught between horror and amusement.

I disentangle myself from Luke and get to my feet, giving Charlie a very serious look.

"Apologies. I just think that brilliant suggestions should be enthusiastically rewarded," I explain.

"Remind me to tamp down my own genius around you then" she snorts.

"That won't be a problem," Luke tells her with a grin.

She hurls a pillow at him in righteous indignation and he hurls one back as I pull the laptop back onto my knees and navigate to Coop's Facebook page. He is far from being an avid social media user, but there are sporadic pictures of him, drinking in gardens with friends, posing with mum, smiling with me and Olly. My chest feels tight looking at them. They're all so familiar. I know this life, it's happening right alongside mine. There are more and more pictures the further back I go. When Olly was a toddler the numbers were astronomical and when he was a baby there were almost a dozen a day it seems. Before that, there are some pictures from Coop and mum's wedding- a small event, not much pomp or ceremony, but lots of love. I pause a long time on a picture of the three of us, me in the blue dress that I helped mum pick out, embroidered with flowers and stars. I felt so beautiful and special, and Coop held my hand at the very front of the ceremony because he said that this wasn't just a wedding, they weren't just becoming husband and wife, we were becoming a family.

"You alright Pen?" Charlie asks.

"Yep. Course!" I say quickly, scrolling on and smoothing whatever expression it was that made her concerned.

There are less pictures now, just the odd one of him on work nights out or him golfing with a friend. Then I see it. A picture of Coop and another man leaning against a car. He looks relaxed and confident, I'm sure that it must be his. My heart swells. It's a red four-door the same sort of shape as almost every other car in the world. It's not a convertible and it's not silver. It looks to be in good condition and fairly new.

"I might have something!" I say quickly.

Luke and Charlie both gather around and peer at she screen.

"This would be from right around that time! Look at the date! It's just days before!" I say, my excitement building.

"What does the caption say?" Luke asks eagerly.

"Coop and Reg. That's his brother's name, it must be him. He lives in Australia so I've never met him," I explain, looking closer at the other man's face. Now I know to look for it I can see the resemblance. Reg is taller and darker haired but they have the same baby face

343

and the same blue-grey eyes and easy smile.

"If this was his car, then he couldn't have been driving the silver convertible, right?!" Luke asks, his own voice filled with excitement.

"Exactly! This could mean that it wasn't Coop at the house that day! If this was his car–" I break off, catching sight of Charlie's face.

"What?" I ask her, my stomach already sinking.

"Look," she says, pointing at the screen.

I follow the line of her finger and my breath thickens in my lungs. The car keys. The car keys are visible in the picture, clutched in Reg's hand. It's not Coop's car.

Disappointment hits me like a truck. I keep scrolling back and forth but there are no other pictures of Coop near any kind of vehicle and nothing else helpful from around the right time.

"Would it have killed him to post more pictures?!" Luke exclaims in exasperation as I flop onto Charlie's bed and hold out an arm to welcome Caesar into a consolation hug.

"He's not much of a social media person to be honest," I mumble into the dogs flank.

"Why?! People love photos!" Luke complains, totally hypocritically, as he scrolls through the same pictures I've studied and discarded.

I sit up.

"What?" Charlie asks.

"Well he does have photos. He just doesn't post that much," I say thoughtfully.

"Did he take more pictures than he posted back then?" Charlie asks, following the line of thought with me.

"It's possible," I shrug not wanting to let my hopes rise too high.

"Where would they be then?" Luke asks, setting aside Charlie's laptop.

"On his old laptop I guess. He has a couple in the loft. All the pictures since Olly was born he backed up onto a separate hard-drive, but from before that I'm pretty sure he just kept the old laptop that had them on, just in case."

This is the first step in the plan. Get into the loft without arousing suspicion and find Coop's old laptops. Step two is to check them for pictures and anything else from the time Rose disappeared. I need to confirm the affair one way or the other.

I write these two steps down on a blank piece of paper and slip it into the back of my science book. Just seeing them in ink makes me feel more grounded. I need more steps of course, but depending on my findings my course will diverge, one route leading me deeper into Coop's life and the other taking me away.

Luke walks me home and he spends those few minutes talking about TV shows and books and things that feel deliciously normal. I hold his hand tightly in mine and tell myself that everything is going to be normal soon. Every interaction will be like this one, with no sleuthing and no awful conversations over Sunday lunch. We'll talk about Star Trek and Lord Of The Rings and no one will leave roses in my locker.

"I'll see you tomorrow morning," he tells me with a kiss, "I still plan to escort you to classes. With Coach Dan roaming the halls I want-"

"PENNY!"

Luke and I both turn as mum flings herself into my arms, shaking and sobbing.

"Mum?! What happened?!" I ask frantically, trying to get a look a her and see if she's hurt.

"Paula! She's fine! I told you she was alright, see? She was just at Charlie's house with Luke, just like her message said," Coop croons softly, pulling mum back into his arms as she continues to reach for me.

"What happened?!" I demand.

"It's just a bad spell," Coop murmurs in an undertone.

"It's not just a bad spell! She's terrified!" I hiss, not letting go of my mother's hand as she sobs and tries to clutch me to her.

"I don't know what happened, she's been getting

347

worse since she got home today, she's just..." he trails off, shrugging my concerns away and tenderly tucking a lock of hair back behind my mother's ear.

"Penny?" Olly whimpers from the doorway.

"NO!" mum shrieks, turning on Olly in a flash, "you need to get back inside! It's not safe!"

Olly whimpers again and shrinks back. I dart around mum and Coop and gather my brother into my arms.

"It's alright Olly, mum's just not feeling well again, but it's going to be fine. I'm home now," I tell him, stroking his hair as I feel him shake with sobs of his own.

Coop firmly guides mum back inside as she wails and clutches her hair.

"They're fine love, the kids are fine, Penny and Olly are both here, they're both safe," he repeats over and over while she keeps crying.

"*My baby! My baby!*"

I'm about to follow after them with Olly when Luke's voice stops me. I'd let myself forget that he was here, witnessing this.

"Is there anything that I can do? Do you want me to stay?"

I love him for asking. I really do. But I want him as far away from this scene as possible.

I tell him that we're fine even though he can't possibly believe me and I even manage a smile when I tell him that I'll see him tomorrow. It's a relief to close the door behind us and shut the world out. Whatever I may hope for the future, we're not normal. Nothing about this is normal.

"Olly, what happened?" I ask intently.

"I don't know, mum just started getting upset and then she was crying," he weeps.

"It's alright, it's going to be okay, but what made her upset?"

"I don't know, I was doing my legos and then mum came in. She'd been talking in the kitchen," he recounts.

"Talking in the kitchen? To Coop, to your dad?" I press.

"I don't know, I could only hear her, she was loud," he explains.

"Could you hear what she was saying?" I ask, studying his face.

He squirms and tries to bury his face in my shoulder.

"Olly, it might be important," I say in a hushed whisper.

"She said it was her fault. That she was punished."

He breathes the words, his eyes so wide and fearful that I pull him into my arms and hold him so tight he barely draws breath.

"What did she mean Penny? What was she talking about?" he asks when I let him go.

I wait a long time before answering.

"I don't know Olly. But I'll see if I can find out."

Coop takes care of mum and I take care of Olly, helping him with pyjamas and tucking him into bed like he's half his actual age. By the time he's settled enough that I feel comfortable leaving him, mum is asleep. Dead to the world.

"Did you give her a sleeping pill?" I ask Coop in a flat voice, looking at my prone mother from the doorway.

"I had to give her something, you saw what she was like," he responds with a sigh.

I don't answer, I just walk away.

I wake early the next morning and check on Olly. He's still sleeping but I go downstairs and make him some pop-tarts, a treat usually reserved for weekends. I fell asleep still playing his words over and over in my head.

She said it was her fault. That she was punished.

What does that mean? There are so many ways to interpret those words and they all scare me to death. I can't even be certain of who mum was talking to, but I'm pretty sure it was Coop, he was the only one I know was in the house. One thing I am certain of is that I don't want either of them near Oliver. I take the pop-tarts up to him and wake him gently, sitting on the edge of his bed.

"Penny?" he asks blearily, his eyes widening in alarm. I'm not usually the one who wakes him for school and I can see him wondering what's wrong.

"I made you some breakfast," I whisper with a reassuring smile. I give him a conspiratorial wink too and put a finger to my lips like this is some secret treat.

"Pop-tarts!" he exclaims in a whisper of his own, shuffling up to a sitting position and receiving the plate from me with delight.

"Yesterday was a bit... rubbish," I say evenly, "sometimes you just need a treat."

He nods solemnly at me and looks at the pastries with increased respect.

I hover while he starts eating but eventually I need to go and get ready for school myself. I race through getting washed and dressed and resume my position as sentinel on the landing while Olly puts on his uniform and gets his school things together. I keep glancing at the door to mum and Coop's room, where sounds of movement and low voices emanate but no one has yet appeared. At the last moment mum steps out, dressed and ready but looking anxious and harassed.

"Olly are you up?! Breakfast time!" she calls, checking the time with a worried expression.

"I fed him," I say, folding my arms and gazing at her coolly.

"Oh! Thank you Penny," she replies uncomfortably.

I just shrug and keep watching her. She looks tired but she's dressed for work so clearly she's planning on going.

"So what's the plan?" I ask in clipped tones.

"Same as always, we'll drop Olly off first and then..." she trails off and a silence hangs in the air, thick and stagnant.

Olly is the one who breaks it, rushing out of his room with his backpack swinging behind him.

"Careful!" I laugh as the momentum of his bag causes him to bump into the wall and then into me.

I catch him against me and keep my hands on his shoulders.

"Alright then, shall we go?" mum asks with an uneasy smile from across the hall.

We trail downstairs and out to the car where I decide to sit in the back with my brother. He's thrilled and spends the whole journey to his school talking a mile a minute about a new movie that's coming out soon. Things are mostly normal until we pull up outside the gates and he goes to open his door. It doesn't budge.

"Mum?" I say as Olly continues to lift and release his door-handle.

"Mum, the child-lock," I say louder.

She doesn't move. She's twisted in her seat, facing Olly with wide, slightly vacant eyes. I can see her breathing becoming faster.

"Mum!" I snap.

She still doesn't move and Olly sits back in his seat uncertainly, looking between me and mum with a scared, unhappy expression. I unfasten my belt, and clamber to the middle of the car, reaching past mum to the controls and hitting the child-lock button. Then I lean across Olly and swing his door open with a smile.

"There we go, open sesame," I say brightly.

He slips out of the car without a word and hurries across the playground without a backward glance. I slump back into my seat and watch mum's face as she gazes at the empty space where her son sat.

"Mum!" I snap when she doesn't move.

She jumps and straightens in her seat.

"What was your fault?" I ask the back of her head.

She starts the car and pulls away as though she hasn't heard me, and I'm too much of a coward to ask again.

"Good morning mi'lady" Luke says with a small bow that sends colour rushing to my face.

"Dork."

"Is *dork* a thing? Do people say that?" he replies pensively.

"If they don't, I'm bringing it back. I have no choice, you are absolutely a dork."

"How were things after I left?" he asks, dropping his voice, suddenly serious.

"Awful. But Coop drugged mum into unconsciousness, so she wasn't much trouble," I recount bitterly.

"Well, that's... one way to go I suppose," Luke comments doubtfully.

"Maybe the right way," I mutter.

She said it was her fault. That she was punished.

What did you do, mum?

"So, not to change the subject, but are you going to Cross-country today? Please tell me you're not. I mean-there's no reason to now, right?" Luke asks anxiously as we wander towards the school doors.

I feel a sharp pang in my chest. I hadn't thought about it, I hadn't given myself the chance, but I suppose he's right. There's no reason to go now that I know Dan Cosford had nothing to do with Rose, and Tina is safely far away. Going would just be tempting fate.

"I guess not," I agree slowly.

"You like running though, don't you," Luke replies with a deep sigh.

I stick my bottom lip out in a pout and nod. I'm making light of it, but I really do enjoy running and it was thrilling to do so well at something.

"I'm not going to say a word," he sighs again and wraps an arm around my shoulders.

"PENNY COOPER!" a voice shrieks and heads turn.

"Never subtle, is she?" Luke comments with a grin.

Charlie storms over to us with an expression of absolute outrage on her face. I'm still desperately trying to think what I could have done to incur her wrath when she reaches us.

"You had a fist fight with Claire Netherhall and you didn't bother to tell me?!" she demands in her attempt at a whisper.

"I did not have a fist fight," I grumble, squirming.

"What would you call it then?" she asks, hands on hips, "because *I'm* hearing fist fight."

"A minor altercation?" I attempt feebly.

"A minor altercation?! I heard you tackled her into a bank of lockers!"

Luke turns towards me now, his eyebrows lost in his hair.

"What's this now? Where was I when this fist fight took place?"

"I'd just got back from Janet. And it wasn't a fist fight!" I repeat.

"Tell us everything. It's the only way," Charlie announces with a flourishing hand gesture.

I sigh but I give in.

"Mr Danes called her cruel and malicious?! I mean- he actually said the words? Cruel and malicious?! Go Mr Danes!" Charlie comments happily once I've given them my account.

"Very McGonagal," Luke agrees.

"Ooh! Great comparison!" Charlie approves.

"Really? I don't see it. Maybe we should get him a pointy hat," I suggest.

"You know what we mean," Charlie insists, "he protects you! You're his teachers pet! You always have been! Does this make Claire Netherhall Umbridge?"

"Now *there* I can see a resemblance."

"Claire definitely crossed a line. Mr Danes wasn't just protecting me, he was protecting mum and himself too," I explain.

"Because Claire dared to mention the world's most obvious crush?" Charlie asks sceptically.

"His wife definitely wouldn't like it," I point out.

"Hmm... I still think he was looking out for you. He's been protective since your first day," Charlie counters.

"I say take the protection. Maybe it'll balance out some of the more obnoxious teachers," Luke suggests.

"Is that a reference to first period double English by any chance?"

Luke walks us to our form room for registration and promises to be back to walk us to English too. Apparently thanks to my incredibly minor altercation with Claire, I will still be being escorted to classes for the foreseeable future. I'm not complaining.

He's as good as his word and the three of us make our way to class together and select our customary seats, with me in the middle flanked by Charlie and Luke.

"Maybe you should tell Mr Danes" Charlie hisses when Ms Gittings accidentally drops my work book onto the floor rather than placing it in my outstretched hand.

"Tell him what exactly?"

"Tell him about this!" she hisses back, gesturing with her pen towards Ms Gittings' hastily retreating back.

I just sigh. I don't think there would be much point in complaining, except perhaps to increase my teacher's existing animosity. I'm not sure why exactly Ms Gittings hates me, but I am sure that she won't be the last person who does. It's probably best that I develop a thicker skin and learn to tune her out. By the end of the lesson I'm thinking that my skin might need to be thicker than I'd ever realised.

"Who knew that Machiavellian literature could be used as a weapon," Charlie marvels as we trudge along the corridor to get some lunch.

"I was noting down the veiled references and the significant looks, but eventually I lost count," Luke tells us, shaking his head in wonder.

"It didn't even make sense! Most of it had nothing to do with abduction or crime or anything!" I complain.

"So you're most annoyed by the inaccuracy of her insulting literary parallels?" Luke asks, an eyebrow raised.

"It did sound more like she was calling you a slut," Charlie agrees thoughtfully.

"Exactly!" I agree.

"Who's a slut?" a voice asks from behind us.

I turn to find Chris just catching up to us and shift over to make room for him to walk alongside.

"Penny is apparently," Charlie tells him.

"I'm missing something here, aren't I" he responds, looking between the three of us for enlightenment.

"Penny is not a slut," Luke clarifies.

"Though she could be if she wanted to be! If men can whore around all over the place then women can too!" Charlie declares, holding up a fist in what I imagine is meant to be some kind of feminist power move.

"But I don't want to be a slut," I tell her helplessly.

"Well that's fine too, sweetie," she says comfortingly.

"We just had a weird English class," Luke adds when Chris looks no more clued-in than before.

"Oh, someone in English called Penny a slut?" he asks.

"Ms Gittings," I confirm.

"*Ms Gittings* called you a slut?!"

"Can we all please stop saying slut?" I beg.

"Is she allowed to do that?!" Chris demands.

"She did it very subtly," Luke explains.

"At least at first," Charlie says, quirking her brow upward, "It was all very sneaky really."

Her tone is almost admiring and I scowl at her to remind her what side she's on.

"That's crazy! You almost make me wish I'd taken English!" Chris remarks, shaking his head.

We purchase our sandwiches and chips and again Charlie buys me a treat to commiserate.

"If that woman keeps being awful to you in lessons, you're going to get fat," she tells me as we leave the dining hall.

I'm about to point out that Charlie is the one buying the cookies, but Luke interrupts.

"Are we heading back to our grassy corner for lunch today?"

"Actually, I have a different idea," I tell them, blushing slightly.

"Well this is nice," Chris comments, looking around at all the rose bushes.

"It's a memorial garden, for my sister," I tell him.

"Hence all the roses. Nice. And kind of morbid," he

replies.

"Thank you!" Charlie cries victoriously, settling onto a bench and tucking her coat around her.

"It isn't morbid, it's beautiful!" I tell them stubbornly, sitting across from Charlie.

"It was morbid how *fast* the garden was made after Rose went missing. The police were still looking! The case was red hot! And here this *memorial garden* got built," Charlie argues.

"People wanted to *do* something. They wanted to help and there was no way that they could. I think making the garden gave people the chance to volunteer and feel like they were helping my family. Besides- the case was never red hot," I point out.

It's true. Rose vanished into thin air. One minute she was in the woods with me and the next she disappeared into the trees and was never seen again. There was no trace of her. They scoured the woods, they talked to everyone, they desperately hunted down leads, but there weren't any.

Until Charlie told me about the car on my driveway, it seemed like there was no one known to be near the woods that day who hadn't already been cleared. My dad spent a decade creating a list of people who had ever met my sister or been involved in any kind of child related crime and then determining where they were that day. It was a laborious and soul sucking way to investigate and he hadn't found any answers.

"I still think it's a bit weird," Charlie maintains.

"And I still think it's beautiful," I counter.

The garden is open to everyone and it's supposed to be a space for community. It was built and maintained by volunteers though only Mr Danes still tends the plants regularly. He started the garden and he still comes here to look after it and to get away from his wife. When I asked him for permission to come here during school hours for lunch, he was only too happy to say yes.

"It's very nice," Luke agrees loyally, settling beside me on the bench and lifting his coat collar.

"It is a bit cold though," Chris adds, tightening a

scarf that's definitely overkill.

I glare at them all in turn and they hastily adopt expressions of comfort and satisfaction with their surroundings.

"It was a really nice idea Penny!" Charlie finally agrees.

I allow myself to be satisfied with that and turn my attention back to my fries and ignore the cold seeping into me from the pretty wrought iron bench.

"So are you going to cross-country today?" Charlie asks.

"She's not sure yet," Luke tells her when I sigh.

"What?! I thought you'd be staying as far away as possible!" she exclaims.

"Because of smarmy Coach Dan the psycho killer," Chris comments, slowly nodding his comprehension.

"Turns out not a killer, but definitely still a psycho," I correct.

"I take it you wont be signing up for one-to-one classes then?" Chris asks Luke.

Charlie and I both look confused by this question. Luke is by no means weak or out of shape, he's actually a pretty wonderful shape, but physical education isn't exactly one of his interests.

"Coach Dan is trying to convince all the guys to sign up with him as a Personal Trainer," Luke explains.

"Marcus Kain has weekly session with him, doesn't he? And he's being given time in school hours to meet with him too," says Chris.

"Really? How is that going to help him with a career in finance?" I ask.

"Finance? Marcus?" Charlie snorts.

"That's what Claire says he's going to do," I tell her.

"Well then Claire is delusional. There's no way Marcus is going to work in finance unless his life takes some seriously unexpected turns. He doesn't want an office job at all," she explains.

"What does he want to do then?" I ask.

Charlie just shrugs and eats another fry. I'm actually a little comforted that someone else in our year doesn't have a plan for the future, even if it is Marcus Kain.

"Seems to me like he's on track to be the next Coach Dan. They're very chummy," Chris suggests.

Chris doesn't know exactly how chummy Dan Cosford has been with a student in the past but Charlie, Luke and I exchange looks while he unwraps his sandwich.

"So if he's not a psycho killer, why are you going to cross-country?" Chris asks a moment later through a mouthful of tomato mozzarella panini.

"I like running," I say simply.

"And cross-country would look good on a uni application," Charlie adds thoughtfully.

My french fry turns ashy in my mouth. I give a slightly jerky nod and force myself to swallow.

"I don't like it. Dan isn't going to be happy with you," Luke says firmly.

Chris looks interested at this but the conversation sweeps along.

"Maybe not, but he doesn't know anything for sure

and I don't want to miss out just because he's a jerk. I can stick with Sophie and the other girls anyway," I tell him.

"Only if you're prepared to hustle! Sophie is *fast!*" Charlie comments.

"I'm faster," I tell her, allowing myself a small smile.

"Seriously?!"

I could be offended by her incredulity but honestly it came as a surprise to me too. Fear and adrenaline had forced me to push myself and find new limits. It turned out I was a damn good runner.

We continue to chat about inconsequential topics until our food is gone and then a silence descends as everyone tucks their hands into their pockets and turns to look at me with imploring expressions. It takes a full minute of shivering for me to work out what they're hinting at.

"Fine!" I announce eventually, "we can go inside!"

We practically jog back to the main doors of the school and even I breathe a sigh of relief when we gain the warmth of the entryway.

"Maybe there's a staircase somewhere we can hide under," Charlie suggests, rubbing her arms.

"Very Harry Potter," Luke comments.

"It's only September, it shouldn't be this cold," I grumble.

"Global warming," Chris tells me, nodding wisely.

"That sounds counter intuitive," Charlie tells him.

"Alright, climate change," he concedes.

"Thank you, that's much better."

We opt for strolling the corridors and hoping that mine and Charlie's fame will be enough to get us a reprieve if we encounter a teacher.

"I don't know why they think fresh air is so healthy anyway!" Charlie mutters, casting a dark look out of a window.

"To be fair, we do have the Sixth Form Common Room," Chris reminds her.

"Yes but that's full of Sixth Formers. And the younger years are still forced outside for the whole lunch hour," she reminds him.

"My old school let people stay indoors through lunch," he tells us.

"Really?! I thought it was a national phenomenon, that all teachers think fresh air and sunshine is healthy in literally any weather!" Charlie tells him.

"Nope. Your teachers are just sadistic."

This debate continues until a flash of blonde hair at the end of the corridor stops and backs up at the sight of us.

"Penny!" Sophie calls out and jogs up to us.

We all exchange greetings before Sophie turns her attention back to me with a frown.

"I was looking for you, have you heard?" she asks.

"Heard what?"

"Cross country practice is cancelled today," she tells me.

"Really? Why?" I ask quickly.

Is this it? Has word gotten out about Tina? Is Dan going to be taking time off work after the collapse of his marriage? Do people even do that?

"Apparently Marcus Kain's muscles are more important than the whole girls' cross-country team," she tells me hotly.

"What?!"

"He's having a private weight session today. No other explanation! I tried to talk to Mr Danes but he said there's nothing he can do. It's ridiculous! Coach Dan has been acting really off this term, and now this!"

I could tell her why he's been acting off. I could probably even tell her why he's cancelled our practice, but I won't.

"That's rubbish!" I say instead.

"You can bet they wouldn't just cancel the *boys* practice like this," Sophie comments, shaking her head in disgust.

"So true! Girls' sports are always treated like an afterthought! Second class!" Charlie agrees enthusiastically.

"I thought Penny wasn't sure about going anyway,"

Chris queries, earning himself a look of hostility from three quarters of his companions.

"I bet if *you two* wanted to do cross-country practice-" Sophie begins grumbling at Chris and Luke.

"Hey! I don't even do any sports! I am clearly not the enemy here!" Luke hastens to remind us.

"Why weren't you sure whether you were going?" Sophie asks, switching her focus back to me.

"Oh that, I'll explain in science," I tell her with a shrug that I hope says - this explanation is very boring and mundane, but too long to provide right now.

She seems to accept it and hurries off to inform more of the cross-country girls about the cancelled practice.

"What are you going to tell her?" Charlie asks curiously.

"No idea. She likes Coach Dan, or at least she did before today. I don't think I can tell her that I'm avoiding him."

"At least it looks as though he's avoiding you too.

That should make it easier," Luke tells me with a broad grin.

"Ever the optimist," I comment with an indulgent smile.

"Yep that's me - Mr Bright-side-of-life," he agrees, pulling me towards him and pressing his lips slowly to mine.

A charge runs through the length of my body but Charlie's voice cuts through the moment like a knife.

"You two and your canoodling! If you get us sent outside into these arctic conditions I am going to be livid!"

I step back with a sheepish expression and a deep blush, but Luke looks utterly unrepentant. His eyes stay fixed on me for another moment in a way that does absolutely nothing to cool my cheeks.

We resume our walking and manage to avoid being caught by any teachers or staff before the bell rings for afternoon registration. At this point Luke and Chris go one way, and Charlie and I the other.

An afternoon of double science lays ahead of me and I trudge there with Luke's hand clasped in mine. He's still escorting me to each class, though it must be making him late. I selfishly linger, stealing one last kiss before slipping into the classroom and hurrying to my seat between Sophie and Abed. The slight curve to Sophie's lips tells me that she knows exactly what I was doing, and once again I feel colour flood my face.

"Ah! Penny! Good!" Mrs Haskins calls from the front, making my stomach lurch. Am I really that late for class?!

"I have the information for you three about the open evening!" she continues brightly, holding up some sheets of paper.

I draw a blank. Open evening?

"We agreed last week," Sophie mutters in an undertone when she sees my vacant expression, "to help out. You, me and Abed."

Oh God, it does ring a vague bell, though everything else that's happened had driven it out of my mind. I briefly contemplate backing out - just telling Mrs Haskins that I can't be there after all, as I'm too busy trying to figure out whether someone close to me is responsible for my sister's death.

She said it was her fault. That she was punished.

But I know that I won't.

"Brilliant!" I say cheerfully, holding out my hand for the papers when she reaches us.

It's a brief run through of times- when to arrive and help set up, when the event opens to the public, what experiments we'll be demonstrating, then what time it ends and we start clearing up. It all looks fairly simple and it might actually be fun to show some small people some science.

"Looks good," Sophie agrees happily, scanning the sheet.

Abed nods his agreement and carefully puts his copy in his bag. I follow suit and we turn our attention back to today's topic in our text books, ready to learn.

Two hours later I have a headache and a text from

mum saying that she headed home early. I forgot to let her know that cross-country was cancelled, so I can't really blame her. Still, I feel a twinge of unease that she's going to be home with Olly for any length of time without me. Luke is waiting outside the classroom when I leave and we head together towards the buses. We make it as far as the main lobby before a raised voice catches my attention.

"I just want to get that *definition*, right?"

"Absolutely. That's what everyone wants now."

"It's not about size, I don't want *huge* muscles, I want that *defined shape*."

Marcus and Dan are performing for a group of adoring girls. They're both holding up their arms so that their biceps can be admired more easily and Marcus is even lifting his shirt to display his abs. I see Claire in the group and her face is a picture of conflict. It's clear that she's enjoying everyone admiring her boyfriend, the adoration and the envy in their faces is like a drug, but she also shows an underlying layer of doubt. I wonder if

377

she's starting to realise that Marcus has no plans to go into finance and make her rich, or if maybe it's something deeper. Does some small kernel of self preservation in Claire make her wonder whether Dan Cosford may not be the role model she'd choose for Marcus?

"It's all about those defined V-shaped abs, right Dan?" Marcus asks.

"Oh absolutely. I have some killer exercises for you to work on those. We need to up your weights too. If we can get you bench pressing a bit more-" Dan begins but the fluttering, breathy voice of Rosemary cuts in.

"Do you think you could bench-press *me* Coach Dan?" she asks sweetly, making my stomach roil.

Claire casts her a sharp look but Dan and Marcus both laugh so Rosemary doesn't even see it.

"How's Tina, Dan?" Marcus asks loudly, shifting his gaze quickly to Rosemary with a look of condescension, and then back to Dan with amusement.

"Oh she's fine, you know Tina," Dan responds

lightly.

"Oh yeah, Tina's always *fine*," Marcus replies with a laugh and a significant look.

Dan laughs wolfishly and Rosemary wilts. The laughter continues as Luke and I slip out into the cold air, but despite Dan's apparently jovial mood I couldn't help but notice that the laughter never reached his eyes.

"He's not telling people she's gone then?" Luke murmurs in an undertone.

"Doesn't want to be humiliated I expect."

"He didn't look happy though, did he? When Marcus brought her up, he looked... I dunno," he trails off uncertainly.

"No. No, he didn't look happy at all."

I run all the way home from the bus stop. It's just a few streets but it's enough to trigger the itch to go further. Soon- I promise myself. Soon I'll make time for a real run, as fast as I can go.

For now however, my place is very definitely here.

"Olly?" I call as I push open the door.

"Penny!" he calls back happily, tumbling into the hallway to meet me.

I feel a wave of relief that he's here, safe and happy. I don't know what I was expecting, but- well- I feel relieved.

"How's mum?" I ask him quickly in a low voice.

"I think she's okay," he responds a little uncertainly.

"Have you had a snack?"

"No, not yet. She-" he begins but breaks off.

"What?" I ask in a whisper.

"She keeps standing in the hall," he murmurs.

"Standing in the hall?"

It's not what I would have expected him to say if I'd even begun to guess.

"Penny! I was just about to toast come crumpets! Do you want some?" mum asks, coming down the stairs towards us with a broad smile.

"Um, yeah, that sounds good," I tell her, wrapping an arm around Olly's shoulders.

"Wonderful! Wonderful. Crumpets all round," she confirms with a sharp nod.

"We'll be in the lounge," I tell her, steering Olly back through the door and towards the sofa.

Her wide smile and bright eyes didn't look quite right. I wonder if she's just taken her medication or if maybe she's on the wrong dosage now. If, like she told me, it's all a balance of the right medication and the right amount, she definitely doesn't seem balanced now.

She said it was her fault. That she was punished.

"I'm going to help mum with the crumpets," I tell Olly once he's settled in front of Wallace and Gromit.

I open the door from the lounge to head to the kitchen but I stop in my tracks. Mum is standing in the hall. She's opened the door to the back porch and she's just stood back, staring.

"Mum?"

She doesn't react. Not a flicker of recognition, not a single sign to show that she's heard me.

"Mum!" I try again louder.

This time she almost jumps out of her skin and wheels round wide eyed, to look at me.

"Penny!" she exclaims, her voice harsh and brittle.

"Do you need a hand with the crumpets?" I ask her, trying to keep my face passive.

"Crumpets?" she murmurs vaguely, her eyes slipping back to the porch.

"I'll do them. Why don't you go and rest," I suggest helplessly.

She nods dreamily and I wait until she's taken a small step towards the stairs before I go into the kitchen and dig out the crumpets from the cupboard, shoving a few into the toaster while I find the honey and butter. I wolf down my own stood at the counter and assemble Olly's on a plate for him, with just the merest sliver of honey since I know that somehow he's going to manage to cover himself in it. I go to deliver his food but when I leave the kitchen I find that mum never made it out of the hall. She's one step further towards the stairs but her eyes are fixed on the porch and her expression is somehow both vacant and anxious at the same time.

"Mum?"

She doesn't move, barely even her lips, she just breathes the words.

"I am *so sorry.*"

"Mum?"

She doesn't respond.

"You're sorry for what mum?" I press.

She breathes out a small sigh but still seems frozen.

"Mum is there something you want to tell me?" I try desperately, "did something happen?"

"She keeps not walking through that door," she mutters, her voice coming from far away. Her head on one side, body limp, a marionette held in a slack hand.

"Is that my crumpets?!" Olly's voice calls from the lounge, sending a jolt through mum like an electric charge bringing her back to life.

She spins round to look at me, her face a mask of panic.

"Sometimes I don't know what I'm saying," she tells

me in a frantic whisper.

"But what were you talking about?!" I insist.

"It's been such a long time," she mutters in her strange, dreamy voice, her gaze wandering away and back towards the porch.

"Mum!" I snap, making her flinch.

"I think you're right," she says suddenly.

"Right about what mum?"

"I think- I think I'll go and rest."

She hurries to the stairs and up, her steps barely seeming to make a sound. I feel dampness on my cheeks and it takes a moment to realise that I'm crying. Tears are flooding down my face and I try my best to wipe them away with my sleeve but they're falling faster than I can keep up with.

"Penny?" Olly's small voice from the door to the lounge brings my head up.

"Sorry Olly Wally, I have your crumpets here," I tell him, handing him the plate.

"Penny, what's wrong with mum?"

"I don't know," I admit.

"She seems scared," he says.

"She does, doesn't she."

"Is she scared of the person who took Rose?"

The words are a punch to the gut, a knife to the chest, a bullet to the head.

"I really don't know. But it's going to be alright," I tell him.

The words sound small and insufficient to me, but then- Olly *is* small.

"Alright," he whispers, taking his crumpets and going back to the sofa and the comfort of a predictable plot-line.

No creaking sounds overhead. I wonder what mum is doing. Is she in bed? Is she pacing her room? Or is she in Rose's room perhaps, replaying old memories?

She said it was her fault. That she was punished.

I am so sorry.

I'm going to clear out the porch.

Chapter 14

Dust seems to have resettled since my last cleaning session so I begin by going over the same ground, spraying and wiping until things look fresh again. The sharp lemon scent of the cleanser is soothing compared to the musty stench of stale air that had settled into everything. I'm going to make the porch look how it used to. Whatever memories are haunting mum, I want details. I want to know what she's thinking of when she stands hopelessly in the hallway looking at the back porch. I want to know what she's sorry for.

She said it was her fault. That she was punished.

I am so sorry.

Olly's words and mum's, loop round in my head. What was her fault? What happened to Rose? In what way was it her fault?! Could she actually have-

I don't let myself finish the thought. The statistics are all there, when a child goes missing or is killed, their family are always the most likely perpetrators. I just never considered it in my case. I thought my family was a happy one. Shows what I know.

But there's still the car that Charlie saw. And there's still Coop.

If he was already in a relationship with mum then he may have been here that day, close to the woods, without anyone knowing. I just need to find out what car he drove ten years ago.

Slowly, I stack one shoe bucket on top of the other and hoist them up into my arms before making my way out into the hall.

"Penny?"

Olly's voice is small and hesitant as it so often is

these days.

"Hey Olly Wally, I'm just going to take these up to the loft and sort them out, alright?" I tell him reassuringly.

He nods and goes to turn back to the television but I stop him.

"I might be up there a little while, so, if mum comes back downstairs will you come and get me?" I ask him, trying to keep my voice level and calm.

He nods again and this time I let him go. He didn't question it. I wonder if he realises that I'm scared to leave him alone with her. I wonder if he's scared too.

I carry the baskets upstairs, setting them down on the landing while I pull down the concealed ladder that leads to the loft. Getting them both up and through the hatch is tricky, but with some careful balancing and a scrape to one elbow, I manage it. I hope I've bought myself enough time.

I scan the attic quickly in the measly light of the one naked bulb that swings gently in the centre of the room.

There are boxes everywhere. A lot of these look as though they predate Coop coming to live with us, they might even be from mine and Rose's baby years, but along one wall is a selection of boxes that might be what I'm looking for. They're more organised and localised than the rest. Most of the room's contents looks like a sprawling mass. Piles and stacks look as though they grew organically over time. These boxes however, are all the same age and the same size. A few look as though they might have seen activity in the last few years, but they're still grouped together, separated from the debris of a family living their lives for over two decades.

Coop's boxes.

I start with the boxes at the front, the ones that look as though they've been opened at least semi-regularly. In one I find office things, spare business cards, a hole punch, some empty ring-binder folders. Another has a few pairs of jeans that I know Coop can't fit into any more and a jumper that mum gave him last Christmas that I could tell he hated. Unbidden a smile tugs at my lips. I still remember the broad smile on his face when he opened it, concealing the faint look of dismay. Mum couldn't understand why I was laughing and her confusion set Olly and Coop off too. We'd all been in hysterics, my sides aching as I shook with laughter.

Please, tell me he didn't hurt Rose.

The third box I check contains two old laptops. Perfect. I quickly pull them out and plug them in to the closest socket to charge. Neither of them is switching on right away and I decide to keep checking boxes while I wait. It's just as well that I do, since I find a third laptop in an older box, further back and more encrusted with dust. There are only two sockets on this side of the loft so I have to dig around before I can find another one. Eventually I locate a viable power source behind a pair of doll prams that cause a pang of nostalgia deep in my chest. I plug in the last laptop and I wait.

The boxes are all just old clothes and school books and mementos. There aren't any photo albums or framed pictures. No helpful images of Coop in front of an old, rusted convertible with a fabric roof. The laptops are my best chance.

I hear a ding and hurry back to the first laptop I'd plugged in. It's finally switched on but it has about a hundred updates waiting to be downloaded and it isn't going to let me get any further until every single one is complete. With a sigh I begin the process, watching as the counter ticks up to one percent, then two. It's going to take an age. The second laptop is better. It must be newer because it doesn't need half as many updates and the ones it does require must be less crucial because it lets me skip them and navigate straight to the 'photos' file instead.

I trawl through them but quickly realise that I was right. This laptop is newer, it could only be a couple of years old, the pictures don't go back anywhere near far enough. I skim the other file names quickly, but there's nothing, just work documents and the odd list or two. No car insurance information or anything else that might be useful. I turn my attention back to the first laptop, waiting for the uploads to finish. The third one is still struggling to come back to life and I'm uneasily doubtful of its ability to do so. I watch the percentage bar creeping up, sometimes fast, sometimes slow. Eventually, with a series of chimes and pings it resolves into the 'home screen' and I can get to work. There are multiple folders of images so I decide to start with documents, looking for anything at all referencing a car. I try different key word searches but nothing brings any result. The folders of photos are all unnamed and don't seem to be in any particular order so I start with the last one and work backwards, hoping that they're at least roughly chronological and that I'll find some sort of temporal landmark that I can recognise to figure out when they're from.

The first picture I open is of me.

I'm sitting on Coop's shoulders, a wide expanse of blue sky above me, my expression utterly joyful. My chest tightens and I have to fight the urge to slam the laptop shut. I have to remember that I am not betraying Coop.

If he had something to do with Rose's disappearance, her death, then *he's* the one who betrayed *me*. If he's responsible then the last ten years have been a betrayal. Is that what mum's so sorry for? For bringing him into our lives? Does she suspect him? Surely if she did, she would say something. Surely, if she had any doubts at all she would take me and Olly and she would run.

I want to believe that she would, but her shaking hands and her vacant expressions rob me of any certainty. Is he the reason that she seems so afraid?

I force myself to keep scrolling back through picture after picture. I stare at our smiling faces, trying to pick out the lie. Oliver starts out a small, chubby little thing with dimpled cheeks but he gets smaller and smaller as I go, reverting back to infancy and then to a swell in mum's belly. There are wedding photos before that, and then pictures of the three of us, living our lives as a newly forged family unit. A ring sparkles on mum's finger but her face is drawn, her expression more wistful than happy. I've always remembered Coop's arrival as bringing happiness and stability back to our lives. Before him there was sadness, and with him there was joy. But looking at these photos tells a different story. Coop and I are smiling, our faces decorated with broad grins, but mum... she looks like a wounded animal. Her eyes are a little too wide and strain shows in the lines of her face. She looks broken and traumatised and I don't know how I didn't see it at the time. Coop might have saved me, but she was clearly still haunted. Did she already suspect the man beside her of harming her child?

Reluctantly I admit to myself that there aren't any pictures of the car. I scroll back to the very beginning, the first photo on the device, a picture of Coop and a group of friends out drinking together in a pub garden. There isn't a beat up old convertible or anything else that looks as though it may belong to Coop, but in that pub garden photo I do find mum. The difference is astounding. I knew that she'd changed of course, and I thought that I remembered the way she used to be, but I suppose over time it had become hazy, the image of her losing detail and definition. In this photo she looks- I don't know how else to describe it- she looks alive. She seems to radiate energy and vitality. Her eyes are so bright that I'm amazed they don't cast everything else into shadow. She's talking to the woman sitting across from her and they're both laughing, her hair is curling wildly and her skin glows. She's barely recognisable as the woman who stood in the hall downstairs, apologising for undisclosed sins. I stare at the picture for another minute, taking the time to note Coop's expression. He's watching mum with a look of almost slavish devotion. A look that sends shivers up my spine. Finally, I tear myself away, shutting the laptop down and stowing it back in the box. The pictures covered the early part of Coop and mum's marriage and extended back to the time before Rose went missing. If there were any pictures of that car, they should be here. Still, I cast another look at the third and final laptop. I could shut it down now but it would feel like leaving the job unfinished. I turn the screen towards me and see that it is lit faintly, still battling to return to life. I'll give it another minute.

I settle down more comfortably, but with nothing to do my eyes are drawn to the baskets that I abandoned by the loft hatch. Perhaps I should sort through the shoes, they've been locked away for ten years but maybe some of them will be in good enough condition to be donated. I fetch the baskets and set them out beside the laptop. One by one I lift out the contents, methodically pairing them up in neat rows.

A last, broken pair of dad's trainers that he didn't bother to take. Sandals of mum's. Loafers. Heels. Tiny shoes of mine- the pink ones that were too small but too loved to let go of. Sandals and boots and plimsolls and school shoes. For each pair of mine, a corresponding pair for Rose, still in the baskets that we dumped them in every single time we entered the house. I line them up. Two pairs of winter boots side by side. Two pairs of school shoes, never worn. We had to buy me some new ones when I was finally given the all-clear to attend. Two pairs of sandals, with butterflies on the straps.

But it's the last pair-

One pair of shoes.

White trainers with pink edging, with no corresponding pair for me.

Because I was wearing them.

I was wearing my pair that day in the woods, and so was Rose.

She said it was her fault. That she was punished.
I am so sorry.

What does this mean? What does this mean? What does this mean?

One fact has dominated my existence for ten years. One single fact has eclipsed all others- it changed my life, it tore apart my family, it cleaved my world in two.

Rose disappeared in the woods. She stepped away from me into the trees and she vanished.

I stumble to my feet and stagger to the loft hatch, almost tumbling down the ladder head first in my haste. I just barely make it to the bathroom in my room before my stomach heaves, vomit spattering the inside of the toilet with so much violence that drops are sprayed back at me. I keep retching, bringing up wave after wave, so hot it burns my throat.

Rose made it home.

I collapse onto the tiles in a sitting position, not able to care about the sick in my hair and speckling my face and my shirt.

Rose made it home.

I want to scream or run or set the house on fire. I want to tear it down brick by brick and demand that it tells me where my sister is.

Rose, what happened to you? Where did you go? *What happened?*

I force myself up onto my knees and crawl into the shower, my limbs shaking too much to stand. I turn on the water and only once I'm soaked through do I peel off my clothes, dropping them into a heap on the floor of the shower. I gradually pull myself to my feet and breathe slowly as I shampoo my hair, desperate to get rid of the acrid smell, scrubbing so hard that surely I could erase this knowledge.

"Penny?"

My head snaps up, my heart pounding. I can feel the adrenaline course through me as my shaking redoubles.

"Coop?"

Even to my own ears my voice is trembling.

"Are you alright, love? I thought I heard you being sick."

I try to think fast but my mind is still screaming at me to run.

"No- no, I just got some dust in my throat in the

loft. I'm fine now."

The words are spoken in my voice, but I didn't choose them. A feeble lie given on auto pilot while I fight the urge to flee.

"Are you sure? You don't need anything?"

"No I'm fine. I'll be out in a minute."

I turn off the water and hear him hurriedly leave the room, giving me my privacy. So considerate.

Only the thought of Olly downstairs with mum and Coop gets me out of my room.

"Penny!" he exclaims cheerfully upon seeing me.

I ruffle his hair and smile as Coop gives me a suspicious look and mum stares vacantly across the room.

"I whipped up a stir-fry," Coop informs me, gesturing to the plates already set out on the table.

"Great," I manage as my stomach rolls in protest.

Olly is into his chair in a moment and happily digs into his food but I can only pick at mine, doing my best to look unconcerned as I watch Coop and mum across the table. Coop looks normal, though definitely wary of me, and once or twice I catch him watching me closer than I'd like. Mum on the other hand, looks as though she doesn't even know where she is.

"Are you alright mum?" I ask, my voice a touch too harsh.

She doesn't respond, just continues to gaze aimlessly across the room.

"Your mum's just tired," Coop tells me when it becomes clear that she isn't going to speak for herself.

"Not sleeping well?" I press, unable to let it go.

"Mum has tablets to sleep," Olly pipes up unexpectedly.

"That's right bud, she does," Coop agrees flatly.

"Mum has lots of tablets but they don't seem to be working," I snap.

"It's complicated," Coop tells me with a long, drawn-out sigh.

"Really?! This doesn't seem that complicated to me! She's a zombie! Mum? Mum?" I keep trying, my voice raising, but she does nothing but murmur vaguely under her breath, not looking at me.

"Do you want to go and lie down Paula?" Coop asks her gently.

"Mum? Do you have something to say?" I press, my voice sharp.

Her eyes drift slowly towards mine and eventually she seems to see me.

"Penny," she mutters.

"Do you have something to tell me?"

"I'm sorry. I'm so sorry. I can do better," she whimpers, her voice raised to a whine.

"You're doing just fine love, you don't know what you're saying," Coop croons, lifting mum to her feet and sweeping her from the room.

Part of me wants to go after them, to force a confrontation, to demand answers. Part of me is too afraid.

"Penny, what's going on?" a small voice asks from beside me.

I turn and look at my little brother for the longest

time, tears stinging my eyes but I won't let them fall.

"How about a sleepover?" I ask him in a would-be bright voice.

He agrees.

To give me the best chance of actually getting some rest, I decide that Olly and I will both sleep in my room since my bed is a double. I'll have him right there, safe beside me, but I'll hopefully have enough space to be out of reach of his night time thrashings and acrobatics. I go to bed when he does, reading him a few chapters of The Hobbit until he looks as though he's really dropped off. It might be cowardly but I don't want to give him the chance to ask me any questions- I don't know how I'd begin to go about answering them.

I lay beside him in the dark, my thoughts in my locked desk drawer, now home to two decaying roses and a small pair of white shoes. I press my eyes shut and will answers to come but sleep overtakes me before I have the chance for any kind of epiphany.

Chapter 15

A small, warm body wriggles beside me, waking me up.

"Penny?" he hisses in a whisper.

"Hello Olly," I murmur back, not opening my eyes.

"Can we have pop-tarts?"

A smile tugs at my face but I grumble and groan as I check the time and drag myself out of bed. The alarm hasn't gone yet but it wasn't far off and I'm feeling well rested for once after my unusually early night. I toast four pastries and take them back upstairs to bed where we eat them while I read one more chapter of The Hobbit aloud.

"Can we have sleepovers every night?" Olly asks me sincerely.

I chuckle but when I turn to him the look on his face brings me up short. There's an awareness there that I didn't want to see. He looks wistful and wise and I'm reminded again of how much he sees and hears in this house that isn't explained.

"Come on Olly Wally, time to get ready for school."

I usher him to the bathroom and rush through my own preparations until I hear a voice calling from downstairs.

"Come on you two! We don't want to be late!"

I hurry to the top of the stairs, looking down to where mum is waiting in the hall.

"You're driving us?" I ask flatly.

"Of course."

"You're going to work?"

"Yes Penny, I'm going to work," she confirms with a sigh.

I just stand there, looking down at her. She does

look better today but I've learned not to trust that too far.

"Come on, we need to go," she adds briskly.

"Are you sure you should be going in? That you should be driving?" I ask bluntly.

"I'm fine Penny, I'm having a good day. The mornings seem to be my best time at the moment. It must just be the change in routine, going to the school first thing every day that's making things harder."

"Then don't go."

"It's my job Penny. Sean- Mr Danes- he's very understanding, but I've caused enough problems there already, I need to be reliable," she tells me.

She's talking about her very public and humiliating meltdowns. God forbid they make her seem *unreliable* to her boss.

"Mr Danes wouldn't mind," I tell her, "I could go and talk to him-"

"No! I'm going to work Penny!" she snaps.

"But-"

"Get in the car!"

We drive in awkward silence until we reach Olly's school. I watch her closely but she looks alert and she keeps her eyes on the road. I try to tell myself that I have nothing to worry about, that everything is fine, that I'm being irrational, but then she won't unlock the door.

"Mum?" Olly's voice pleads.

"He's going to be late," I say firmly, reaching for the child-lock button, but she slaps my hand away. She presses her palm over the control panel and her breath quickens into short, panicked gasps.

"Mum? What's going on?" Olly asks.

"It's not safe! Nowhere is safe!"

The words seems to be snatched from her against her will and she grimaces with the effort of falling silent.

"School is safe mum. He'll be safe," I insist, wrapping my fingers around her wrist and relentlessly prying it away.

As soon as it's exposed I press the button and turn to Olly.

"Go! Now Olly! Everything will be fine!"

He's out the door in a flash but then he stops, looking back at us, the fear obvious in his expression. I make myself smile until, reluctantly, he turns and hurries away.

A sigh brings my attention back around to mum and I'm surprised to find that I'm still holding her wrist clasped tight, her fingers paling. I push it away, shuddering, and run my hands over my face.

"What is going on?! I need you to tell me the truth!" I hiss.

She slowly turns her head from side to side as though clearing water from her ears.

"I'm sorry sweetheart, just a wobble. I'm fine now."

"Just a wobble?! Mum! You can't be serious! You're cracking up and I want to know why! What did you do?!"

She doesn't respond, just keeps her eyes fixed firmly on the road in front, her lips pursed. I keep asking right up until we pull into a space in the staff car-park and she climbs out of the car away from me.

"This isn't normal! It's not healthy!" I hiss, climbing out after her.

"Have a good day sweetheart!"

Just like that she's gone and I'm left staring after her, unanswered questions ringing in my ears. I wait a minute, ignoring the sound of students shouting and laughing, ignoring my phone chiming in my bag, ignoring the cold bite of the wind, willing myself to walk towards the school and go inside, to put everything else on hold for a few hours and just be normal.

Charlie's waiting for me out front looking distinctly disgruntled.

"I should have got a ride with you. These bus journeys are becoming less and less enjoyable," she grumbles.

"Better than driving in with mum, wondering if she's going to steer us into oncoming traffic any moment," I shoot back.

"What?!"

We were walking towards the doors but at my words Charlie grabs my arm, pulling me to a stop.

"Nothing," I tell her with a sigh.

"Penny, are you serious?"

"Maybe. Maybe I come from a whole family of psychos," I say with a shrug and a grin that she doesn't return.

"What's going on Penny? Do we need another extra-curricular team meeting?"

I think of every terrifying thought that's been swirling around in my head for the last few days. I picture a small white pair of shoes. The problem is, these new fears, as awful as they are, they don't drown out the love.

"Not yet- I- soon."

She's still studying my face intently, searching for answers in my eyes, but that's the one thing I don't have.

"Soon," I repeat, willing her to trust me.

"Alright," she replies grudgingly, "But I expect full disclosure when the time comes."

The trouble is, that's exactly the reason that I'm not ready to talk.

It's not until I'm settled in my first class that I remember my phone chiming in the staff car-park. I pull it out and see the icon for a picture message at the top of the screen. My breath catches when I open it.

One eye is still swollen- deep purples, burgundy and scarlet giving way to a rainbow of sickening hues, but her eyes are bright. The passing days have allowed her face to take on the shape of itself once more, healing back into recognisable features. I can see stitches in her bottom lip, pulled taut by a wide smile. She looks tired but happy, more like the photo in the wardrobe than I ever saw her look in real life. And clasped in her arms is a small pink form swaddled in a blanket.

Tears prick my eyes and I fight to keep them at bay but a sharp prickle in my throat warns me that I'm fighting against a tidal wave.

I shove my hand into the air and as soon as permission is granted I race into the corridor and to the nearest bathroom. Locked inside a stall I let myself go, sobbing so hard that tears blur my vision, obscuring Tina and the baby completely. I feel a rush of emotion that leaves me trembling. Fear and hope and anger and joy all rolled into one, as I watch Tina in that frozen moment, smiling out of her broken face. It takes a long time to piece myself back together and even longer to make myself presentable again before I can brave leaving the bathroom, but eventually I slip out into the deserted corridor with nothing but red-rimmed eyes to give me away.

"Peeenyyyy!" his voice is soft and musical, filled with mockery.

I don't turn around, I just keep walking but Marcus is tall, long legged and catches up with me in moments.

"Little Penny Owens, didn't your mother ever tell you that it's rude to ignore people?"

The use of my old name coupled with the mention of mum sets me instantly on edge and I know that he can see it in my stance and hear it in my breath.

"Go to hell Marcus," I snap.

"Well that's not very polite either!" he exclaims in tones of exaggerated dismay.

I grip my phone tighter in my hand, trying to call to mind the image of Tina and the baby, to fix it front and centre in my thoughts and tune him out.

"Just go away," I mutter, still trudging relentlessly towards class.

"You know, someone should really teach you some manners. Clearly you're not learning them at home," he says thoughtfully, "I suppose it's only to be expected, being raised by nut-jobs and killers. I can tell just by looking at you that you're a psycho too."

He rakes his eyes up and down me, his face twisted into a sneer but I surprise us both with a harsh bark of laughter.

"Because you're such a good judge of character?" I ask before I can reign the words back in.

"What the fuck does that mean?" he demands, his voice cold, his expression dark.

"Nothing," I say quickly, shrugging and starting to walk away again.

I pray that he'll leave it at that, walk away and let me go, but that's not who he is. Within a few strides he's level with me again and then suddenly he slams his hand into the locker in front of me, forcing me to stop. He leans in close and drops his voice low.

"I said- what the fuck does that mean?"

I don't even think about it. My adrenaline is surging from the sound of his hand making contact with the metal locker and his proximity fills me with fear. I shove him backward and he stumbles, but my phone slips out of my grip and topples to the floor, skittering away across the linoleum.

His expression, angry at first, shifts when he sees the raw terror in my face. His lips curve into a sickening smile and he makes it to the phone before I can reach it, holding it aloft with glee.

"What's this then? Something you don't want me to see?" he crows in a singsong voice.

"Marcus, please!" I mutter, low and urgent.

His face seems to freeze.

"What is this?"

His voice sounds wrong.

"Is this Tina Cosford?!" he demands, still in a voice that sounds nothing like his own.

"Is this Tina?! What the fuck happened to her?!"

I just look at him in disbelief. Incredulity.

He stares back at me, his expression inscrutable. I make the most of the moment and snatch my phone out of his hand, stowing it deep in my bag and then walking away. He doesn't call after me.

My stomach is churning so much that by lunch I can barely stomach anything. I head towards the dining hall with Charlie, Luke and Chris but the very thought of food makes me queasy.

"What's wrong with you?!" Charlie demands, seeing my pained expression.

"I feel sick," I mutter back.

"Why? Did you eat something bad?"

"No, I just did something stupid."

"Explain," she orders with an exasperated sigh.

"I inadvertently ensured that Dan is going to find out I helped Tina escape," I say in a rush.

"What's that now? You did what?!"

"His best buddy Marcus saw a picture Tina sent me this morning. She had the baby, they both look good, but..." I trail off, worrying my lip between my teeth.

"She had the baby?!" Charlie exclaims in a shrill whisper, her face breaking out into a broad smile.

"She did-" I begin but Charlie cuts me off by throwing her arms around me and jumping up and down with me tightly squeezed in her arms.

"That – is – such – good - news!" she says, each word punctuated by another little jump.

I can't help it, my own lips curve in response, a small laugh escaping my affectionately crushed chest.

"What's got you two so excited?" Chris asks.

We've ground to a halt and our celebrations are

blocking the corridor but Charlie doesn't care. She pulls back and I see her eyes shining with tears.

"They're safe!" she whispers, her face close to mine. "*You* did that Penny!"

"*We* did that," I counter.

She rolls her eyes but her face is flushed with happiness and pride and I feel my stomach settle.

"PENNY!"

My insides freeze, my breath catching in suddenly icy lungs. Charlie's smile has gone, her head whipped around to find the source of the shout but my body is locked in place, frozen solid in the middle of the corridor. All around us people have stopped and are up on tiptoes looking back and forth to see what's happening.

"PENNY!"

With another wild shriek she's on me, clinging to my face and sobbing with wild abandon.

"I lost you! I couldn't find you!" she sobs.

"Mum- mum, it's alright, I'm here, I'm fine," I assure

her hastily but her hands continue to clasp my face her eyes searching desperately, frantically within my own.

"I couldn't find you! You were so small! I couldn't find you!" she repeats over and over.

Her voice is still a shrieking wail, bouncing off the hard floor and walls as it carries along the corridor and through to the canteen where people are starting to congregate, watching the spectacle with horror and glee. We're a car crash and everyone gets to watch.

"Mum, what happened?" I try but she just keeps repeating herself.

"I couldn't find you! I couldn't find you! I couldn't find you!"

"Mum, lets get outside, get some fresh air," I suggest, raising my voice so that she can hear me over her own frantic words.

"NO!" she screams, "IT'S NOT SAFE! NOWHERE IS SAFE!"

I hear some nervous laughter picking up around us but I stay focused on her, trying to will some calm into her.

"Mum. It is safe. I am safe. I'm right here."

I try to keep my voice from shaking but I can still hear the tremble.

Mum's eyes are roving my face but suddenly they seem to catch and a small spark of reality lights her eyes.

"Where- Penny? Where are we?" she whimpers, folding herself into my arms like a little girl.

"We're at school mum. This is my school. But it's alright, we're going to go home now."

I lead her trembling form outside after handing my phone to Charlie. She calls Coop for me and in just a few minutes he's outside, gently guiding mum into his car.

"I'm coming with you," I tell him.

"Penny, you have school. I've already cleared it to work from home this afternoon, you should go to your lessons, it's an important year," he argues.

"My teachers will understand. I'm coming home," I tell him wearily.

Suddenly I feel exhausted. I am tired right down to my very bones. My head feels too heavy for my neck and my eyes are already drooping.

"Penny!" Charlie cries, hurrying over to us.

"I'm going home," I tell her, already shaking my head and going to open the car door.

"I know. I understand. I just brought your bag and your phone," she tells me, pulling me in for a quick hug.

"Thank you," I whisper into her mass of curls.

"People will have stopped talking about it by tomorrow," she tells me, her smile not reaching her eyes.

"What's one more thing for them to talk about me, hey?" I reply with a shrug.

I climb into the back-seat and lean my head against the window, enjoying the cool seeping into my skin. I allow myself a minute, my eyes pressed tightly shut. When I open them I find Coop's gaze on me in the rear-view mirror and I almost laugh.

Here I am, heading home with my murder suspects. What could possibly go wrong?

I try to feel afraid but I just feel tired. I try to sort through my thoughts but they keep on slipping away. I look from Coop to mum and back again, wondering if I really believe that one of them is a killer, but I can't hold either possibility in my mind. I need to sleep.

Coop takes mum inside and I drag myself along behind them. She's still crying quietly and muttering under her breath but I can't even summon the energy to care about what she might be saying. I just trudge up the stairs and go to my room. The bed is still a mess from Olly and me this morning and I lay down on his side, breathing in the smell of him as I let myself slide into oblivion.

Chapter 16

I only manage an hours sleep before I wake, feverish with fear. My heart is pounding and I could have sworn that someone was standing beside the bed, looking down at me, but the room is empty and the door is still closed.

I'm the only one here.

I flop back onto the pillows, drawing deep breaths that do nothing to slow my racing heart or calm my mind.

She said it was her fault. That she was punished.

I am so sorry.

Olly's words and mum's hum beneath my skin.

Mum couldn't have hurt Rose. Coop couldn't have hurt Rose. But someone did and the facts are all starting to point the same way, back towards this home and this family. I allow myself to seriously consider going to the police and telling them about the shoes. I have incontrovertible proof that Rose made it home that day, a possibility that no one seems to have even considered before. The narrative had been fixed from the first moment. Rose vanished in the woods.

It bore all the hallmarks of a fairytale, something the brothers Grimm might have penned to warn children against the dark. These are the stories so ingrained in our histories that we don't question where they came from. A beautiful child disappears in the deep dark woods- everyone looks for a monster.

I pull myself out of bed and splash cold water on my face. It helps, grounding me to the feeling of damp, icy skin. I change out of my school uniform and into leggings and a sweatshirt. The house feels cold even though I can hear the heating humming with life. It's the only sound I can hear, there's nothing from mum or Coop. Assuming that they haven't left, Coop must be in the tiny office room downstairs and mum is probably asleep. I let my feet carry me along the corridor, keeping my steps light to avoid the creak of the floorboards. I gently ease the door open to mum and Coop's room. She's tucked up in bed like a child, the covers pulled up to her chin. Her breathing is a little too heavy for sleep though, and I'm not surprised to see the pill bottle on the bedside table. I edge closer and pick it up, reading the meaningless name of the medication, all consonants and soothing vowels. Clonidine. I remember talk of something beginning with 'z' before, so this must be one of the new medications that was having such a good effect for a little while. There's a note on the label warning against taking the drug with any other medications and the sight of it almost draws a laugh out of me. Mum has been on so many meds for so long that it's a miracle her doctors can keep track. She's a delicate balancing act of antidepressants, anti-anxiety meds and sleeping aids. She's just a milligram in any direction away from total collapse. I set the bottle back where I found it and gently slide open the top dresser drawer. As I expected, there are more pill bottles inside. Four more bottles of identical white tablets. Sertraline, Benzodiazepines, Dapoxetine and Vortioxetine. A full medley of medications all to quiet her mind. I study her sleeping face.

What are you hiding? What truth are you trying to medicate away?

Meds in her bag, meds here, meds in her desk at work. She's never far away from something to smooth the jagged edges of her panic, and yet she's still imploding now. The past is creeping up on us and even if I wanted to, I'm not sure I could stop it. If dad's case goes to trial this whole situation might be taken out of our hands.

She looks so peaceful in the bed, even if it is an artificially induced moment of calm. My stomach twists as I wonder what she'll be like with the truth laid bare.

"Penny?"

I almost leap out of my skin at the sound of Coop's voice.

"What are you doing in here?" he asks, his voice soft and even.

"I- I thought I heard her. I was just checking she's alright," I hastily stammer.

He just looks at me, not disbelieving but his expression sad.

How did we get here?

"When did you start seeing mum?" I ask in a small, pleading voice.

"You already know that."

Then he just walks away.

I make sure that I'm the one to pick up Olly from school even though it means walking there and back. It's not that far and I wrap up warm despite still being indignant that it's so cold in September. Some years it still feels like summer at this point, but a cold front has chased away the last of the summer's warmth and the chill permeates everything, leaving even my hands in my pockets numb.

"Penny!" Olly is delighted to see me, hurrying over with his nose pink and his arms extended.

I fold him into a hug and glare at a passing boy who dares to snigger at the sign of affection. I know that soon my cuddly, soft, Pokemon obsessed Olly Wally is going to start pulling away. I know that ten becomes eleven and secondary school boys grow more obnoxious every day, but I'm not ready for it to happen yet. It's hard not to see a chubby toddler when I look at him. It's hard to believe that he's the same age now as Rose was when she was taken. Somehow, she still feels older than me. It's not as though she's aged along with me, it's more that whenever I think of her I'm still eight years old.

"Come on," I tell him, "let's go home."

As we walk, Olly gives me a detailed though somewhat jumbled account of his day. As always, his clearest recollections are of what he had for lunch, but he also tells me about a book they're reading as a class and some phonics they're learning.

"Are we having another sleepover in your room tonight?" he asks when our house comes into view.

"Yes we are," I reply carefully.

He's quiet, his eyes fixed on the floor in front of him.

"Is that alright?"

"I like sleeping in your room," he agrees with a nod.

"What's with the long face then?"

"Is mum alright? And dad?"

"Why do you ask that?" I query, my heart-rate picking up.

"Everything feels weird at home."

How do I explain this to him? I can't tell him that I suspect one or other of his parents committed a murder!

"You know how Charlie went missing for a bit?" I ask slowly.

He nods his comprehension.

"And then my dad got arrested? He went to prison?" I continue.

Again, more nodding.

"Well, it's made me think about things. And I think it's made mum think about things too. It made lots of people think about things, and that's making everyone weird." I explain.

"What are the things they're thinking about?"

"Mostly about Rose."

"Because she went missing too?"

"Yeah, I guess so."

That and her killer started leaving flowers for me to find.

"Rose is why mum's so sad?" he asks bluntly.

"Yep, pretty much."

"And she feels guilty."

"So it would seem, yeah," I agree.

Olly falls silent and I wish I'd had more to offer him. I should have seen this conversation coming and had some better answers ready, but I honestly don't know if there's anything I could say right now to help. Looking down at him, feeling his hand clasped in mine, I feel as though I'm being split in two. I want desperately to stop all of this, for him. I want to let it go and keep his life intact as much as possible. At the same time, I think about picking a university, any university and leaving him behind, alone with the two people he should most be able to trust...

I have to see this through.

Mum doesn't make an appearance at dinner, keeping to her darkened room and the comfort of her medicated slumber. Coop whips up a quick meal for us and we eat in silence before Olly and I retreat to my room. We keep going with The Hobbit and Olly is out like a light after just two chapters. The tension is taking a toll on him.

I try to sleep too but after crashing out in the afternoon my brain just isn't ready to shut down. Instead I set my screen brightness as low as it'll go and delve into the copious notes I made on my laptop. There's a growing feeling in the back of my mind, that this might all be too much for me to handle. I wonder how easy it would be for the police to confirm what type of car Coop drove ten years ago. They would probably have an answer by the end of the day tomorrow. I consider what they might be able to do if they knew that Rose, or at least her shoes, made it home the day of her disappearance. If something happened to her here, might there still be evidence to be found? Could there be microscopic traces of violence in the back porch? Bloody clothes stashed behind false walls?

A body?

I try to shake the thought loose but it snags on something. An inconsistency never addressed. Mum always claimed that she was right here, at home, doing laundry, the whole time that Rose and I were in the woods that day. She was preparing Rose's school uniform ready for her to start on Monday. If Rose had come home, she would have known about it. She couldn't have missed the fact.

The trouble is, I know now that Rose came home.

I try to reason it out and find the snag. Mum couldn't have hurt Rose, she couldn't have killed her and hidden her body and cleaned up leaving no trace, could she?!

Cleaned up.

Those words send a chill through me and I'm not sure why. I go back to my notes, scrolling until I find mum's account to the police of her movements that day. Nothing. Nothing but laundry. Why does that seem wrong to me?

I lay back on the bed and close my eyes, slowing my breathing the way I've practised.

I feel the sharp sting of my knee, worsening with every step. The trickle of blood runs down my leg and I can't stop worrying about getting blood on my trainers and the friendship bracelet tied to my laces. I'm so relieved when I reach the house, whimpering as I step through the back door and see mum there. Her expression holds so much love and concern as she looks at my knee. My stomach tightens as her face changes when she realises that Rose isn't with me. I don't know what it is yet but I know that something is terribly wrong. I can feel her arms around me, holding me and the cling of her damp hair, still smelling of lavender from her shampoo.

Oh. There it is. The inconsistency.

I recovered those memories more than a year ago. I've thought about them again and again, playing them back in my mind and never once noticed that they don't match up with mum's account. She didn't mention taking a shower in the middle of the day to the police. She didn't tell them that she showered, she didn't tell *me* that she showered, it isn't mentioned anywhere. I search my notes for any reference to a shower at all, but I find nothing. Maybe she just forgot, or didn't think it was important. I try desperately to believe that that's the case. Maybe she just didn't see any relevance.

A shower. Something that could be so small. Or the biggest thing in the world.

I slip out of bed and tiptoe downstairs with my phone. I gently shut the kitchen door behind me- for some reason we always think of the kitchen as being the natural room for phone calls even though there hasn't been a corded phone in there since I was a baby, and even then it was a relic. I'm not expecting dad's lawyer to answer at gone eleven, but I leave him a voicemail asking him to get dad an urgent message to call me. I keep the phone clasped in my hand, willing him to call as I sneak back up to bed and settle in beside Olly. I slide my phone under my pillow and it lies there silent, as I wait for it to ring.

I'm still waiting when dawn starts to cast the room in shades of grey and I finally drift off.

"Penny?" a gentle voice asks from the warm lump beside me on the bed.

"Hm?"

"Are you awake?"

"Hm."

"Can we have pop-tarts again?"

My eyes fight to remain closed. I drag them open and stumble out of bed, colliding with the door-frame on my way out of the room. I'm tired. So tired that I feel a little bit sick. Still, I clasp my phone tightly in my hand.

I boil the kettle and pull out the pop-tarts, already hearing signs of life from mum and Coop's room. I wonder if she's going to appear again, acting as though everything is normal and drive us to school. The thought sets my blood simmering. I make myself a very large coffee to go with my breakfast pastries and take everything back up to my room again.

I stumble over a few of the words but Olly doesn't mind. He listens happily to my reading as I trudge through the book and he only spills about a thousand crumbs onto my sheets. Checking the time, I send him off to get dressed and head to my bathroom to get ready myself. The view in the mirror is a nasty shock. My face is pale and my eyes are sunken with exhaustion. I pull my hair up into its customary bun and take the time to smear come concealer under my eyes and swipe mascara onto my lashes. I look better but there's no way that Charlie is going to be fooled. Out on the landing I hesitate, not sure what to do. There are still sounds from mum's room but no sign of her yet and if I'm walking Olly to school we'll need to leave now.

"Penny? Olly?"

I let out a sigh of relief when I hear Coop's voice. He's downstairs in the hall calling up to us in a voice of would-be cheer.

"Are you driving us?" I ask as I make my way downstairs to join him.

"I am. Your mother isn't feeling very well still."

This is the understatement of the century and I feel my hands clench into fists.

"Why is that? Why does she feel so guilty?" I demand.

"I don't know what you're talking about. Are you ready to go?" he replies flatly, brushing my words aside.

"She said that it was her fault Rose disappeared," I

tell him in a low voice.

"That's ridiculous. She just feels responsible because she's a mother. She loves you kids. She loved Rose. It's not surprising she feels guilty."

He hisses the words at me with such vehemence I catch my breath.

"How do you know? Were you here that day?" I challenge.

He just looks at me, his expression blank.

"Penny, do you want a lift to school or not?"

"I'm here! I'm here!" Olly cries happily as he bounces down the stairs, his backpack swinging on his back.

"All ready to go, buddy?" Coop asks him brightly.

"NO!" mum shrieks from upstairs, her voice desperate and wild.

Olly blanches and turns back to look up at mum who's finally emerged from her room in a whirlwind of chaos.

"NO!" she cries again, racing down the stairs in a

pyjama top and a work skirt, half fastened. Her hair is escaping from its tie and sticking up from her head in mats and tangles.

"Mum, what's-" I begin but she cuts me off when she reaches the bottom of the stairs and shoves me backward and flings her arms around Oliver.

I collide with the wall behind me and freeze, stunned.

"Paula! Careful!" Coop cries, stepping to my side.

She doesn't even look at me.

"Are you alright Penny?" he asks me.

I shrug him off, still looking at mum as she clings to Olly.

"Mum, what is it?" he whimpers.

"YOU CAN'T TAKE HIM!" mum roars at Coop and I, "YOU CAN'T HAVE HIM! I'M HIS MOTHER! I'M A GOOD MOTHER!"

"No one wants to take Oliver away my love," Coop croons softly.

"I'M A GOOD MOTHER! I'LL DO BETTER

NOW! I CAN DO BETTER!" she wails, breaking down into hysterical tears.

"Better than what? What happened mum?" I ask her.

Coop casts me a dark look but I ignore him, pressing on.

"Mum, what did you do wrong with Rose?"

Rose's name acts like a spell or a curse. Mum immediately focuses on me with a terrifying intensity.

"All my fault," she murmurs.

"How was it your fault mum? What did you do?" I ask quickly.

"I deserved this. It's important that I understand that. All my fault. All my fault. All my fault."

Her eyes glass over and her grip goes slack. The moment it happens, instinct wins out and I grab Olly from her, pulling him into my arms and shifting him behind Coop.

"I'm going to take the kids to school now Paula. I'll be back soon. Just go to your room," he tells her slowly.

She nods vaguely and starts backing up the stairs, keeping her eyes averted from the sight of me and Olly cowering by the front door.

We all half run to the car and clamber in breathing heavily.

"Coop-" I begin haltingly.

He's clasping the steering wheel tightly and his eyes are fixed out the front, though he looks deep in thought.

"I know," he says simply, "I know."

We don't speak again until we've dropped Olly off, shaken but safe.

"I'll talk to her doctor this morning," he tells me.

"I don't understand. She seemed so much better," I say.

"I know. I thought she'd really turned a corner! So did she! That's why she wasn't prepared to give up when she started feeling bad again. We were hoping it was just a blip, but-"

"It's not a blip."

"No," he agrees. "It's obviously a difficult time, but

this isn't just a blip and we don't have it under control."

A difficult time. Made more difficult by me.

"If dad doesn't plead guilty to Charlie's abduction, it's going to go to trial. There might be another police investigation into what happened to Rose. This was all going to come out anyway," I say defensively.

"What was going to come out Penny?"

He sighs as he says it but he doesn't sound exasperated, to me he sounds scared.

"I'm not sure yet. But- but I think Rose might have made it home the day she disappeared. I know she did."

He's quiet and I study his face but it's smooth as glass, I have no idea what he's thinking.

"I had a blue Ford Fiesta."

"Sorry?"

"Ten years ago, I had a blue Ford Fiesta. Is that important?" he asks me as we pull up outside my school.

"Do you know anyone who had an old silver convertible? A friend of mum's maybe?" I ask hesitantly.

"No but- your mum and I weren't that close then, I

wasn't really a part of her life."

He looks so sad.

On the spur of the moment I lean across the car and pull him into a hug for the first time in weeks. Tears prick my eyes but I fight them back.

"Penny, you're a bright girl but you can't be doing all of this on your own. You're- We're going to go to the police. I'm going to arrange for us to sit down with a detective and go through all of your concerns, alright? We'll get you all the answers that are out there, okay?"

I just nod, numb with relief.

"I think that might be a good idea," I tell him.

He manages to give me a smile and I return it shakily. It's time to drag everything out into the light.

My first stop is the school office to report mum absent from work. I probably spend more time traipsing to and from the headmaster's office than any other student and I haven't even earned it through truancy or delinquency or any of the other fun 'cy's.

Mum's desk is empty of course and the sight of it causes me a pang. I knock for Mr Danes but he isn't there and I remember that the whole reason for mum working mornings was to give him more time for his many charity obligations. I slump into mum's chair and absent-mindedly rifle through her things while I try to decide whether I should just leave or not. I could scribble a note to Mr Danes or maybe message Coop and ask him to call in a bit. I've just located mum's spare medication in her draw, once again a completely different drug, when the door clicks open and I look up to see Mr Danes surprised face.

"You're looking younger than usual Paula," he quips.

It's a bad joke since I look nothing whatsoever like my mum, but I force a smile anyway, hoping that it doesn't look too much like a cringe.

"She won't be in," I say bluntly, too tired and worn down to finesse the truth into something more palatable.

He must see something in my face because his manner changes, dropping the cheer and pleasantry.

"What's going on?" he asks me flatly.

It's such a big question that it catches me off guard. I should probably say that she has a cold or something. I should probably lie, but I don't.

"Dad's arrest. The public attention. The threat of a trial, maybe a new investigation... she's just been struggling with everything I suppose," I tell him, running my hands over my face.

"A trial? For your father? She has mentioned it," he admits with a sigh.

I'm surprised but also oddly relieved. It's nice to be vindicated- to find that I was right about her fears, her reasons for unravelling. It makes it easier to keep picking at the threads.

"Has she said anything else?" he queries.

I don't know for a moment what he means, and my confusion must be evident because he follows it up quickly.

"Does she need to take more time off? Maybe a few months until this all blows over? Or perhaps she could work from home?"

I almost emit a savage laugh at the idea of all of this blowing over in a few months, but he's being so kind that I choke it down.

"She's not lucid enough to even be thinking about that," I admit.

"Ah, I see," he sighs.

I give a small apologetic shrug and try to ignore the well of tears.

"Penny, if there's anything that I can do, anything at all that I could do to help you, please just tell me."

"It's fine," I say vaguely before forcing a little surety into my voice, "really, it's alright, Coop's going to get me an appointment to sit down with the detective in charge of Rose's case. Mum might be falling apart, but that doesn't mean everything else has to."

I know that I probably sound callous and he clearly isn't wholly approving.

"Are you sure that's a good idea Penny? Your mother is clearly fragile, and it doesn't sound like the most healthy thing for you to be concerning yourself with," he suggests, frowning.

"The truth is healthy."

He shrugs, clearly unconvinced.

"Well, let me know if there's anything I can do. I didn't get the opportunity to meet your sister, but I like to think that I know you and your mother very well. If I can be of any help, don't hesitate to ask."

"I went home yesterday, with mum. I missed my afternoon classes. It would be helpful if that didn't count against me?" I suggest tentatively.

He smiles.

"Consider it taken care of. Just make sure that your education is your first priority for the time being please? This year is very important, it could affect your whole future!"

I quickly agree and beat a hasty retreat before the talk of the future sends my anxiety through the roof. I wish that someone could understand that my mind, my whole life, is still rooted firmly in the past. Something started ten years ago and it still isn't finished.

I don't see Charlie and Luke until lunch but they both take in my appearance at a glance.

"If you thought that missing registration this morning was going to stop me from seeing what's happening here, you are crazy," she tells me, hands on hips.

"What? Nothing's happening here" I protest feebly.

"Penny, you look like you haven't slept in weeks!" she exclaims.

Luke nods his agreement, his expression serious.

"I have slept, in fact I had a nap yesterday!" I counter, though I know it's hopeless.

"What is going on?!" Charlie demands.

"We're supposed to be a team remember? You can depend on us," Luke says softly, making me feel like an absolute monster.

"I know. I'm sorry," I tell them with a sigh, "how about we meet up on Saturday? I'll fill you both in on everything. I won't do anything else until then, I promise."

"I'd rather you told us now," Charlie shoots back, but Chris is approaching and she gives a small sigh.

"Fine, Saturday, but you better not be keeping anything too big to yourself, missy!"

Luke slips his hand into mine and gives it a reassuring squeeze. Something in his expression tells me that he knows even now that Charlie is going to be irate.

After lunch they all disappear off to their lessons, leaving me to my solitary free period. I've let my school work slide and the resulting anxiety is starting to tug at the edges of my consciousness. We're only a few weeks into the year and I'm already behind on assignments and essays. I decide that since the sixth form common room is definitely still out, the library might be my best bet. An hour of silence and study should do me some good. I plough through a maths workbook, revelling in every straightforward answer, and even outline an English essay for the delightful Ms Gittings. By the time the bell rings signalling the end of the period, things are feeling slightly less out of control. I head to science hoping that I can keep the streak going, but I immediately hit a roadblock and stumble.

"Make sure you're in pristine uniform this evening you three!" Mrs Haskins calls cheerfully when I settle into my seat between Sophie and Abed.

"This evening?" I repeat slowly, looking to Sophie in panic.

"The Open Evening? Tiny humans coming with their parents to look at the school? We agreed to help?" she prompts, smiling at my obvious lack of comprehension.

She reaches over to my book and flips back a couple of pages to the information sheet Mrs Haskins gave us previously. As I scan through it, the bells finally sound and memories slot into place.

"Yes, yes of course, I remember," I insist.

Sophie's face changes, her smile smoothing and

turning down, into an expression of concern.

"If you can't do it- if you have too much going on- I'm sure Mrs Haskins will understand," she tells me in a low voice.

Clearly she heard about mum's outburst yesterday and our dramatic exit from school. At this point I imagine everyone's heard. In one way or another my family is a spectacle and not a good one, but Mrs Haskins still asked me to help out- she's taking a chance on me, making a statement of solidarity and I'm not going to pass it up.

"No. I want to do it, I'm definitely going to be there. In a pristine uniform no less!"

Sophie smiles delightedly and even Abed gives me a happy bump with his shoulder as he opens up his text book and we settle down to the lesson.

Coop picks me up from school and we go together to collect Olly from his after-school reading club. I don't ask about mum and Coop doesn't volunteer any information but as soon as Olly clambers into the car he breaks the spell.

"Is mum alright now?"

Coop sighs and pauses before answering.

"She's been a bit better this afternoon, but she's worn out. Her work stuff was dropped off an hour ago and she only chatted for a few minutes but it's left her so tired, she was practically asleep when I left to get you two."

Olly thinks this through, digesting the information.

"So she's still not very well?" he asks finally.

"No buddy, she's still not very well."

Olly slumps back into his seat and I lean my head against the window, trying not to let exhaustion overwhelm me again.

"I'm going to be out later," I announce, rousing myself, "will you be home?"

I'm not going to leave Olly unattended with mum, whatever else my commitments may be.

"Yep, I should be home. What have you got on?

Something fun I hope?"

"There's an Open Evening at school. I was asked to help out."

"Ah. So not particularly fun then," Coop commiserates.

"I don't know, showing a bunch of ten year olds some science experiments might be fun, or it might be horrendous," I counter.

"Can I go?" Olly asks from the back of the car.

"Sorry buddy, but we already know you're going to that school, we don't need the Open Evening," Coop replies.

"Why don't we need the Open Evening?" he asks.

"Because *I go* to that school! We already know all about it!" I tell him, twisting in my seat and sticking my tongue out at him.

"*Fine*! But I want to see the science experiments when you get home," he insists, sticking his tongue out in response.

I agree and we both grin, even drawing a small smile

from Coop who is as grave as I've ever seen him. We pull up at home and Olly tumbles immediately from the car but hesitates at the front door, waiting for someone to unlock it and standing back, reluctant to be the first one in.

Coop goes in first, the advance guard, but everything is silent.

"I'll just go upstairs and check on mum," he says quietly.

Olly seems inclined to hover in the hall, waiting for a verdict, but I usher him into the lounge and distract him with the offer of snacks.

"Pop-tarts?" he asks eagerly.

"How about something a little more healthy?"

"One pop-tart?"

"How about toast?" I suggest, laughing.

"With jam?"

"Alright, you drive a hard bargain, but with jam," I agree.

I head to the kitchen to rustle up some food and I'm

relieved to hear the television going on behind me. I've just dropped off some toast and strawberry jam with Olly, and started to think about food to last me the evening, when Coop appears looking harassed.

"Is she alright?" I ask quickly.

"Mum? She's sleeping," he says shortly.

"So what's wrong?" I press.

He looks at me uncertainly before responding.

"What?" I demand.

"I just got a work call, they need me to check the IT network at the school, apparently they're having problems. They said it should be a quick fix, but I'm not sure I should leave. What time do you need to be at the school yourself?"

"I need to be there in just over an hour and a half," I tell him, checking the time.

"I don't know... it's cutting it close. I suppose I could check it out and if it's a longer job they'll just have to get someone else out to cover it... but it still means leaving."

"It's fine, I'm here with Olly, so long as you're back

in time for me to go it should be alright. I'll see if I can get a lift with Sophie, it'll be quicker than the bus and buy some extra time for you to get back," I tell him firmly.

He searches my face but he must feel reassured because he agrees and grabs his keys before rushing out the door.

"Where did dad go?" Olly asks, appearing in the doorway.

"Work, but he'll be back soon. I'm going to make myself a giant mish-mash sandwich. You want one?"

The offer works as a perfect distraction and before long we're both sat in front of the TV with huge sandwiches filled with a little of almost everything savoury in the fridge. Olly is happily consuming his while watching Detective Pikachu for the thousandth time, while I sit beside him one eye fixed firmly on my phone. I'm not sure why, but I feel the hairs pricking to attention on the back of my neck.

Something's wrong.

After half an hour I message Coop just asking whether the problem looks like a quick fix or not.

He doesn't reply.

Ten minutes later I message him again, asking when he's going to be home.

Nothing.

The room seems to hum softly around me, vibrating at a higher and higher frequency the longer my messages go unanswered. I try calling but his phone just rings out.

This brings my total up to two fathers, radio silent.

Coop was supposed to be the one adult that I can trust. He answered my questions about the car, he told me that he and mum weren't together until after the divorce, he promised to take me to the police.

So where is he?

With a sickening swoop of my stomach I realise that I only had Coop's word for anything he told me. He could have been lying through his teeth and then left at the first opportunity he got.

No.

No, I look at the little boy next to me on the sofa and I refuse to believe it. Coop wouldn't leave Olly, he wouldn't just abandon him.

Right?

If he did, if he ran, I don't want Oliver here if he comes back.

"One minute Olly Wally, you stay here, I'll be right back," I say quickly, running upstairs.

I go to his room and grab a bunch of his things, his pyjamas, his school uniform and some of his books. I stash them all inside a bag and then do the same for myself. I don't have a clear plan, I just know that I need to get us out of here. We can't stay in this house and we can't stay with-

I gently push open the door to mum's room. I can hear her breathing even from the doorway but it doesn't sound peaceful. Her breaths are too short, too deep, too laboured. She sounds like she does after a sleeping pill but amplified.

Have I been an idiot? All the talk of mum's delicate balance of medications and it never once occurred to me that someone else could upset that balance intentionally? She shares a room with Coop, how easy would it be for him to swap some of the new pills for the old ones? Swap some anxiety meds for antidepressants, or swap antidepressants for sleeping pills?

I look down at my mother in the bed. She looks small again. Pale and fragile against the pillow.

Is she a killer? Or a victim?

I hear my phone chime on the landing and rush out of the room, digging it out of my freshly packed bag. My heart sinks when I see that it isn't from Coop. It's not a message apologising, letting me know that he got held up and he's on his way. Instead it's Sophie agreeing to give me a lift to the school for the Open Evening.

Damn. Once again the Open Evening had gone completely out of my head. I pause, indecision freezing me in place. At last, I make a snap decision and promise to be ready in ten minutes. After all, the school was the last place that Coop told me he was going. Maybe he's there, his phone out of battery, still trying to fix some problem with the network before tonight's event.

"Olly Wally! We're going out."

If Sophie is surprised to see my ten year old brother with me, she rallies quickly.

"Hello you two!" she trills as we clamber into her car.

"Could we make a quick stop?" I ask, "Oliver's going to a sleepover."

She agrees readily and within a few minutes we're pulled up outside the house and I'm hauling mine and Olly's bags out of the car.

"Why am I staying here?" Olly asks me again.

"I told you, it'll be fun. And I'll be back here later and I'll sleep right next to you, all night, okay?" I assure him, trying to keep my voice bright.

Openness and honesty have gone out of the window but I don't have time to think about that now. I ring the bell and wait, bouncing on my feet until Charlie answers the door.

"Hellooooo, what's all this?" she singsongs uncertainly.

"Olly is here for the sleepover," I tell her firmly.

"Um, for the sleepover. Of course. That's totally normal."

I usher Oliver inside but Charlie corners me by the door.

"*What is going on?!*" she demands in a hiss.

"I've got this bloody school Open Evening and I can't leave him at home!" I tell her desperately.

"Where's Coop?"

"I don't know," I admit quietly.

"You don't know?"

"I don't know. He said he had to work and he'd be back in an hour, but-"

"But he wasn't back," she finishes for me.

I just shake my head, trying not to let too much of my panic show.

"And where's your mum?" she asks.

"At home," I tell her.

"But Olly can't stay there becaauuuse?"

"He's not safe with her."

Charlie stares at me, her brow furrowed.

"Because she's going through one of her phases and she's out of it? Or because you think she might actually hurt him?"

Her voice is barely a whisper but I still look quickly to Olly, making sure that he can't hear us. He's by the sofa digging through his bag to see what I packed.

"I don't know," I say bluntly, keeping my eyes on my brother's small form.

"Oh Penny," Charlie sighs, burying her face in her hands.

"I'll be back as soon as I can," I tell her.

"He's a ten year old boy! What am I supposed to do with him?!" she asks despairingly.

"Just stick a movie on for him, maybe bribe him with some snacks," I tell her confidently, "just keep him out of the booze, he's a weepy drunk."

That gets a laugh out of her and I use the

opportunity to run and plant a kiss on Olly's head, promising him I'll be back, before hurrying to the door and waving goodbye as I shut it behind me. It's not ideal, but at least I know he's safe. I'll figure out our next move tomorrow.

"Sorry about that!" I tell Sophie as I jump back into the car.

"No problem, everything alright?" she asks.

"Yeah, yeah, just- family stuff."

I'm grateful when she lets it go at that and moves the conversation on to other things.

"Have you heard the latest sports drama?" she asks eagerly.

"Sports drama? I didn't know there was such a thing."

"Of course there is! What, Coach Dan cancelling our cross-country practice like it was nothing wasn't drama?!" she demands.

"Alright, fair point, what's the new drama then?" I ask, though I suspect I already know.

I've been waiting for this bomb to fall since Marcus saw the photo of Tina on my phone. News had to get out eventually that Tina was gone, I'm just surprised it took so long.

"Marcus Kain quit his one to one training with Coach Dan!"

"Wait, what?"

"I know! It was really sudden, he just up and quit and no one has any idea why! Apparently Claire thinks he's going to start studying finance now," she tells me with a snort.

"He doesn't even study maths does he?!"

"He does not. Claire is delusional," Sophie agrees.

I want to puzzle out the Marcus and Dan situation but I don't have time. We're pulling into the school car-park and I can't see Coop's car anywhere.

"You go ahead, I'll be right in," I tell Sophie, affixing a smile to my face.

I do a quick loop of the car-park but I can't see any sign of him, or his car, anywhere. It crosses my mind that he might never have been here at all, I only had his word for it that there was a network problem needing to be fixed, perhaps he just thought of the first place that came into his head and made a break for it. I should have checked his room to see if any of his clothes and things were gone. The conjured image of empty shelves makes me queasy.

"Penny! Perfect timing!" a voice calls, making me spin round.

"Mrs Haskins!" I exclaim, trying to form a smile.

"You asked Penny Cooper to help this evening Jane?!"

My smile fails to appear. Ms Gittings is beside Mrs Haskins and her face is twisted into an expression of outraged incredulity.

"Yes I did, she's going to do delightfully," Mrs Haskins replies calmly.

"You do know who her mother is?" Ms Gittings mutters in an undertone that she must know I can still hear with absolute clarity.

"Yes, I do. She's our colleague," Mrs Haskins replies shortly, her expression darkening.

"I'm surprised at you Jane. I would have expected you to be more respectful of the sanctity of marriage," Ms Gittings crows in a lofty tone.

"I'm not particularly surprised at you Meg," she snaps back, reaching for my arm and sweeping me away with her.

We have to keep up a slightly uncomfortable pace all the way to the doors of the school but it's worth it to make our dramatic exit.

"What does she mean about my mum?" I whisper to Mrs Haskins once I'm sure we're out of earshot.

"She's just being a cow," she tells me consolingly but not particularly helpfully.

"But why is she being a cow? What does she have against my mum? I expected people to think badly of me because of my dad, but what did mum do that's so—"

"Penny," she cuts in, halting our progress along the corridor and turning me to face her, "I want to be clear about this. You are neither one of your parents and you have nothing to be ashamed of. You are the perfect choice for this evening and you are going to do brilliantly."

With that, she turns and sweeps on, leaving me hurrying after her, my heart in my throat. I still wish I knew what Ms Gittings was talking about but I'm more glad than ever to have teachers like Mrs Haskins and Mr Danes on my side. Between them maybe they can get me through the year unscathed.

It's strange being in the school after usual hours. The lights are all on and the classrooms are set up as though for lessons, but there's still a feeling of surreal unreality, like leaving the cinema in the afternoon and finding it's still light outside. The science classroom that we'll be using for the evening is all set up with a range of simple experiments around the outside counters, and a selection of year seven and eight work laid out on the centre tables. Sophie is already there of course and Abed arrives just a few minutes later. We have time to familiarise ourselves with the experiments and test them out, and then parents and children start trickling in. There's a fairly steady flow with just the occasional lull, but I still manage to text Coop a dozen more times, with no response.

Should I call the police?

If Coop is on the run, would that be enough cause on it's own for them to chase after him?

As the evening wears on, I feel increasingly tense and it becomes harder and harder to maintain my bright smile and cheery, professional voice. I make more than a hundred mobius strips of paper, with the help of hundreds of little hands. My pen trails their never ending loops again and again.

At last we're left alone and the silence of my phone rings loudly in my ears.

"Penny? Help me carry this box down to my car?" Mrs Haskins asks, snapping me back to myself.

"Of course," I tell her, hurrying forward and lifting

the box into my arms.

We head back through the school and out towards the car park, and that's when it happens. Just as I shift my grip on the box to set it into the boot of the car, a couple of mobius strips fall to the ground and are snatched up by Mrs Haskins before they can blow away.

"Your sister loved these," she says gently, holding them up and looking at them affectionately.

"Sorry?"

"The mobius strips. She loved them. Though really, she seemed to love everything. She was so excited," Mrs Haskins elaborates, shaking her head sadly.

"Rose- Rose came to- to one of these evenings?" I ask, sure that I must be misunderstanding but not sure why it's so important.

Static is buzzing in my ears.

"Yes, your mum brought her. That was a few months before she disappeared of course. It's such a shame she never got to attend. She was such a bright, happy girl. I remember her joking and teasing as she was shown around, no hint of shyness even though it would have been understandable in the company."

"What company?" I manage.

But I know the answer even before she gives it.

"I need to go," I tell her shortly.

I just walk away, slowly breaking into a run as I get closer to the school. My footsteps are gunshots bouncing off the walls as I race along the corridor and up the stairs. I know this route so well.

When I try the door I'm relieved to find it unlocked. I don't take the time to think about what that might mean, I just walk over to mum's desk and settle into her chair.

It's all here. Everything I needed to know. All the details pull together.

I should have seen it before, but I let dad get to me, I let his suspicions and bitterness infect me.

I replay Janet's words when I asked her about how someone motivated by guilt might behave. She told me that they might constantly be trying to earn redemption-

trying to make up for what they did.

I slide open the bottom drawer and reach to the back, fingering the ring with two keys attached. Keys that could let someone into our house to leave a rose on my pillow. That's not all that's there, there's mum's bottle of meds too, safely stowed away. The meds that were helping until suddenly they weren't.

A door creaks slowly open.

"Penny."

"You swapped out her medication, didn't you." I say softly. It's not a question. I already know the answer. It occurred to me that Coop might be messing with her drugs, but I didn't carry the thought all the way to its conclusion. I didn't think about the fact that Coop wasn't the only one who had access to her meds.

Coop.

"Where's Coop?" I ask, my eyes still fixed on the pill bottle and the keys.

"He was going to take you to the police, to get all of this opened up again," he replies quietly.

"What did you do?" I demand, my stomach roiling.

"I had no choice, you have to see that-"

"What did you do to her?" I cut in, forcing my gaze up to rest on the man in front of me. A man I had trusted. A man I thought was kind.

"She wanted me to say that I was at the house that day. She wanted to admit to the affair. She didn't understand what she was asking me to do! I just needed her to let it go. I just swapped some of her pills around, nothing that she hadn't been prescribed at some point-"

I meet his gaze full on and he trails off.

"Mr Danes, what did you do to Rose?"

His expression closes off and he doesn't reply.

"You said mum wanted to open up about the affair. She didn't know what you did?" I ask, trying to think through everything he's told me.

"I don't know what you're talking about. I didn't do anything."

"She wanted to say that you were at the house that day, but she didn't realise that you couldn't. You couldn't admit to being there without becoming a suspect. They would have realised in no time that you did it."

"I DIDN'T DO ANYTHING!" he suddenly shrieks, his voice high and furious.

Silence follows his words. A silence that crawls up the back of my neck on pincered feet.

Someone should be coming. Someone should have heard that shout. The only reason that no one would come, is if there's no one here any more. Why did I come here?

"I am a good person Penny. I help people," he tells me, his voice suddenly low and breathy, "I've made up for what I've done."

"What have you done?" I ask, forcing my voice to rise.

"NOTHING!" he shrieks again

"What have you made up for?" I demand, slowly edging one hand towards the pocket that holds my phone.

"I'm a good person Penny. I help people. I've helped

your family, haven't I? I've looked after you at school. I gave your mother a job when she needed one. I've helped your family!" he insists.

"Tell that to Coop!" I spit.

I move my hand another inch closer to my phone.

"I have no choice about that. I have to do what's necessary. I help so many people and I need to keep helping them. That has to be my priority! Cooper was going to get in the way of that!"

"So what have you done to him? What are you going to do? How do you plan to get away with it?!" I demand.

"It's not me who's going to do anything Penny, it's going to be your mother, everyone will see that. She's not well. Everyone knows that, they'll all see that she must have been responsible for what happened to her husband. And to you."

My gut twists.

Of course. Of course, we all have to disappear, to stop digging and let it drop. More than that, he needs someone to be responsible for whatever he did to Rose, he needs someone else to take the blame. Mum is the perfect choice. If Coop and I turn up dead, could she even be sure that she didn't do it? Could she trust her own mind? Could anyone else? Or will he just slip her a few extra pills? After all, the police can't question a dead woman. Certain assumptions would have to be made. I can almost picture the look on Detective Benson's face when she finds Rose's shoes in my desk drawer. When she realises Rose made it home the day she died, she won't have any doubts at all as to what happened.

I need to get out of here.

I slip my phone into my hand and try to dial without looking at the screen. Mr Danes is pacing back and forth, his attention isn't fully on me but he is between me and the door.

"I thought you loved mum," I say, hoping against hope that my fingers are unlocking my phone and pressing the call button.

"I do," he tells me "I did. But she's broken Penny. It's

a tragedy, but there it is. She wouldn't survive a trial anyway, we both know that. She's been ruined by what's happened," he tells me seriously, turning to face me again.

"Ruined by what you did, you mean," I insist, my voice hard, "what did you do to Rose?"

He freezes, his eyes fixed not on my face but on my hand in my pocket.

"What are you doing Penny?" he asks, his voice low and dangerous.

"Stop saying my name," I whimper.

In a second he's over the top of the desk, his body crashing into mine and tearing my arm upward. When he sees the phone he hisses and scrabbles for it, his nails cutting into my fingers, his face twisted into a snarl. He grabs it from me and switches it off before clambering to his feet, leaving me on the floor, panting and sobbing. He crushes my phone under one foot, his eyes wide.

I draw in one ragged breath after another, desperately hoping that he's already too late. The call screen was active when he wrestled the phone from me. I was trying to call 999 but I have no idea if I managed it. I didn't get a good enough look at the screen to tell.

"Who did you call?" he demands, his voice a hiss.

"I don't know," I admit, tears clouding my vision.

"WHO DID THAT NUMBER BELONG TO?!" he screams.

All I can do is flinch pathetically, curling into a smaller ball on the floor. It sounds as though my phone was calling an actual number, but not one I have saved. For all I know I was on the line with a call centre in India, but my god I hope not.

"I'm going to need to leave you here for a little while Penny. It seems we don't have much time, and I need to get some things ready."

He sounds suddenly calm, like his usual self, but honestly that scares me more than the screaming. I scramble to my feet, shaking but clear headed. My tears have stopped in the face of my fear.

"No, don't leave me here, please," I mutter, moving

towards him and towards the door. I let every ounce of my fear show in my face and will him to underestimate me.

"I'm sorry Penny. I have no choice. I had no choice in any of this. I hope that you can see that." He's backing up as he speaks, moving through the doorway with the handle gripped in his hand. I keep moving closer, muttering pleas to him, begging him not to leave me here. He already has the key in his free hand, ready to lock me in. I escaped from an abandoned, derelict house, but this is a third floor office in a school. Every door is a fire door. Every window is safety glass reinforced with wire mesh. I can't let him lock me in.

Just as he goes to slam the door shut, I move. I have no idea what to do so I act on impulse. A terrible impulse.

I shove my hand into the swiftly diminishing gap between the door and the door frame. I scream at the impact but it doesn't block out the sickening crunch of the bones in my hand. The door bounces back, still driven by the force of the slam and I push through it, ramming into his chest with my shoulder, driving him back into the wall and pushing past him in one movement. I don't wait. I don't hesitate. I run.

My footsteps are loud, roaring down the corridor, and all too soon he's up and after me, his own footsteps adding to mine in a cacophony. I glance into rooms as I pass them but everywhere is dark. The Open Evening only finished minutes ago, surely someone must still be here somewhere! Surely someone must have forgotten something, or been a few extra minutes packing away! I can't be alone here!

I try to scream but I'm running so hard that it's nothing but a wheezing yelp emitted from labouring lungs. I try to think of Coop and of mum and of everything that might happen to them, or have already happened, but all I can think about is the next step and the next and the one after that. I have to get out of here. I have to get away.

I can hear Mr Danes breathing behind me, harsh

and ragged but unceasing. As we take a sharp corner his hand grazes my arm but I manage to pull away and he overshoots, colliding with the wall harder than he intended and having to catch himself before he can keep running. It only buys me a couple of extra seconds but I'll take them. I'll take anything I can get. I get to the first flight of stairs and take them two at a time, catching the railing at the bottom to propel myself around at an almost one hundred and eighty degree angle and down the next corridor. My right hand is throbbing, stuck in a useless claw. Even through the adrenaline I can feel the sting and ache of broken bones and torn cartilage.

"PENNY!" he roars from behind me.

He's further back than I expected, not taking the turns as fast I am and failing to catch up on the straights. I give silent thanks to Dan Cosford for my improved running pace and the irony barely even stings. One more flight down and I'll be at ground level and can start looking for a way out. There must be a door or window somewhere that I can get out of. Two more turns and the stairs come into view. I race towards them, my legs pumping and my breath coming in sharp bursts. I'm going too fast, I need to grab the hand rail to slow myself down but it's on the wrong side. Desperately I reach out with my contorted fingers, but it's a mistake. The pain bends me double, bringing me to a clumsy stop, losing precious time. I look back to see how close he is and find us face to face, his breath hot on my skin.

I manage a feeble, "no," before he shoves me backward.

For a moment I'm in the air. Weightless.

But just a moment. The first impact is beyond my comprehension. It is a wave crashing over me in the water, but a wave of stone and steel. Another wave hits, and another, turning me in somersaults. I can't draw breath.

At last I'm lying on flat floor. I think I must have blacked out because I don't remember landing, but when I force my eyes open, Mr Danes is only one step down, looking at me in horror. I try to move my arms, my legs, to turn my head. Everything at least twitches at my command, but the pain is immense.

"What did you do to my sister?" I croak.

The frozen look on his face is sharp with recollection. He has been here, or somewhere very like here before.

"What did you do?" I say again, slightly louder.

"I am a good person Penny. I help people. I'm needed," he replies, taking another step down towards me.

"What did you do to her?"

"I have to do this Penny. Don't you see that?"

"How did you kill her? Why?"

"It was an accident."

My breath catches. I can't believe that he actually answered me. I can't believe he gave me any kind of explanation at all.

"An accident?" I repeat.

He looks down at me and takes another step, gently nodding his head.

"Just an accident. She- she came home. She wasn't supposed to be there. Your mother was in the shower and I was still getting dressed and she just... walked in. She stood there looking at me and I didn't know what to do. Before I could say anything, do anything, she ran. She went straight out the door and I went after her. She was in the street so I jumped in my car to follow, to catch up. At the end of the road she went into the woods so I turned left, following along the edge of the trees, hoping I'd see her. I was going to find her and explain. I was going to ask her not to tell anyone. I was just going to talk to her! But she ran back out of the trees, doubling back to get home I suppose. I couldn't stop in time. She was so small. And she was already gone, there was nothing I could do. I'm sure, she was already gone. I just put her in the boot of the car and drove away. The car barely even had a dent, she was such a little thing. But I still got rid of it, just to be safe. I waited a week and then I drove three hours to a scrap yard and sold it for cash. It was like it never happened. And no one knew I'd been there. No one saw me and your mother begged me to keep it quiet. She didn't want anyone to know what she'd been doing when her little girl disappeared. So I looked after her, and then I looked after you. I've helped so many people Penny, and so many people still need my help. There's so much more good that I can do. You do see that, don't you? It was just an accident. One accident shouldn't destroy my whole life!"

He's begging me to understand. His voice is pitiful, cloying and desperate. I turn my head to the side and vomit, my ribs screaming in pain. When I've stopped heaving I take a shaky breath.

"You're a monster."

His expression closes off. The desperation in his eyes is replaced by cold anger, like a switch being flicked. He would have liked for me to understand and condone his actions, but either way, he's not going to let me stop him.

He's at the bottom of the stairs now and slowly he bends down, bringing his face close to mine.

"I have to do this," he whispers.

Then his hand shoots out and grabs my wrist at the same time as he rises, jolting me half off of the floor. I scream with pain but he just marches along, dragging me behind him. The screaming of my limbs is unendurable and after a few moments I feel myself turning soft, darkness closing in around me, filling my mind.

I wake in darkness and immediately vomit again. It's coppery and metallic. I don't need light to know that it's mostly blood I'm bringing up. I'm not entirely sure what that means but I know it's not a good sign. I try to push myself up onto all fours but the pain and effort leaves me panting. Eventually I push up enough to look around and make out shapes in the dark. It's a classroom. I see tables and chairs and the floor is linoleum. There's a smell too, something familiar and even stronger then the tang of blood. Turpentine. I must be in one of the art rooms, in its small separate block.

Not I, we.

"Coop!" I sob, dragging myself forward and collapsing across the prone figure.

He's not moving but his chest is rising and falling steadily beneath me. He's still alive.

"Coop? Coop can you hear me?" I ask frantically, touching his face and feeling his head. I think about all of mum's sleeping pills, but then my hand finds a large lump and my fingers come away sticky.

"Coop. Please wake up," I beg, tears stinging my battered face.

He doesn't so much as stir. I take a breath and check his pockets. I need to get us out of here. His phone is gone and he doesn't have anything else except his house keys and a couple of pound coins. At the edge of my consciousness the smell of turpentine is getting stronger.

"I'm sorry Penny!" Mr Danes' voice calls.

"Stop saying my name," I whimper under my breath.

"It won't be long now. I hoped you wouldn't wake up," he calls.

He really does sound regretful, but then I hear the click of a lighter and for a moment I wish I had stayed unconscious too.

I wait, hardly daring to breathe, but nothing happens. More clicking follows, but no flames appear. I hear the faintest noise, what might have been a sigh, and then retreating footsteps. My heart pounds. How long do I have? How long will it take him to find a new lighter or a box of matches, anything he can use to generate a spark? I heave myself onto unsteady feet and stumble towards the door. It's locked of course, but my feet splash into a puddle of clear liquid. I look around, hoping for dry rags, anything I can use to get the liquid away from the door. There's a paper towel dispenser on the wall, full of those stiff green monstrosities that can only be found in schools. I grab as many as I can in my one good hand and start sweeping the liquid away from the door. I go to the sink, knocking paint brushes flying in my haste. I soak some of the towels and then shove them under the door. Will it be enough? What else can I do? I look around frantically, trying to find something more I can use. There's the art supply cupboard, a huge floor to ceiling construction with a flimsy door. It's locked but I pick up one of the chairs and send it crashing against the front. On my second try the door splinters and breaks. There's a mop. I fill the bucket with water and start trying to mop up the sea of turpentine, before just upending the bucket. I don't know if I'm making things better or worse. I tip myself back onto the floor beside Coop, my many cuts and scratches burning on contact with the wet linoleum.

"Coop! Coop wake up! Please wake up!" I cry.

A sound at the door tells me that I'm too late. Any second now I'm going to find out if my efforts have made any difference at all.

The lock clicks and the door swings open to reveal the last person in the world that I expected to see.

"Marcus Kain?" I mutter incredulously.

He looks around swiftly, taking in my broken body, Coop's unconscious form and the smell of turpentine hanging thick in the air.

"Is it Dan?" he asks quickly.

Just then a shadow steps into the doorway behind

him, one arm rising to strike.

I go to shout but there isn't time. The arm starts to fall but Marcus ducks swiftly, spinning round and bringing up a fist in one fluid motion. He connects with the side of Mr Danes' jaw, sending him flying backward.

"FUCK!" Marcus cries, seeing what he's done. He starts forward, leaning down to Mr Danes in concern but I call him back.

"No! No, it was him Marcus! It was all him!" I sob, cries shaking my body.

He looks from Mr Danes to me and back again, clearly uncertain.

"I saw Sophie when she was leaving. She asked if I'd seen you because she hadn't seen you leave. I thought- I thought Dan- I waited and you didn't come out so I tried to call you, and then I called Charlie, but- I thought maybe Dan. Charlie said you were here. She said she couldn't reach you."

He's babbling.

I can't help it, I just keep sobbing. I'm ugly crying,

so loud that I almost don't hear the sound of sirens.

Marcus' head snaps up, his eyes widening in panic.

"Am I going to be arrested?" he asks me, looking down at the writhing figure of Mr Danes, just starting to come to himself.

"No," I sob, "No, you'll probably get some kind of award."

He looks unconvinced, but he takes a step toward me, a small sign of allegiance.

"Penny Cooper?!" a voice calls. It's a voice that I know. I can't call out. My ribs are aching and I feel blood trickling from the corner of my mouth. I can't even lift my hand to wipe it away. I lean down again, resting my weight on Coop so that I can feel each rise and fall of his chest.

In, out, in, out, alive, alive, alive.

"Penny Cooper?!" the voice calls again.

"Um- she's here!" Marcus calls back lamely.

Detective Benson appears in the doorway, stepping over Mr Danes and moving swiftly into the room.

"I'm going to need EMTs in here immediately. I have three down," she barks into her radio before dropping down into a squat beside me.

"Penny Cooper, we have got to stop meeting like this," she says softly.

I manage a weak smile but her eyes are sweeping my face and body and concern is etched into her features.

"You just hang in there Penny. Stay still."

"Mr Danes killed Rose. Drugged mum. Attacked us." I breathe the words and she nods her understanding, her eyes only widening very slightly in surprise.

"I didn't do anything bad," Marcus interjects awkwardly, still standing to the side like a lost child.

Detective Benson looks to me for confirmation and I give a small, painful shrug.

"Saved us I suppose," I mutter.

"Alright. You just stay still. EMT's are coming in now. We'll get you to hospital. I just got off the phone with a PC Chalmers of the Devonshire Police, who insisted that I get to you immediately and save your life.

If I lose you now I think she might hunt me down."

At that I do laugh, blood bubbling from my lips and choking me.

I hear a whispered "*fuck*" from Marcus and Benson pales perceptibly, but I don't care. I know who I called. I know whose the number was that I managed to dial without having it saved in my phone. It was Tina. My blind thumbs must have opened the picture she sent me and called the number it came from. She saved me back.

That's my last thought before it all goes dark.

Chapter 17

The next thing that I'm aware of is a steady beeping. After that, is pain.

After another period of darkness, I wake to the same beeping, more pain, and mum's face.

"P-Penny?" she chokes my name out in a ragged sob.

I try to nod or answer her but the darkness is too quick for me, sweeping up and dragging me down without warning.

The next time I wake, I feel different. Clearer. The beeping is still infuriating and the pain is still alarming, but my eyes focus and I can look around without the intrusion of dark clouds.

"Penny?" mum asks weakly.

"Mum?" I mumble back, my lips barely moving and my tongue so dry that it tries to cleave to the roof of my mouth.

Hearing my hoarse croak, she jumps up and pours me some water from a plastic jug. I have to drink through a straw, only taking tiny sips, even though I suddenly feel parched.

"You have to go slow, sweetheart," she tells me gently.

I study her face. She looks a mess- her hair is wild, her skin is pale and she looks as though she hasn't slept in weeks. However, the eyes that rest over dark pouches of skin are clear and bright. She looks alert and alive in a way that I haven't seen in weeks.

"Coop?" I croak between sips.

She gives a small smile.

"He woke up before you did. He was badly hurt but they don't think there'll be any long-term effects."

Her words make me wonder whether *I'm* going to have long term effects, but I'm too afraid to ask. I try to assess the damage, but it's too extensive to catalogue and whatever medications they have me on have left the pain feeling diffuse and hard to pinpoint. I can see that my crushed hand is in an elaborate metal frame and that's enough to stop me from investigating further.

"You were hurt so much," mum whimpers, tears flooding down her face.

"I'm alright," I tell her, with no idea as to whether I'm telling the truth or not.

She sniffs and pulls herself upright, gathering her wits.

"It seems like there's a lot of healing to do all around," she announces with a smile that breaks my heart.

"Where's Olly?" I ask.

"He'll be here soon. Charlie's picking him up from school since Coop hasn't been cleared to drive yet. He's been here every day. Lots of people have."

"Every day?" I murmur, confused.

Mum's face twists.

"How long has it been?" I ask her.

"Almost two weeks. For a moment there they weren't sure if you were going to- but- you're here now," she tells me, clasping my unbroken hand and gazing at me intently, drinking me in.

"You know- you know what happened?" I ask.

"Only some of it. I'm afraid you're going to have to fill in a lot of gaps. Sean isn't talking."

At his name her expression darkens and hollows out for a moment but then she's back.

"The police want to talk to you. They've been champing at the bit but the doctors couldn't tell them any more than they could tell me," she explains with a half shrug.

Right on queue, Detective Benson appears in the doorway, knocking politely on the frame but coming into the room without waiting to be asked.

"Penny," she breathes with a relieved sigh.

"Not dead yet," I quip in a feeble voice.

She doesn't respond except to come to the bed and give me a once over.

"Up to giving a preliminary statement?" she asks.

Mum starts to object but I cut across her.

"Yes. There's things you need to know," I say definitely.

"There are indeed. Before you very sensibly lost consciousness, you made certain claims. That was wonderful of you, but I would like some more details."

The model of efficiency, she has things set up in no time and I'm able to give a statement then and there. I ask mum to stay. It's not easy, but there are a lot of things that she needs to know and I'd rather she heard them from me.

When I get to Mr Danes' confession about Rose's death, mum breaks down. The tape is paused. Tissues are produced. Water is sipped.

The situation in the art classroom was fairly clear. Assault, kidnapping and attempted murder are the charges that Mr Danes is currently being held on, though Detective Benson assures me that Rose's murder will shortly be added to the list.

By the time we're done, Charlie, Luke and Olly are waiting outside and causing something of a commotion as they insist on being allowed in.

"Penny Cooper, you rat!" Charlie cries as she runs into the room with every intention of flinging herself upon me.

To my relief, Luke snatches her practically out of mid-air and is able to restrain her.

"Please don't jump on me! I am very seriously injured!" I tell her sternly.

"Yes Penny, I'm aware of that! I've had ample opportunity to see exactly *how* injured you are!" she weeps, still evidently angry but overcome with relief.

Luke too is looking misty eyed and even wiping at his cheeks with the back of his hand. Only Olly is standing well back, his face frozen.

"You alright Olly?" I ask him.

He nods quickly, still standing by the door.

"Come give me a kiss then," I tell him, holding out a cheek in offering. It's the best I can do since so much of my body still doesn't seem to be moving.

He edges closer, still looking completely panicked.

"It's alright my love," mum tells him gently, "she's going to be okay."

He takes a final step forward and kisses me fiercely on the cheek before his feelings erupt and he bursts into tears. Mum sweeps around the bed and gathers him into her arms, letting him cling to her as tightly as he can, with all the love that I'm still too delicate to receive.

"How about we go get some hot chocolate," she suggests to him, "I bet Penny would like one."

"Try to find me some marshmallows!" I call after them as they go, leaving me with Charlie and Luke, flanking my bed like expectant sentries.

"You had a dramatic Open Evening then," Luke comments once the three of us are alone.

"You promised nothing else would happen until

you'd filled us in," Charlie reminds me with a frown.

"But then you go charging off into danger, and worst of all you let Marcus Kain rescue you!" Luke adds.

"Yeah, that might be the worst bit," I agree.

"How was he there?! What actually happened with that?!" Charlie demands.

"It's a bit complicated. After he saw the picture of Tina all beat up, he must have realised it was Dan. He started to worry that Dan might be coming after me. He was at the Open Evening I suppose, and Sophie mentioned she hadn't seen me leave. I think he said he tried calling me, and you too Charlie, but then he came inside to try to make sure I was alright. He thought Dan might be pissed off with me and take the opportunity to do something about it. He got there just as Mr Danes was about to burn me and Coop alive and he punched him in the jaw," I tell them.

"Bugger! That means he's actually *almost* as heroic as he's been making himself sound!" Charlie cries.

"Yeah, I guess he's not a total waste of space after

all," Luke comments thoughtfully.

"I do appreciate not being set on fire," I agree fairly.

"I bet Coop does too," Luke adds.

"Is he really alright? Coop, I mean. Mum mentioned that he can't drive. And is she alright too?" I ask quickly, almost tripping over my words.

"Coop had a really bad head injury. It was dicey for a while but he's going to be fine. The doctors are pretty sure about that, it's just going to take some time. Your mum is doing... well she's doing great," Charlie finishes with a shrug of mystification.

"I suppose now that she's not being drugged she's feeling much better," I comment darkly.

"Drugged?" Luke queries simply.

"Mr Danes was messing with her meds. He wanted her to seem unstable so that she'd be blamed for mine and Coop's deaths," I tell them.

I'm not sure how much of this I'm really allowed to be sharing, but I don't care in the slightest. They've been waiting almost two weeks to find out whether I'm going to die or not. They deserve the truth.

"So Mr Danes was like a real villain then," Charlie comments wonderingly.

"That's two people you've had crushes on Charlie. Actually three! Penny's dad, Mr Danes and Coach Dan!" Luke remarks brightly.

She pursues him around the room until she manages to land a couple of good hits and then perches carefully on the edge of my bed.

"Does everything hurt?" she asks tentatively.

"Yeah, pretty much."

"But you're going to be alright," she replies.

"I've not talked to a doctor yet," I admit.

"No not that, we know you're going to be alright physically. You had to have two separate operations to resolve the internal bleeding, and your hand is a complete mess and you probably have months of physio ahead of you, but I mean *you*."

I take a moment, mulling it over, pushing past the physical pain to the traumatised psyche within.

"I mean, it's over now. You found out what happened. You found out who did it. The police will get him talking and they'll find Rose. You're free now, right?" she presses on, looking at me intently.

"I am. I'm free. I'm not really sure what that means yet, but it's true. And I know where Rose is," I tell them.

Two sets of eyes widen in surprise just as my own start to droop. I'm not prepared to lay all of my cards on the table just yet. I want to make sure that I'm not trapped in a hospital bed when all of this draws to a close.

As it is, I manage to be there, in a wheel chair and still looking pale and interesting, but at least I'm there.

I watch as the diggers carve out every single rose bush, splintering stems and sending leaves and petals cascading down like rain. Mr Danes' pride and joy. The memorial that he built and pruned and tended, to the little girl that he killed and buried beneath the soil.

We finally brought her home.

Acknowledgements

Thank you to my wonderful family for taking such good care of me.

Thank you to my lovely husband, for inspiring me and supporting me.

Thank you to my amazing mum for editing and reading my work, and for taking such good care of me.

Thank you to my readers for making all of this worthwhile.

BV - #0008 - 260325 - C0 - 203/127/29 - PB - 9781739571825 - Matt Lamination